FLASHPOINT

MATTHEW H. WHITTINGTON

Published by CLC Publishing, LLC, Mustang, OK
www.clcpublishing.com

ISBN: 978-1-7363318-5-9

FOR GAMBLE. THE HERO I NEEDED.

PROLOGUE

Sorrento Hotel. Seattle, WA

Congressman Ray Tinsley reclined in a plush armchair. He kicked off his immaculately polished Oxfords before setting his feet on the matching ottoman. A long, whirlwind of a day drew to an end as he loosened his designer tie. He rubbed his temple as he received a neat whiskey from his campaign manager, Marvin Miller.

"So, Marvin, how'd we fare today?" His eyes slowly opened and closed as the whiskey warmed his throat. With each passing tip of the ridiculously expensive crystal ware, the tensions of the day eased.

"I would say our message was on target and well received here in the city, Congressman. I think we can say with some confidence that Washington State is yours." Marvin paused a moment to glance at his iPhone. Finding the talking points he needed within the device, the phone disappeared into his slacks' pocket and he continued. "The major news networks are lauding tonight's speech as a bold step in your Presidential campaign that may have you in a comfortable lead by November. As we expected, the message is getting mixed reviews throughout the South. Mostly mixed against us."

Tinsley eased his head back and let his eyes close. He allowed himself a moment to indulge in imagining himself giving an inaugural address. He returned to the moment and set his gaze on Marvin. "What about the swing states?"

"Ohio, Florida, and Virginia are trending our way nicely. Looks like we'll sweep the Northeast and carry the states around the Great Lakes. Texas isn't likely to go our way. Outside of Austin, the Texans aren't keen on our gun agenda. With Florida, Pennsylvania, and Virginia though, I don't think it will matter." Marvin sat down on the small couch opposite the congressman and sipped from his glass of ice water.

"Marvin." The congressman paused to take another pull from his whiskey. "About the guns. I want to talk about how I'm going to get this thing through Congress. I don't want just four years; I want a lasting legacy. I want to go down as the President who made the Second Amendment a history lesson. I want to make it a failed experiment of society. I do *not* want to be yet another President who promised these changes and fell short because of the NRA lobby." Tinsley paused before he continued, "Marvin, I want this gun thing to be the flagship of my legacy."

Marvin savored the ice-cold water as he drank it down and used the excuse of crunching an ice cube to formulate his response. They had worked through versions of this conversation countless times over the months since Tinsley had announced his candidacy. Could they push through a legislative package that all but dismantled the Second Amendment? Would an aggressive political power play of this nature require a

Constitutional Amendment to do the job of outright abolishing the Second Amendment, as the Congress of 1933 had done to end Prohibition? Failing those options would the congressman try his hand at utilizing Executive Orders and taking his chances with the Supreme Court as President?

Finally, Marvin framed a candid response, "Congressman, the only way guarantee your agenda stands the test of time is the Constitutional Amendment, as we have discussed previously. While an amendment would be able to withstand court challenges, this is of course the most difficult to achieve. We will need to pick up a *lot* of seats. We'll have to go back through seats up for re-election in both Houses, re-evaluate seats we had previously considered going to the other side. We can add campaign stops in those districts hoping to swing sentiments back our way. We may be able to call in some favors for the promise of Cabinet and lower level appointments as well; sway others to our way of thinking in other cases."

Pausing a moment, Marvin poured another glass of ice water from the pitcher room service had set on the lavish bar. He glanced at the congressman; no longer reclined and relaxed, but sitting upright with his fingers tented and eyes closed. Tinsley seemed meditative. He frequently had this look; as if the man were trying to visualize and conjure his future desires.

Marvin continued, knowing Tinsley was waiting for him to fill in the rest of his picture. "Congressman, that said, you know this is an uphill battle. The gun lobby has powerful friends and the last time enough politicians agreed to ratify an Amendment was 1992, and the 27th regarded their own compensation. Before that, we have to go back to 1971 when the 26th Amendment was ratified giving 18-year-olds the right to vote."

Congressman Tinsley nodded his head very slowly, the only sign he was listening and not lost in a trance.

His campaign manager pressed on. "I know we talk about this a lot on the trail, my gut says without the Amendment, the other legislative options are probably not tenable. Our best chance after that is to hope for a few Justices to retire or die so we can stack the court to lean our way, preferably with those we can count on to rule the way we want. Then you can try some Executive Orders. This approach is the weakest overall and is probably doomed to be reversed down the line. We need a major shift in public opinion to rally the people behind this from the middle and undecided voters. In that case, I believe we can compel a vote that stands a chance."

Tinsley opened his eyes and met Marvin's gaze. "So, Marvin, we need a tragedy," he stated. "We will have the cataclysm we need. At some point, there will be another convenient shooting we can hitch this thing to." Tinsley downed the remainder of his whiskey and set his jaw.

Marvin waited. Again, his candidate seemed to be gazing at nothing in particular until Marvin brought him back. "And then sir?"

With a half-smile, Tinsley replied, "Then, Marvin, we strike."

Marvin Miller, a lifelong activist and political player in D.C., felt his skin prickle at the disturbing and chilling certainty of his candidate's choice of words. *We strike.*

PART 1

CHAPTER 1

The Mayo Clinic – Rochester, MN

Jake Thornton's shoulders slumped as the doctor delivered the diagnosis. Across the table from Jake and his wife, Jocelyn, sat a formidable medical team of neurosurgeons and specialists. A dream team, as it were. The very best and brightest minds the medical community had to offer, at least in the upper Midwest, worked at Minnesota's Mayo Clinic.

Inoperable, grade four glioblastoma.

Lead surgeon, Dr. Amin broke the news gently, "Mister and Misses Thornton, the best our team can do at this point is to treat your daughter's tumor with radiation and chemotherapy. She will be uncomfortable, she will be sick, and there will be pain. A lot of it. You can expect changes in her behavior and moods that are not representative of the child you are accustomed to. Only about 5% of patients with a brain tumor of this nature live as long as 5 years. More often we see timelines of 12 to 18 months."

Dr. Amin paused a moment to re-group his conclusion. In his experience, parents hearing a diagnosis like this one often held their breath while the terrible news was delivered. He found that these pauses allowed parents the opportunity to breathe again.

Continuing, he finished the delivery he had mastered over countless years of tragedy. "I would love to tell you that Hope will make it to her 13th birthday, yet the statistics and nature of progression in this specific tumor bear that out as very unlikely. We'll give you a few minutes before discussing what comes next. Again, you have my most profound sympathy, I'm very sorry." With a soft touch to their entangled arms, he stood up. He and his team and left them to their grief.

Through blurred eyes Jake turned to his wife. They fell into a puddle of inconsolable grief. Jake had known Jocelyn since the day she had bounced a ball off his forehead playing four-square, a lifetime ago.

Jake's emotions rolled over him; as waves approaching a beach rise and fall until they swell to a crest before crashing ashore. His thoughts raced through his past and tumbled in chaos. The benchmarks that led Jake and Jocelyn to bring Hope into the world, and by extension this horrible day. Finally culminating in the tragic conversation, they would soon need to have with her.

Going back to middle school he remembered fondly the boyish crush he had developed for Jocelyn. Little had he known that she admired him, too. That silent mutual admiration lasted between them until Jake had finally worked up enough courage to overcome his shyness and ask her to the Chatfield High School prom in their sophomore year. She later told him that her insides were bouncing with excitement while her outer demeanor was a coy, "Yes."

Jocelyn had done well enough with her grades in school to keep her parents happy and reasonably free of her business.

Jake, however, lived a bit on the edgier side. He would graduate on time, there was no fear or drama on that front. High grades weren't a priority for him though. Jake Thornton found more joy in playing left field on the varsity baseball team and then helping out the coach of his younger brother's little league team. When he wasn't living baseball, he took short-term or part-time work for gas and date money for Jocelyn. Jake had many distractions pulling on him, in the end though, he always made time for Jocelyn. He believed her to be his person.

By graduation, Jake and Jocelyn found themselves at a crossroads. Jocelyn wanted to attend school to be a nurse. Beyond studies, volunteering at their community church in town made her happy. Jake's scholastic resume wasn't strong enough for advanced education and while he was a good baseball player, nobody was beating down his door for scholarships to play at the next level. Furthermore, both of his parents were hopeless drunks. Jake feared becoming his parents; stuck in a small town with a job he hated, addicted to alcohol and mediocrity. He needed to get out of town.

So, Jake had picked up Jocelyn and they drove east to a quiet spot overlooking the Mississippi River to talk about their future and what was next for them. There they sat with the old river slowly crawling along in front of them as they talked. Jake poured his heart out. He wanted to get out of town to see what else was out there, though the thought of being without her destroyed him. Jake wanted her to follow him wherever the road led. Having just enrolled in school in Rochester, Jocelyn wasn't ready to leave, she wanted to see her schooling through. At least for a while. She didn't want him to go, they talked about different jobs Jake might work to keep them together, but the wanderlust was strong. Jake shared with Jocelyn that he felt joining the Marines might be best for him. He said the recruiter had promised that Jocelyn could join him to live in base housing once all his training had been completed.

Just the thought of Jake in combat terrified her, but the logic sounded as though it could work out for them. Jake's time in training would overlap nicely with the time commitment to school Jocelyn desired, she could focus on those studies with little distraction. At the very least, pushing decisions about the future of their relationship or family down the road seemed like a great idea.

Best laid plans often seem to fall apart, especially when the Marines get involved it seemed. What should have been a year turned into two and a half before they were together again. Upon Jake's graduation to a fleet Marine, he was sent to Iraq where he took part in the First Battle of Fallujah. While clearing a room with his teammates, Jake took an AK-47 round through his left shoulder. A Corpsman was able to staunch the bleeding and got him evacuated to safety. A Blackhawk got him from Fallujah to a field hospital where the wound was stabilized. Then he caught an Air Force C-17 to Germany for surgery. Once well enough to fly again, he was moved back stateside for recovery. After months of painful recovery from the gunshot wound, Jake found himself struggling with PTSD. Anytime a door swung open or slammed he jumped, grasping for his weapon. The Marines decided they didn't need a jumpy grunt back in the field with weapons, so they gave him early separation.

Jake was finally able to go home to Minnesota and Jocelyn.

After a rocky five years of acclimating back to life in America and learning to co-exist with a woman who desperately desired to understand him, Jake was able to settle and find himself a steady job mowing grass for the local golf course and tending the grounds. Once the grounds maintenance was done, he would head to the local animal shelter to volunteer. There he learned the therapy shelter dogs provided him while out on their walks. The shelter had an old black lab in hospice nobody seemed to want, named Doober. Doober was a sweet old soul that Jake loved. He agreed to bring Doober home with him where the old fella would enjoy some real love in his twilight years.

Doober's passing was a devastating loss for Jake. In a stroke of divine timing, the loss was only eased when Jocelyn told him a week later that Jake would be a father.

Nine months later Jocelyn delivered a healthy girl. In the recovery room a nurse laid the infant on Jocelyn's chest. She cried tears of joy as their tiny girl laid there heart to heart. After a few minutes Jake asked to hold her. Cradling the baby, he lifted her up to his own chest and in that moment all that had been troubling Jake; alcoholic parents, combat trauma and the death of a special canine companion fell away. In his arms, in that moment was renewed hope. Her name would be Hope.

In Hope, Jake found his second love.. Jocelyn never had to plead for his help with things some husbands seemed to dodge, such as late-night feedings or diaper changes. Jake wholeheartedly jumped in to help with his little Hope. Jake would often hold her close to his heart and walk around the house with her before settling into a rocking chair and easing her to sleep. Each night as he put her to bed, Jake would kiss her forehead and tell her, "Good night, my sweet little Hope." He immersed himself into being her father

As the years went on, Hope followed Jake everywhere. When Jocelyn was working, Jake would sit Hope on his lap while they rode the mower all over the golf course. She would then of course be delighted around all the friendly dogs and cats at the shelter. Hope felt she must take on the responsibility of naming some of the strays. Both the animals and the shelter staff adored Hope. No one adored her more than Jake.

As Hope got a little older, she began to share a passion for some of Jake's favorite things. Hope loved to listen to Vikings or Minnesota Wild games with Jake in his ice fishing shack. Sometimes they reeled a few Walleye in. Other times they just sat together talking about how football and hockey worked. Talking about hockey led to Hope's desire to play it. Jake put every extra dime he could wrangle towards Hope's improvement in the sport. He made sure she had all the best gear and coaching that he and Jocelyn could afford. When she wasn't busy with coaching or practices, Jake would go through drills with Hope, sometimes until it was dark outside.

During a game in the most recent season, Hope had checked another girl into the boards. Suddenly collapsed on the ice. When the coaches reached her, they noticed she was having a seizure. After what seemed like minutes the seizure passed and she was taken to the hospital. Hours and several tests later, Jake and Jocelyn were told their daughter had a tumor on her brain that was probably causing the seizures. All of that led them to this moment.

Jake wondered how he would tell his one and only Hope that she was going to die.

CHAPTER 2

CNN Presidential Election Night Coverage

"Good evening, America! This is Megan Kincade coming to you live with our award-winning election night coverage. As many of our experts have predicted, Congressman Ray Tinsley is expected to soon clinch the final electoral votes needed to win the Presidency. According to exit polls out in California, we may be able to call that state, which will be more than enough. No word on a concession speech forthcoming as of this report. We will bring that to you live when it *does* happen. Stay with us all night for complete, ocean to ocean election results. We'll see you after the break."

CHAPTER 3

The Thornton Home – Chatfield, MN

Looking through Hope's bedroom window, Jake could see the serenity of an early winter day. Snow laid gently upon the grass as if Mother Nature had placed it there like a blanket over a baby. There was not a breath of observable wind to disrupt the calm. Meanwhile, his body ached with grief. His mind was a tempest of anger, despair and, hopelessness.

Hopelessness.

Hope.

Jake slumped into his rocking chair; the same chair he had rocked Hope to sleep in countless times. The pain Dr. Amin had mentioned, came much sooner than either he or Jocelyn had thought it would. As the tumor swelled, it pressed on nerves and blood vessels which, in turn, manifested as headaches that grew in intensity. Seizures were also increasing in frequency. Jake felt moving himself and the rocker into Hope's bedroom to be necessary. He was determined that Hope wouldn't suffer alone.

As Jake leaned forward, trying to rub the dreadful hours of the previous night from his mind, he realized his suffering had only just begun.

In the time between that awful day at the Mayo Clinic and this morning, Hope's final days had been an awful thing to behold. Pain management techniques were only marginally effective if at all. She moaned in pain every night, slept restlessly, and cried until late hours out of anger or fear. Sometimes both.

Jake never left her. When she broke down in tears, he would simply hold her to his chest. Sometimes she vented in anger, sometimes she just sobbed. If she didn't cry out too loudly, he would cradle her like he had when she was a baby. Hope often fell asleep this way. No matter how uncomfortable the weight of her frail body made him, Jake wouldn't move. He just rocked while she slept.

Now, he would never hold Hope again.

Jake couldn't make out the conversation in hushed tones between his wife and the clergy from the church. Clearly, he and Jocelyn mourned differently. Barely an hour had passed between Hope's passing and Jocelyn's phone call to the pastor. He recognized that his wife needed the support of the church's fellowship and the God she embraced. While Jake never fully embraced faith the way Jocelyn had, he understood his wife well enough to know her needs would mean having lots of people around her.

Jake knew a God that was far less merciful from the one his wife worshiped. The God Jake knew, stood by as a friend had his legs blown off in an IED explosion and bled out crying for his mother. The God Jake knew, blessed him with two drunk parents. The God Jake knew, allowed a murderous tumor to grow in his daughter's brain. The only God Jake knew, allowed him a glance at Heaven with Jocelyn and his beautiful sweet daughter, Hope, before yanking the rug out from under his life.

That's the God Jake knew.

After a few minutes, Jake heard their voices getting closer. Muffled at first and then he could make out the words as Jocelyn and the pastor approached. Jake had assumed it was the pastor earlier when the doorbell rang, and now with the two just outside Hope's bedroom, he knew it for sure. This was the last conversation Jake wanted.

Please just stay out there. Don't. Please, just don't.

Briefly Jake thought about hiding in Hope's closet. How would that look? Maybe he could slip out the window or something. Deciding that none of his escapism options were valid he resolved to kindly receive the pastor and nod his gratitude at the man until he was left alone. Despite his lack of faith Jake said a quick prayer of his own. *God, please just have him say some sympathetic words and leave me alone. I don't need this right now.*

Hope's bedroom door opened slowly. Pastor Brown followed Jocelyn in. Looking around, the man decided that there were no good seating options. He just stood there with the Bible pressed to chest waiting for his cues to speak.

Jocelyn spoke first. "Jake."

Jake pulled his hands away from his face and met his wife's eyes, "Yes, sweetheart." His heart ached again with the visage. Jocelyn had obviously been crying. Her face was fatigued and heavy with anguish.

"Jake, Pastor Brown wanted to check on you."

Jake had expected this moment would come when he'd heard the doorbell. He wished his wife would just understand that he simply functioned differently. Relenting, Jake faced the pastor.

"Listen, Pastor. I appreciate the sentiment, I really do. You can't understand where I'm at right now. You just can't. We are different people; you haven't lost what I've lost. So, please just respect my need to handle this my way. Please, I don't want to hear about God right now."

Pastor Brown tilted his head slightly to one side and put a kindly smile on his face. "Jake, our Heavenly Father blessed us with His one and only son, Jesus Christ, who died on the cross for our sins. God understands your pain, Jake. Put your worries on his shoulders now. Hope is with God and our Savior, Jesus Christ now. She was called home, where God needs her in Heaven above."

Jake blinked in disbelief while looking at the pastor's smug righteous face. *Did he really just say Hope was home? Did he really just insinuate that God needed my daughter MORE?*

Jake closed his eyes and then slowly reopened them with a renewed focus and strength. Meeting the pastor's eyes again Jake finally responded, "Get out."

Caught off guard the pastor visibly recoiled at the rebuke. Collecting what remained of his pride the man quietly left the room with the Thorntons still in it.

Having dispatched Pastor Brown, Jake looked again at his wife. Rather than understanding, her face was shrouded in anger. Jocelyn turned and left the room. Finally, Jake broke.

The anger.

The frustration.

The grief.

The loss.

The hopelessness.

Hope.

Jake quietly sobbed until the complete devastation couldn't be pushed deep inside any longer, the part of him that kept the steely exterior simply broke and nothing could stop the flood of anguish from spilling out. Jake openly cried out loud until it hurt to breathe. Then there were no tears left. All that remained to him now was anger. Anger at a God that Pastor Brown believed, needed Jake's Hope more.

CHAPTER 4

CNN Presidential Election Night Coverage

"Welcome back, America! This is Megan Kincade anchoring your election night coverage. As expected, Congressman Ray Tinsley has won the Presidency in a landslide victory. Perhaps more stunning are the gains his party has made in Congress. The House of Representatives has swung to his party with tonight's results. We will have a new Speaker. Additionally, the Senate is now heavily weighted in his favor. A near supermajority at 51-49. Surely the President Elect will frame this as a mandate where, for at least the first two years of his term, significant legislation proposed during the campaign should pass with ease. Stay with us all night. We will bring to you both concession and victory speeches as they happen."

CHAPTER 5

President Elect Ray Tinsley's Campaign HQ

Standing at the podium, Tinsley's smile seemed to be touching each of his ears. He nodded and pointed to people throughout the mass of assembled supporters. Confetti fell upon the crowd as they heartily applauded and chanted his name.

The President Elect raised a hand to quiet them so that he could make his remarks. "America, you have spoken!" Another raucous round of clapping and cheering while Ray Tinsley chuckled and raised both hands.

"My fellow Americans, you have bestowed upon me the greatest privilege any person could ask for. I spoke with Governor Redd moments ago, where he graciously congratulated us on this groundbreaking night." Tinsley was interrupted with another round of standing adoration. He took in the moment while reveling in the thrill of victory and nodding his approval.

"The Oklahoma Governor ran a spirited and hard-fought campaign, yet you have made your desires known. America has spoken and, with this election, made a very clear statement about the future. You have had enough of centuries old dogma and antiquated tradition. You have had your fill of the status quo. We move to a new generation of leadership. We move to a new generation of ideas. It is time for the genesis of a new government! Together, we move forward. Together, we build a new America. This is day one. I look forward to working with our overhauled Congress to effect real and lasting change for this country. Thank you, America!"

An uproarious ovation followed Ray Tinsley off the stage where he met Marvin Miller's greeting, "Succinct and powerful, sir."

Ray Tinsley shook his hand. "Thank you, Marvin. Enjoy the night. Tomorrow we get to work. I want to hit the ground running on the first day of the next legislative session. Start working all the angles on the Amendment right away. Let's get this thing out there while the people and media are behind us. I'll announce in the next press release that you will be Chief of Staff. That should give you a bump in clout while working those phones."

Marvin nodded and replied, "Of course, sir. In my highest hopes, I didn't expect so many Senate seats to go our way. We only need to bring over one from the other side now if our people vote true. I would think that even the slightest media events in our favor could do the trick."

The President Elect returned a half grin before turning to exit with the new First Lady. "This is an emotional time in our country, Marvin. There is bound to be someone out there; charged up, on the verge of imploding. When he does, that will be more than we need to get that vote."

As Tinsley pointed his wife towards the celebration hall, Marvin asked his boss, "Sir, you said, "When he does." How do you know that 'he' will be a he?"

Over the presidential shoulder came the reply. "It's always a 'he', Marvin."

CHAPTER 6

Chatfield, MN

Jake subconsciously considered road signs and terrain features as he drove. He'd just left Jocelyn at their house following a heated argument His head was still there. Jake replayed their fight in his head, turning over the words they shouted back and forth at one another. Hope's death was not a unifying force in their relationship. Rather, the tragedy was eroding it as a flooding river does to house foundations. Their lives were wobbling on the verge of oblivion.

Jocelyn was incensed with Jake's harsh dismissal of Pastor Brown. Rather than accepting Jake's frustration and allowing her husband some grace, she politely walked the pastor to his car and apologized profusely. When she returned to Jake in their daughter's bedroom, Jocelyn unloaded her exasperation and anger on him.

"Jake, what is wrong with you?" She shouted at him. "Pastor Brown is a good man and he was only trying to help you. How could you be so rude and hateful?"

Jake, having just moments earlier completed a breakdown of his own, looked up at her from his rocker. He struggled to see her through the clouds of his emotions. "Jocelyn. The last thing I need right now, the *LAST* thing I want, is for that man or any other to tell me, "God needs Hope." I don't want to hear it! I tried to stop him. I tried kindness. That man needed to push his vengeful God on me. I didn't ask for that." He paused a moment, "Jocelyn, you don't push an angry, scared animal into a corner. That is *exactly* what the two of you did. How can you be surprised or upset about the outcome?"

Jocelyn waited a long moment, weighing the effect of what she wanted to say. As Jake looked at his wife, he could tell the words were heavy on her mind. Her carriage looked as if the pain of whatever it was might eat her up if it went unsaid. Finally, she looked Jake in the eye. "I think the only way I, we, can make it through this, Jake, is to wrap our arms around the idea that God has called her home. I think the only way to avoid having this destroy us is to think of Hope's death as a necessary addition to Heaven. I don't think we're made to understand "why?". I think we just need to have faith that it was God's will."

Jake's anger flashed as he bolted out of the old rocker, shoved his way past Jocelyn, and stormed out of the room. She followed behind him. "Jake, I'm wrestling with all this too! I'm not saying I fully understand it all. To keep from losing my mind I *have* to believe God has plans for Hope."

Jake spun around to face her. "Until now I have kept my mouth shut, I have given you the space to believe what you believe. Since you deemed it necessary to shove your pastor on me, despite my expressed desire to not talk to him, it's my turn now. There. Isn't. A. God, *Jocelyn*! At least not a merciful, bearded man in the clouds pulling our strings like a bunch of damned puppets! If there is a God, then why is there so much evil and devastation in this world? If there is a God, why do you think he favors one set of people over another? If there is a God, and he gives a damn about you, then why did he put the tumor in Hope's brain? Maybe you think His vengeance isn't about you. Maybe deep down you think this is punishment for *my* sins. Tell me, Jocelyn, why would you need or want to believe in such a hateful sadistic God? No, Jocelyn, there isn't a God. Just death. Hope is gone; there is no reason. There is no *plan!"*

Jocelyn fired back. "Clearly I don't understand *why*; it's called faith, Jake. It's messy and imperfect to us. Chaotic even. Where we see a mess, God sees His divine plan. Hope is part of that plan. We don't understand it, Jake, only He does." She pointed at the ceiling. "As for vengeance, we can't say. Maybe it is. He is vengeful, that's in the Bible."

Jake looked at his wife incredulously. "I want no part of your God."

Jocelyn quietly uttered, "I'm sorry you feel that way, Jake."

With those words, Jake did another about-face and made for the door. Jocelyn didn't follow him.

Now he drove. He didn't know where he wanted to go, just away. Away from the home his daughter just died in. Away from fighting with his wife. Away from his problems and despair.

Just away.

With his left hand steering the wayward escape, he glanced down to his right hand on the truck's center console. Inside the console, he knew, rested his loaded firearm. Jake opened the console and looked down at the cold steel. In the grip rested 9 hollow point 9-millimeter rounds while a tenth was seated snugly in the chamber.

Emotion washed over Jake all over again as he thought about putting the barrel in his mouth and pulling the trigger. It would be quick, he thought, that is if he could keep his nerves and do it.

While working out the how and when of the decision to take his life, Jake realized he couldn't kill himself just yet. He had to see through Hope's final arrangements. He had to say good-bye to his little girl first.

CHAPTER 7

Presidential Inauguration – Washington D.C.

President Tinsley surveyed the crowd from the inaugural platform. An ocean of supporters, politicians, and well-wishers from across the nation spread out in all directions before him. The Chief Justice had just issued the Presidential Oath, Tinsley stood at the podium where he would give his first remarks as President.

Just behind him sat the new First Lady, Elizabeth Tinsley. New Vice President, Adam Whitmore and his wife Natalie sat next to the First Lady. Other dignitaries on the stage included General Seth Adams, the new President's Chairman of Joint Chiefs, and William Smithson whose name had been put forward as a candidate for Secretary of Defense. One of the President's staunchest supporters in the Senate, Crosby Moffitt was also on hand along with many counterparts among senior Senate leadership. Congresswoman Madison Regan, who many believed would take over as Speaker of the House, rounded out the political power of the President's new government on stage.

The crowd noise ebbed as the President stood poised to deliver his prepared remarks. Outside the periphery of cameras trained on the President, was his Chief of Staff Marvin Miller. Marvin glanced at the President as he opened his speech the same way countless Presidents before had, "Thank you, President Collins..."

Marvin pulled the iPhone from his suit jacket inner pocket and read the text.

'Will the President turn to center or stay true to the message we discussed?'

Marvin looked over to the President as he had finished the traditional courtesies and began laying out his new direction. "Now America we stand together at the dawn of change...." The Chief of Staff returned to the text and responded.

'The President is committed, no fear on that part. We move forward as planned.'

An immediate response flashed and Marvin read it.

'We have never been so close; keep him in line.'

Marvin smiled and locked the screen before sliding the device back into his pocket, freeing his hands to clap along with thousands of his fellow believers. The elation he felt at that moment was intoxicating. With each powerful declaration from the bully pulpit echoing like the staccato of a rifle's report, the crowd swelled in emotion until they were all on their feet in an uproarious standing ovation. Marvin felt an enlightening sense of pride for his part in engineering his country to this moment.

CHAPTER 8

The Thornton Home – Chatfield, MN

The golf course had sent Jake away for the day. Freezing temperatures across Southern Minnesota were still at least a month away from lifting, the snows of winter still clung to the greens. Mower and cart maintenance had been caught up for weeks, there just wasn't any work for Jake to do. Other volunteers at the shelter had already covered Jake's walks and responsibilities there as well. With nowhere else to turn, Jake decided he would go home to Jocelyn; it was her day off and he hoped to find his wife pleasantly surprised.

As Jake turned the corner onto his street, he saw Pastor Brown's Mercedes sitting curbside in front of his house. The car sitting there wasn't necessarily alarming, he had been visiting Jocelyn to pray often in the weeks following Hope's death. Jake mostly just kept his distance from the man and gave his wife the respect of mourning Hope in her own way. What he did find odd was the fact that he was at the house so early in the day. Most of the visits Jake had been aware of took place on Saturdays or occasionally in the afternoons when the pastor had finished his duties at the church during the week. Jake had assumed that Pastor Brown was simply stopping by on his way home.

Jake looked at the dashboard clock. 9:24 A.M. He second-guessed himself and checked the calendar app on his phone. It was a Thursday. Jake recalled that Jocelyn told him she liked to attend Bible study with the pastor at church every Thursday between 9:00 and 11:00 A.M.

So, why was the pastor here? Was something wrong with Jocelyn: If so, why hadn't she called *him*?

Panic crept into Jake's mind; maybe Jocelyn was suffering some kind of crisis. Then he slowed his mind down enough to reason, if this was an emergency, where is the ambulance?

He slowed to a stop a few houses away. Something inside Jake, an intuition, told him something wasn't quite right. Numerous patrols in Iraq, his experience in Fallujah, had trained his brain to subconsciously look for incongruous details. Jake had developed an inherent knack for noticing small details that could indicate danger. It had probably saved his life. The last time he ignored the instinct, a round of 7.62 had penetrated his body.

That car *should not* be here. Something is *very* wrong.

Jake steered the truck into his driveway. He hoped that Bible study had been canceled and his wife was simply inside praying with the pastor. If that was the case, he didn't want to cause a racket with the garage door. Rather than open the garage door and go inside as he normally would, Jake elected to walk through the front door. Jake held the doorknob, put the key in, and quietly turned it until he heard the bolt retract. He eased the door open and stepped inside.

Jake stilled himself for a moment in the foyer to listen. Expecting to hear a faint conversation, all his ears detected was a startling silence. Moving further into the house Jake looked into the living room where he expected to see the two sitting in prayer on his couches. There was nobody there.

Confused and a little worried he moved to the kitchen, also empty. Jake's insides fluttered with paranoia and fear. *Where could they be?* Although temperatures were still below zero, and it made no sense for anyone to be outside talking, Jake checked the back patio. Nobody. Next, he opened the door going to the garage, maybe the pastor came over and they left together for the church and Bible study? Jocelyn's car sat right where he last saw it.

He knew which rooms of the house hadn't been checked yet, a voice inside told him to just leave. The little voice told him; *you're better off not knowing.*

While Jake's little inside voice told him one thing, his feet operated independently. He slowly climbed the stairs to the second floor. Near the top of the steps, puddled on the floor was the top his wife had been wearing when he had left for the golf course hours ago. As Jake numbly walked down the hall toward the master bedroom, he passed Hope's room. A black pair of men's dress shoes had been kicked off; one came to rest with the toes touching the door. The Marine's face reddened with anger.

Jake steeled himself and forced his mind to quiet the raging storm within. He forced himself to listen. The sound was faint but unmistakable. Jake knew the sound of his wife making love.

Jocelyn was making love at that very moment; without him. Slowly, Jake made one foot go before the other until he was just outside their bedroom door. He stopped and looked down.

Heaped at his feet was a pair of pants he knew very well. Jake always loved the way Jocelyn looked in those pants. From the other side of the door, Jake could now hear a man moaning and grunting.

Jake's hand reached for the doorknob and turned it. Pushing the door open, he saw everything he never wanted to see. The Marine spun on his heels and walked away.

Jocelyn saw the back of her devastated husband as he disappeared down the hall. She didn't follow.

***

3 Days Later

Jake had heavy bags under his eyes, his palms were clammy, and he hadn't shaved since the day he discovered the betrayal of his wife with her spiritual leader. Mostly he had been at a local bar, drinking in hopes of drowning the problem. What little sleep Jake managed was in his truck. The abundance of alcohol and grief mixed with almost no sleep served Jake poorly, he was exhausted.

When alcohol failed to do the trick, he tried his hand at road therapy. Jake didn't know exactly what he was looking for or what he hoped to find. One moment he thought about driving the truck into a snowdrift, hoping to get buried and forgotten until spring. A few miles later, taking a bullet through his mouth sounded better.

Jake's wanderlust had a final destination. A parking spot at Pastor Brown's church, three days after he had walked away from his duplicitous wife. The parking lot around him was full; all the cars empty. Everyone was inside the church for the Sunday service. Except for Jake.

A few hours before, the devastated shell of a man had come into a frightful moment of clarity. He realized the last piece of himself that had any direction died with Hope. She was his rudder. The lifeboat Jake should have been able to cling to, was his first love, Jocelyn. That had was swept away when Jake saw her legs wrapped around Pastor Brown. He was sinking now.

Hope

Jake, she is home now.

He closed his eyes. His fingers wrapped around the grip of the loaded pistol sitting on his console. *Home?*

"God called her home," Jake muttered. "God *needs* her. What about my needs, *Pastor*? What did God have to say about you taking Jocelyn from me?" Jake looked at the front door to the church. He closed his eyes tighter, envisioning the look on Jocelyn's face the moment she realized her husband was going to kill himself in her place of worship. What would her God have to say then? What would her God say about His grand plan when a devoted father and husband blew his brains out in His house? What would be the "Why?" in that? How would that fit into the "Plan"?

Jake slowly opened his eyes to a renewed sense of purpose. Resolved, he deftly opened the truck door. Stepping out, he felt the ice melt crunching under his feet. Jake didn't bother concealing the pistol still in his right hand, he simply walked toward the church. Once inside he would find his cheating wife. Upon making eye contact with Jocelyn, Jake would put the gun barrel in his mouth and pull the trigger.

With his left hand, Jake pulled the front door open. He stepped through the entrance and crossed the threshold, clicking the door's locking mechanism as the doors shut. The contrast of sub-freezing temperatures outside to the well-heated room hardly phased him. Two ushers turned to greet whoever the latecomer was. They were very welcoming; that is until they saw the right hand of the new arrival.

The first usher to notice stood 12 feet in front of Jake and slightly to his left. As the man turned to confront Jake, the bedraggled Marine instinctively raised the weapon to meet the usher's gaze. Jake shook his head in discouragement, but the man took a step toward him. Before the second foot left the ground, a hollow point 9mm round blasted the back of his skull off. Pivoting a few degrees to the right, Jake dispatched the second usher in a similar fashion.

Now fully committed to his end goal, Jake made snap decisions to achieve it. In front of Jake, the mob of people scrambled to find shelter among the pews. A cacophony of screaming and crying broke out; the entire building spiraled into bedlam. Two tall men halfway between Jake and the altar developed a case of let's-play-hero, and charged the determined Marine. Subsequently, they collapsed with matching gunshot wounds to the chest.

In the fog of chaos, Jake lost track of how many rounds he had squeezed off. He deftly dropped the partial magazine to the floor and replaced it with another. During the tactical reload, another hopeful thought to seize the moment to exploit Jake's vulnerability. He wasn't fast enough. Jake leveled him with the round still seated in the chamber.

With the latest victim crumbling to the ground, the outbreak of hero syndrome ended. Jake purposefully made his way up the center aisle, past scores of cowering church patrons until he finally reached his destination. Shrunk behind the altar Jake found Pastor Brown sitting with his knees pulled to his chest, arms wrapped around them, sobbing.

The terrified pastor looked up at Jake and blubbered. "Jake, I'm so sorry, please don't kill me. Have mercy, Jake. I have a wife and kids! I'm too young. I don't want to die. Please don't kill me!"

Jake met the terrified eyes with firm resolve. "God is calling you home, Pastor." Before Pastor Brown could utter a protest, a hollow point round penetrated his left eye and exited through the back of his skull.

Jake turned to the mob of hysterical and sobbing worshipers, looking for one more person. He scanned the faces and quickly found the one he was looking for in the front pew.

Jocelyn.

Jake's wife was frozen in fear, her face streaked with tears. He took a few steps towards her. In the distance, Jake heard the growing wail of sirens. He looked down at his terrified wife. Seeing her now, soaked in fear brought Jake back to that day at the Mayo Clinic, the day they learned Hope was dying. Jake began sobbing. Just as fury had carried Jake through the church, despair in their shared loss washed it away. Jake couldn't think of anything profound to say. All he could muster was a whisper. "Why?"

Jocelyn looked up and saw the boy she once knew, not the murderer standing there now. She murmured, "I don't know, Jake. I'm sorry, I don't know. I'm so sorry, Jake. I was wrong and I'm sorry."

Past the pews and sea of humanity, Jake saw flashing blues and reds refract through the stained glass windows. Over the swell of sirens, Jocelyn heard Jake say, "God didn't take our daughter; cancer did. All I had left was you, Jocelyn." He paused and met her gaze again. "You were all I had left, and you betrayed me." He looked up from his wife toward the door where the carnage had begun only moments ago.   He heard cars come to screeching stops in the parking lot, and he knew that he only had a few more seconds before it was all over.

Jake looked down at Jocelyn. "God isn't real, but this is."

Before she could form a response, Jake put the hot 9 mm barrel in his mouth and pulled the trigger.

CHAPTER 9

CNN Prime Time Coverage of Amendment Debate and Public Response

"Good evening, America. I'm Megan Kincade reporting from the CNN news desk. We are only 12 weeks into the Presidency of Ray Tinsley yet, tonight in Washington debate over the proposed 28th Amendment rages on into the late hours. As you would expect, drama and tensions run high on the debate floor. Meanwhile, a vast throng of protestors has assembled across the National Mall. Images coming into CNN tonight have shown a crowd that stretches from the Capitol building barricades as far as the reflecting pool and Lincoln Memorial. As yet, the enormous crowd seems to be mostly peaceful with conflicts being resolved quickly by Capitol Police. Some arrests have been made for small skirmishes; we will take you to that scene for a detailed report in a moment. First, let's check in with our congressional correspondent, Christina Walker, for an update. Good Evening, Christina."

"Good evening, Megan. After some early procedural maneuvering attempts, the day has been a procession of representatives laying out their prepared remarks regarding gun control. Many of those who have fought to kill this Amendment have pointed to the purpose of the Second Amendment, detailing that it was the one safeguard Americans have to keep political extremism at bay. Of course, the other side has countered with volumes of case files detailing countless, *pointless,* murders that could have been prevented had guns been kept out of the public's hands. Most notably, dare I say *emotionally powerful,* was the testimony of the recent atrocity in Chatfield Minnesota. Representatives from Minnesota each read different statements from survivors of that senseless slaughter. Claims abound that laws meant to keep weapons from the hands of mentally unstable individuals such as Jake Thornton are ineffective and lack the teeth to bring meaningful change. Outstanding community leaders such as Pastor Brown have been needlessly killed because of outdated notions of government tyranny in America. A vote on the Amendment is expected to be called tomorrow morning by Speaker Regan. Our experts expect that it will pass by day's end."

Megan Kincade looked thoughtfully into the camera, shuffled a few papers, and pressed the correspondent. "So, Speaker Regan expects to have the votes she needs for passage?"

"Megan, many opinion polls, including Reuters and the New York Times, indicate overwhelming support for this Amendment. Additionally, Senate Majority Leader Moffitt has been making the rounds on both broadcast networks and cable news. He's laying out the case for passage in an attempt to gain public support. Those who oppose this Amendment seem to think all this PR is an indication that President Tinsley and his party feel they may be just short on the votes they need. Our experts here at CNN, however, believe that the Amendment has the votes it needs in the House, with a dozen or so to spare.

While in the Senate, the way seems more clear-cut. Only one defection is necessary to gain the supermajority needed for Amendment passage. Many evangelical Senators are at a loss over the senseless murder of Pastor Brown; a man the community considered high caliber. Remember, Megan, they only need one. We think they will get that vote from a defector out of the Bible Belt."

Megan nodded. "Thank you for your report, Christina. Keep us posted." She paused a moment while the screen switched Christina Walker's camera shot to the protests across the National Mall. Megan transitioned. "Now we take you to live coverage of the protest growing outside the Capitol building. Percy, what can you tell us?"

Percy Arrington, an award winning journalist, had covered a myriad of world events for CNN in his career. He had been among the faces Americans became familiar with while embedded among the Army's 3rd Infantry Division in their push across Iraq toward Baghdad during Operation Iraqi Freedom. He had covered war, natural disasters, and civil unrest. America knew him as the man CNN put in dangerous situations to get the story. If you saw Percy on your television, there was danger afoot.

With his poised baritone and a hint of dramatic inflection, Percy opened. "Good evening, Megan. I report tonight from the front lines of this historic march for gun rights. While much of the day has been a sea of humanity holding signs with clichés and fear tactics, I can say there is a sense of anticipation in the air. Good sense and organization at this time may yield to violence. An anti-gun faction clashed earlier today near the Washington Monument with a group of gun rights advocates.

What began as shouting and finger pointing spiraled into a virtual rumble. Arrests were made and since then, the massive gathering of mostly pro-gun Americans has become increasingly hostile. I have personally overheard some chant about a revolution, Megan. I fear that at some point all the guns I cannot see will be drawn and I will be reporting live from the scene of a mass murder."

Megan Kincade drew a rehearsed look of concern across her face and pressed on. "Percy, Capitol Police have provided a press release to CNN that they are diligently monitoring the situation. They claim to have checkpoints all around the mall where they are screening for firearms. Further, they have fortified many barricades and crowd control points with beefed-up security and crowd control assets; or so they claim. Are you reporting at this time that you believe this protest is, in fact, an armed revolutionary militia?"

CNN's danger man struck a defensive posture then looked assertively at the camera. "Megan, I believe something very serious is happening at a checkpoint not fifty yards from where I am reporting to you! Suddenly the mob of people gathered there became very loud and seemed to be pressing up toward the barricades. I'm not sure, but I caught in my peripheral something flying toward the security officials; it may have been on fire! Megan, I believe I just witnessed some incendiary device being used!"

The lead anchor sat higher at her news desk as if her posture reflected the alerted moods and anxieties of human beings around the world witnessing something truly extraordinary. She could almost see herself accepting the Emmy now. Before she could continue her award winning coverage, Percy Arrington was visibly shoved about as the wave of the crowd moved around him in all directions. He grunted to stand tall against the chaos. Just as it appeared he had endured yet another brush with mortal danger on live T.V., there was a pink spray. The man crumpled below the view of the camera.

CHAPTER 10

Ground Zero, National Mall Washington D.C.

Smoke hung heavy on the twilight air. Everywhere it floated across the National Mall, it carried an awful confluence of odors. David Barrett, a retired aircraft mechanic from Texas, had flown in to make his voice heard to those debating his rights in the Capitol. He now found himself hunkered among the dead and dying in the expanse of misery around him. Murderous gunfire erupted only moments ago, yet to David, it seemed to have lasted hours. He had seen a man only feet from him hurl a lit Molotov cocktail at the security checkpoint. David followed its awful trajectory through the air toward the law enforcement standing sentry.

Time seemed to slow as it fell. David held his breath. Horrified that a person in his midst had resorted to such a vile act, he hoped that the flaming projectile would fall harmlessly to the ground. He hoped the man's aim was as awful as his judgment.

David's hopes were all in vain.

As the deadly weapon fell among the crowd of armed guards, it struck one of them on his exposed neck. A wrenching scream of agony preceded the unmistakable, nauseating odor of burning flesh. The unfortunate soul screamed and flailed on the ground as he attempted to roll out the flames.

David wanted to help the man, yet feared what running at the line would mean for his own safety. In that sad and helpless moment, he observed some of the officers raise their weapons and aim in the direction of the attacker. David thought it was an intimidation tactic at first.

It wasn't.

The line had opened fire on the crowd as a whole. All around him, where living, breathing Americans had been standing only a few moments ago, were bloody bodies. David had the sense to dive to the ground in hopes that he would be missed. His clothing and hands were slick with fresh blood while the rank odor of humans letting go of their bowels mixed with the iron-rich tang of blood in the air. His ears ached from the percussion of rifle reports which were constant and ruthless. Moaning and screaming among the panicked only added to the fog of confusion and fear.

David dared not move as the rifles fell silent, he didn't know if the carnage had reached its conclusion or if the men were all reloading. After a brief pause, he heard what sounded like firecrackers a little further away, and felt his gut plunge at the realization that the horrific nightmare he had just survived was repeating itself elsewhere. Even now men and women, Americans, were being slaughtered. He blinked his eyes and hoped that this was all a very visceral, terrible nightmare. He didn't wake up from it. The reality was that he had survived, at least so far, a criminal atrocity. David considered what he needed to do next to survive.

At that moment his eyes settled on the limp frame of a small child. A girl. She couldn't have been more than 9 or 10 years old. Then, he became angry. Very angry. He knew that someone had dragged that girl here to be a part of this day. *Too young to have political motivations or hate in her,* he thought. Her fear was frozen on her face in death.

Something had to be done. He dared to move his head around a little to see if there were other survivors. David was shocked to see a group of men and women around him slowly low crawling toward the gunmen.

He joined the crawling procession. The old Texan didn't know what would happen when they got up on the shooters, or if they would even make it. He did know that he was pissed off and of a mind to do something about it. Locking eyes with another crawler he could see the rage and determination on his face. David and this stranger had contrasting appearances. David was an older, white, tall, and stout man with salt and pepper hair. This man looked to be in his twenties or thirties, Native American, slender, with long black hair. While David imagined their lives were very different, he assumed they had more in common than being caked with blood. They were both very angry Americans with a burning desire to avenge this atrocity.

David nodded at his companion. "Hey, fella, what the hell are we going to do if we get there? There's just a few of us!"

The stranger whispered back with a half-grin, "We're not alone, friend. Look behind us."

David complied. It seemed as if the corpses were crawling immediately to their rear. But the hundreds of angry Americans storming toward them took his breath away. "Oh my God!"

Acknowledging David, the stranger said, "Yeah, man. I'm sick of it, too. They got some guns, but the bastards won't get all of us. We may die today, man, but we'll take some of them with us."

David briefly considered the dead girl he saw just a moment ago, then steeled himself and said, "Alright then."

Moments before the swell of angry Americans reached David, he looked at the stranger. They nodded at each other then stood to join the wave. Accelerating to meet the mob's sprint, they were crossing the narrow remaining distance toward shooters. David glimpsed a body crumple just to his left a split second before he heard the shot's report. It didn't matter; they were committed now. Younger men ran past David on his left and right flanks. His breathing was already growing labored in the short distance he had covered, yet his adrenaline and the fear of being crushed or shot pushed him onward.

Younger and faster protesters reached the objective only seconds before David in a crescendo of violence and screaming. A few brief staccatos of gunfire erupted in protest and self-defense; it was for naught. Easily overwhelmed, the gunfire ceased as quickly as it started. David arrived as the hand-to-hand combat ceased; his companions had immobilized the position. At his feet lay a half dozen plainclothes American citizens and what he determined were a few dozen black-clad security agents.

There were no firearms left on the ground. David assumed that the weapons had surely been liberated from these men and were now serving a new mission in new hands. He followed the crowd and soon determined that he had been correct in his assessment. The old Texan's eyes just happened to glimpse the young man he'd been crawling on the ground beside. He held an M4 combat rifle in a low, ready posture. Approaching him, the man nodded and said, "We're in it now, friend. Did you find any weapons?"

David shook his head.

The man responded, "They all had 9 millimeter pistols still holstered when we overran them. I grabbed one. Didn't think to search for extra magazines though. You want it?"

David numbly nodded. "Yeah ok. But, isn't it done? I mean they're all dead right?"

The stranger shook his head. "No, man, this isn't over. Those bastards were following orders. Someone gave them rules of engagement to follow. Didn't you notice, man? Not a single crowd control munition was used! They jumped straight to live rounds! That's not standard protocol for a protest of any kind. Think, man! You've seen countless protests on the news over the years, anytime a protest turns violent it's all: gas, bean bags, or foam rounds that knock people silly. Hell, I've even seen fire trucks turned on to crowds at a pipeline protest. Not one time, never, did they start with live rounds! An order like this came from way higher than a head of security, chief of police, or a damn mayor, man!" The man nodded at the Capitol building.

Simply imagining what the stranger implied made David's skin crawl. Still, he found his hand reaching for and wrapping around the pistol that had been offered to him. The stranger nodded his approval at David and said, "Might want to sweep back to where I found this and pick up any magazines that are left. They should all be the same caliber; it's issued to them."

David began walking toward the dead officers then stopped and turned to the stranger, "Where are we going next?"

The stranger responded matter of factly. "The congressional office buildings," he pointed at the nearest one. "They are all connected by tunnels. We start there."

David thought a moment and asked, "Ok, but don't you think they'll send reinforcements? Or the National Guard?"

When the response came it chilled David to the bone, "They *will* come. We will probably *all* die. We don't do this for us man, this is for our future. Kids died today; I saw them gun down a little girl back there. It's not about politics anymore, this is about right and wrong. Somebody wants to silence us."

David knew that his moment of truth had arrived. He could simply walk away and let his fellow Americans write the chapter of history that was about to occur all around him. Or, he could follow it through to his own end. He realized that millions of Americans must be watching on live T.V. at that very moment. Some would be at home wishing they could lend their hands to make right what had gone wrong. Others, he thought, sat on their couches in fear and would resign themselves to the sidelines. David decided that he wanted to speak for those who were angry and wanted to do something about it.

"Alright, friend, I'm right behind you. My name is David, by the way. What's yours?"

The long-haired Native extended his hand. "Hey man, I'm Frank. Let's go."

David bent to pick up two magazines from the belt of a dead officer and followed his new friend Frank.

CHAPTER 11

FBI Incident Command Center
Washington D.C.

A makeshift field command center was established mere blocks from where the violence started just hours before. Desean Purnell had been designated incident commander by the director himself moments after the fighting had started. A rising star among FBI agents in D.C., Agent Purnell was thrilled by the opportunity. He glanced about the small room to see if all his appointed liaisons from other agencies were on hand and ready to start giving him updates. In his notebook, he scribbled: *ATF, D.C. police, Secret Service, National Guard* with checks next to all of them. As he looked at the ID badges for the next two people it gave him pause, CIA and NSA.

"Ok everyone thanks for being here, let's get this started. The Director wants this handled on the up and up, airtight prosecutions. Obviously before we start processing the evidence the Capitol will need to be secure. D.C.P.D., situation?"

D.C.'s liaison officer curtly replied, "We're still assessing casualty totals. I can confirm at this moment, 43 of our officers have been killed. At least twice that number injured; some in critical condition, or still in surgery." Shaking her head, she finished, "I can't give you an accurate count or status yet of our firearms."

Agent Purnell scribbled a few notes down. "Thank you. ATF you're up."

ATF's liaison scratched his cheeks a moment and sighed before giving his report. "At this moment I have agents scouring the Mall from one end to the other. As yet, we have not found a single firearm among the dead protestors nor have we found so much as a slingshot among those we've detained on the Mall. Nothing. Seems the screening procedures implemented coming into the city worked well in that regard."

Purnell frowned and looked at his ATF counterpart. "Nothing? Keep looking; for God's sake don't let that out to the media!" He scribbled a few more notes before looking at the National Guard officer, "You're up next, Major."

The major opened a folder on the table in front of him and reported, "We've secured all government buildings. Per rules of engagement, any resistance possessing a firearm was shot on sight as we cleared buildings. I can report at this time any deceased within the operating area have been exclusively security, building maintenance workers, or congressional staffers. We have not identified at this time any Senators or Representatives among the casualties. Furthermore ..."

Agent Purnell held up a hand to pause the major's report and looked at the Secret Service. "Safe rooms?"

Nodding his head Secret Service liaison replied, "Yes, when the shooting started, congressional leadership was ushered into shelter procedures by security."

Agent Purnell nodded and scribbled a note before looking back to the National Guard officer. "Apologies, please go on, Major."

The officer continued, "Furthermore, we have assumed security of all routes into the Capitol. Additionally, I have put air assets on standby."

Purnell raised an eyebrow and queried the major, "Air assets?"

The man nodded. "Apaches and Blackhawks."

Agent Purnell nodded in approval. "Very good. Thank you, Major. Rules of Engagement for use of air assets, I will need you to provide me with everything you have in that regard." He did not wait for a reply. "NSA?"

NSA technician, Annie Nguyen curtly offered, "I have been directed to advise you that our surveillance assets are available to assist. Our full cooperation is at your disposal."

"Assets? You have people trained and available to use on the scene?" Agent Purnell looked at Nguyen quizzically.

Nguyen shook her head. "Satellite intelligence."

"Ms. Nguyen, I think this is just the biggest protest gone wrong in our history. Not sure what we will need to image from space that we haven't already observed."

Annie shrugged, "You think this is over?"

Before Purnell could frame his response, Jennifer Miller from the CIA spoke up.

"Agent Purnell. I think you need to consider the fact that we have only scratched the surface of what is going on here. Tonight was just the beginning. A CNN correspondent was killed on live television. America was watching. Leadership will frame this as a domestic insurgence, the acts of an extreme few.

They will partner with the media to spin this as domestic terrorism. Before this night is over, the media will have America believing that a hostile, armed militia came to the Capitol today to start a revolution. Some will eat that narrative by the spoonful. Still, others will assume, correctly mind you, that we fired on our own people first. In a sense, the revolution angle isn't wrong, they will just cloud who fired the first shots. My job and the jobs of my colleagues is to provide intelligence to our elected policymakers. I am here, specifically, to advise you the threat is real and will be ongoing."

Agent Purnell nodded his head thoughtfully, jotted down a few more notes, and then addressed the room. "Alright, thank you, everyone. Keep me posted as things change. Meeting adjourned. Major, can we have a word in private please, sir?"

As the command center emptied, Purnell pulled up a chair directly across from the National Guard officer.

"Major, let's assume Ms. Miller's alarmist warning to be an accurate assessment. Let's assume for a moment that tonight was the beginning of something bigger. For just a moment we assume that tonight was more than a simple protest gone terribly wrong, that it was, in fact, a flashpoint for a revolution. Could you confidently assure me that you are capable of defending the Capitol with the assets you have at hand?"

Without hesitation, the major offered a simple response. "Agent Purnell, if enough Americans agree on a single purpose and take action, there aren't enough bullets in all the National Guard armories to do a damn thing about it. There's a reason the Japanese aborted thoughts of an invasion on the mainland back in World War II. Admiral Yamamoto famously said, 'I fear all we have done is to awaken a sleeping giant and fill him with a terrible resolve.'" The major took a pull of dark coffee from the mug sitting in front of him and continued. "Not only was he referring to America's industrial infrastructure and abilities; he knew there would be pissed off Americans defending every city block or old farm with hunting rifles from the Pacific to the Atlantic. That was 1941, Agent Purnell. As we sit here today, Americans privately own more firearms and ammunition than the rest of the world combined. So, to answer your question; no, I cannot hope to hold this city with the assets currently at my disposal. We would need to utilize a vast network of force multipliers that I currently do not have access to, along with real-time imaging from space and drone assets. Any force hoping to defeat the American people will need to deny them the use of space assets, which would hamper their ability to communicate and organize. Further, policymakers will need to control the media and deny any potential insurrection the ability to spread propaganda. Finally, should there be a confrontation, the less constrictive the rules of engagement the better. Break their will to fight. Failure to control the high ground, propaganda, and execute violent engagements decisively would almost certainly mean a guerilla style conflict the government isn't likely to win."

Agent Purnell sat back in his chair and rubbed his eyes. Soaking in the major's words he hoped the assessment was just a worst-case doomsday scenario that he wouldn't truly have to worry about. He hoped that cooler heads would prevail and that by morning some version of a normal life would resume. Agent Purnell wondered if a sleeping giant had indeed been awoken tonight, and if so, what would that mean for the future of his country?

CHAPTER 12

White House Situation Room

President Tinsley entered the White House situation room where his cabinet and senior congressional leadership had been awaiting his arrival. Many sitting around the room looked as if they had been up all night. The President himself had spent much of the evening in the White House bunker. Now, as the sun rose over Washington, a scene of carnage was in plain sight for the world to see and the country at large held its breath waiting to see what would happen next.

President Tinsley took his accustomed seat and the briefing started. Speaker of the House, Madison Regan, addressed the President first.

"Good morning, Mr. President. I'm happy to see you are well. Once security gave us assurances that all was secure in the late hours, I convened an emergency meeting of the House. We passed a resolution that grants you the ability to quickly deal with the violent acts of these extremists. Essentially, it sweeps away red tape and oversight committees regarding the use of force against those moving on government buildings and

representatives here at the Capitol. More specifically the resolution streamlines and consolidates National Guard units in
surrounding states to operate by your command to defend the
Capitol. Those who do not disperse and are apprehended will
fall under the umbrella of existing domestic terrorism statutes.
Additionally, we have the votes needed to push the 28th Amendment over to the Senate. I have been assured by Senator Moffitt
that there is support for both the Amendment and the aforemen-
tioned resolution sufficient enough for you to move forward as
needed."

President Tinsley nodded his approval before turning his attention to his National Security Advisor, Savannah Lasser.

"Savannah, what are your people saying?"

Savannah distributed a copy of her brief to everyone in attendance before she offered her prepared remarks.

"Thank you, Mr. President. Our analysts are still working
the situation. I can, however, report at this time on a few key
points. On a normal day, our people pick up chatter on social
media from both home and abroad regarding anti-government
sentiments, conspiracy theories, and low level civil unrest
movements. In the past few hours, signals intelligence has been
flooded with a far higher volume of threat assessments from
within our borders. There is a real grassroots effort in many
states, especially in the Midwest and South to organize protests,
and more, as a direct response to last night. Some of the chatter
is the normal stuff we see daily; just more of it. More concerning, there is talk of actually putting together militias to
commandeer local National Guard assets. Satellite imagery at
this point does not indicate an actual move by these folks just
yet. There is however a large gathering around Fredericksburg

Virginia. Some of the people within this gathering, we have determined, have been among those talking of organizing militias. Further, we have identified many of them to be registered firearms owners. They fall into the group of what we consider to be a higher domestic risk group. These people haven't yet made any overt moves on government assets, but we feel that their proximity to the Capitol bears mentioning."

President Tinsley glanced over the brief. "Savannah, is it your opinion that this Virginia group is a threat to the Capitol? Are they a second wave following up last night's attack?"

"Mr. President, I do not have a smoking gun that these people are a clear and present danger," she said. "I can say that their proximity and known sentiments are factors that should warrant additional monitoring."

"Ok good; stay on it. Matter of fact, get a drone orbiting over that area right now," added Tinsley. "I want constant visuals of those people. Any hint of violence, I want it taken care of quickly. Bill, Seth, what can you have in the area in the event we need a quick response? Can a drone carry enough to neutralize the threat?"

Everyone in the room sat a little straighter and looked around at each other. Senate Minority leader, Susan Brady interjected before the Secretary of Defense or general could answer the President, "Mr. President, couldn't this gathering be something as simple as some Civil War reunion? I mean Chancellorsville is right there."

President Tinsley shook his head dismissively., "No, Susan; these people are a clear threat."

Secretary of Defense William Smithson answered, "Mr. President, a drone flight to surveil American citizens is already pushing the envelope. A strike?!"

Tinsley cut him off. "This is an unprecedented time, Bill; get a drone over Fredericksburg. Now, can we load enough ordnance on it to wipe out the threat or not?"

"Sir, typically a drone carries two Hellfire missiles when deployed to a hostile area," Chairman of Joint Chiefs, General Seth Adams piped up. "It may take some logistical maneuvering to get a drone outfitted for strikes over American soil, maybe hours. Now, it is possible that even when we get the aircraft fitted out to execute a strike, the result would not be the complete annihilation of the target. That would depend on how many threats are on the ground and how tightly grouped they are. One option could be an AC-130. As we speak, a new weapons system is being tested on the platform. We could order the crew to divert from their testing mission to support Capital defense."

"Good. Get the drone loitering over the area and have the gunship on standby. Bill; status report on our stateside military forces?"

Secretary Smithson glanced over his prepared report.

"I've directed senior military leadership to maintain a state of readiness and to cancel all leave. Scheduled training evolutions are being suspended so that units can mobilize quickly. The Pacific Fleet is deployed around the world. The Lincoln is in the Indian Ocean, Roosevelt is in the China Sea, and Vinson is in the South Pacific. Norfolk's ships are also either all deployed or in retrofit. Air National Guards in Hawaii and Alaska have been notified to fly combat air patrols to ensure nobody sneaks up on us while we deal with this situation."

"That's a good start," Tinsley replied. "I want you to make sure commanders are clear on this, they are to stay on their posts and not interact with the communities at all. No aggression or support at all unless ordered otherwise. Lockdown these installations, mission-essential staff are the only ones to be on post. I want these so-called militias as far away as possible from those assets. Also, get the word out to all the National Guard posts that there is intelligence indicating that they are being targeted by these terrorists. Make sure Guard units maintain the highest level of vigilance, Bill."

"Yes, Mr. President."

Tinsley looked around the room and queried, "Anything else?"

Around the room, heads of career politicians and political appointees shook in silence. If there was a dissenting voice in the group, not a soul spoke up. Those who would normally be a voice of opposition had nothing to say. It was as if what had just transpired left most of those in attendance in a state of shock.

"Very good; the meeting is adjourned." Chief of Staff Marvin Miller had been sitting in silence observing the meeting when Tinsley gestured to him. "Marvin, a word please." As the room emptied, Marvin pulled a chair closer to the President and sat down. President Tinsley asked him, "Marvin, what are your thoughts regarding measures the Congress has taken to enable my ability to handle this emergency?"

Marvin considered the President a moment, turning the response over in his head before he answered.

"Mr. President, it's a good start. I found it interesting that there was no mention of latitude regarding how we can surveil the country for threats. The measures seem to be very reactionary. Don't you think it would be more prudent to get out ahead of this before the country lights itself on fire? Maybe I am being alarmist, but I'll refer to Ms. Lasser's report. Terms such as 'grass roots' and 'militias' make my skin crawl. By the time these militias are organized enough to warrant a reaction, I fear the situation will already be out of hand."

"Just say it, Marvin, what did you have in mind?"

"Mr. President, these measures brought to us by Congress don't go far enough. You need to declare martial law immediately; on a national level. We need to unburden ourselves from the massive time waste of obtaining warrants through the court system if we want to end this rebellion before it gains traction. We need to identify those who are promoting this insurrection through social media and other methods and silence their damaging propaganda. The long term wellness of the country cannot be compromised by senseless and prolonged court proceedings that will no doubt be bogged down by technicalities or legal maneuvering. We need to squash this quickly." Marvin paused for a moment to get a drink of water and then continued. "Mr. President, over a decade ago American forces were compelled to conduct a counter insurgency in Afghanistan under senselessly burdensome restrictions. They called it 'heroic restraint.' What *actually* happened in Afghanistan; a shadow government grew under their noses and bled our people at every turn. Do not make the same mistakes, sir. Decapitate this monster before they arrive on the White House lawn."

The President nodded and said, "Alright, Marvin. Draw up the martial law proclamation. I'll talk to Bill and Seth about this situation over at Fredericksburg."

CHAPTER 13

Fredericksburg, VA

A centralized bonfire burned as Americans from all over Virginia, and a handful from other states milled about socializing. Many of them had seen each other annually for years. Men and women would chat about what their families had been up to, who added kids to households, job gossip, and even spirited debates about government happenings. This particular reunion carried with it a different feeling. Nearby, in Washington D.C., the previous night had been one of violence and uncertainty.

Much of the talk centered around news reports they had seen or read regarding the protest and ensuing massacre on the National Mall. Many feared for what the violence would cost the country long term, a few argued the clash was a one-time event, while others argued that actions could escalate. Still, others held their Civil War replica rifles and uneasily joked about the possibility that pulling their modern counterparts out of gun safes may be necessary before all was said and done. Remarks of that sort triggered chuckles and good-natured macho talk followed by a renewed debate over the proposed 28th Amendment.

Nearby, large groups of kids played in a field, chasing each other and throwing balls around. Not a soul uttered words of hate or judgment. All who came to play were accepted as friends.

In the morning, their moms and dads would reenact the Battle of Chancellorsville.

CHAPTER 14

CNN News Update

"Good evening, America. I'm Megan Kincade coming to you live from the CNN news desk. Just one day after the horrible events on the National Mall, where pro-gun extremists launched their attack on the Capitol, CNN has received reports from our congressional correspondent. The House has approved a resolution of emergency powers for the President to deal with threats to the government. We cannot yet confirm how the Senate has voted. The 28th Amendment vote, we have been told, *has* passed the House as well. All eyes now turn to the Senate. In other news, an unnamed source has told CNN that President Tinsley views the emergency powers resolution as 'insufficient'. The source believes a declaration of martial law from the Oval Office is imminent. Stay tuned; we will bring you the news as it happens."

CHAPTER 15

Reaper 01, 10,000 feet over Virginia. 2341 EST. 30 April 2021

Captain Tony Boyton, call sign 'Chavez', keyed his communication link to acknowledge the highly unusual order he had just received. Chavez and his crew had been conducting weapon testing on their AC-130J gunship in the area of Fort Bragg, North Carolina. The Air Force had installed a high-energy laser weapon into the airframe in an attempt to achieve higher precision results than the "Crowd Pleaser", GAU 25 had for decades. Granted, it hadn't quite produced as impressive a site if you were watching from the ground where the laser itself was invisible to the naked eye. Early returns on the accuracy, however, were stunning.

The first directive in itself received by the pilot was not an unusual order per se. Command had ordered an unscheduled diversion for aerial refueling while en route to a secondary live fire target north of their location. Chavez had simply assumed this was all some training the crew had not been briefed on to gauge how well they adjusted to improvisation. He took the diversion in stride, and moments later the aircraft made its rendezvous with the tanker.

After wrapping up a routine refuel navigator 2nd Lieutenant Darrell Song, call sign 'Mo' keyed his internal communications to the pilot, "Sir, data link from the Pentagon with coordinates. 38.3032 degrees North, 77.4605 degrees West."

Chavez responded, "Copy that, Mo." The captain made a slight correction to put the gunship on course, then checked in with his fire control officer (FCO), Captain Charles Masters, call sign 'Chucky'. "Chucky, we have coordinates, confirm targeting information."

Chucky opened his secure data link and read the message out loud to the pilot. "Proceed to coordinates 38.3032 degrees north, 77.4605 degrees west. Make contact with Predator drone orbiting over the target for real-time target locations before commencing attack attitude. Once acquired, eliminate all hostiles. Nearby town off limits. Clearance to engage from POTUS." Chucky blinked a moment as he processed everything. He read it again internally, looking for any words he might have missed such as 'drill'. No, it was a legitimate order for live fire on American soil outside of firing ranges and training scenarios. This was real. "Chavez, they want us to engage...Americans. This order is from the *President*."

Chavez keyed his mike, "Roger that. FCO, standby to acquire drone feed. Should be any minute." His response was crisp, as if he had sanitized the words before they left his mouth.

An order of this sort was unprecedented, Chavez knew that. The officer also knew that a mere 24 hours prior, the Capitol had been the site of a domestic terror attack. This target must be a follow-up threat equal in severity to that of the first wave.

Chavez reasoned they were receiving a lawful order from the Commander in Chief to protect Americans. *Against all enemies, foreign AND domestic*, he thought.

A moment later Chucky broadcasted to the crew. "Drone feed acquired. Large groups of vehicles. A handful of campers; looks like numerous trucks and SUVs. No apparent mounted weapons. Navigation, can you reconcile our grid coordinates with the feed to confirm the target?"

Mo responded, "Copy that, FCO." A brief pause while the navigation officer checked the drone's observed coordinates against their own. "Nav to FCO. Coordinates are good. Coordinates match that large gathering of vehicles and personnel in those fields just outside the town."

Chavez put the aircraft into a left-hand pylon turn in orbit over the field below. He double checked all his instruments and then engaged the autopilot to hold its attack orientation so that he could monitor and confirm targets. He turned to his co-pilot, 1st Lieutenant Sam Wilcox, call sign 'Pigpen'.

"Keep an eye on instruments, Pigpen."

The junior officer nodded in acknowledgment.

Meanwhile, Captain Masters curtly replied to the navigator. "Copy that, Mo. I have large groupings of vehicles and personnel out in the open field up on my monitor." He glanced in the direction of one of the aircraft's sensor operators (SO), Staff Sergeant Sean Patton, call sign 'Deadman'. "Deadman, multiple vehicles in the open field with personnel walking about. Personnel and vehicles are the targets; the nearby town is off limits. Advise when you have acquired the target."

Patton had been flying the AC-130 for over a decade. He cut his teeth supporting Special Forces from high above Afghanistan. In the rugged terrain of Afghanistan, rarely had the vehicles used by the Taliban ever been as closely grouped as these were. He spotted the assembly of vehicles and heat signatures of humans without any trouble at all. Within moments his screen matched that of his FCO. Deadman simply replied, "Targets acquired, sir."

Chucky studied the screen with a critical eye. Like his SO, Captain Masters had thousands of hours flying combat missions in the gunship. What glared at him now, brighter even than the glowing heat signatures on his screen, was how the people below were acting. They didn't appear to *act* or *move* how he would expect a hostile force to move. This particular group on his screen seemed to have no operational awareness at all. They moved as if they had nothing to fear. Not only that, they were just out in the open. These men were making no attempts to conceal themselves or their movements.

Chucky keyed his mike and raised the electronic warfare officer, 1st Lieutenant Danny O'Donnell, call sign 'Irish'. "Irish, you picking anything up?"

Irish's voice filled Chucky's headset with his distinctive New York accent and said,. "Mostly a lot of meaningless noise. I've heard the words 'Civil War' a few times though."

Chucky nodded his head and decided to set aside his reservations to carry through with the mission. He clicked the comms button and said, "FCO to SO."

"Go for SO, Captain," Deadman replied.

Chucky said, "Alright. When command gives clearance, why don't we start with a 105 ground proximity round over the largest gathering of pickups and SUVs to make fleeing more difficult?" asked Chucky. "From there we'll drop 30's on them, starting with the largest groups first and working our way out to the strays. Any vehicles that escape the initial assault we'll target with the guided GBU-39 SDBs (Small Diameter Bombs) to mitigate collateral damage in the areas outside of the target zone. If need be, we can hit single targets with the laser."

Deadman calmly affirmed, "Copy that."

Chucky keyed his radio to make contact with the aircraft's commander.

"Chavez, fire control and sensor have targets on screen. Vehicles and personnel in the field; town off limits. Attack plan in place. Waiting on clearance to fire."

Chavez replied with a succinct, "Copy FCO." He checked his aircraft's data link again, in the back of his mind the officer hoped this was all a very realistic drill. He hoped an order was forthcoming to wave off the attack. When no such message appeared in his queue the pilot switched to his external communication link and checked in with his command. "Reaper 01 to command. On station awaiting clearance to engage."

A low baritone voice answered his call. "Command to Reaper 01; you are cleared to engage targets."

Chavez nodded and copied the sender's message back. Next, he glanced down at his HUD (Heads Up Display) to confirm the target area his FCO and SO were monitoring matched his own. Before Chavez pulled his clear to fire trigger, which would signal the crew to carry out their deadly mission, he made one final transmission over the ship's internal communication network.

"Chavez to crew. Clearance granted to engage targets. Just to be clear, the town is off limits. I repeat you are not to fire at anything within the town." Chavez took a slow breath in and then depressed the button that indicated to his FCO he was cleared to execute their lethal directive.

Within seconds Chucky saw the light which granted him authority to begin directing the aircraft's munitions onto the field 10,000 feet below. "FCO to SO, clear to engage."

Deadman cleared his throat and answered, "Copy. Select 105." He used the joystick at his control station to center the 105 mm howitzer reticle over the largest grouping of vehicles. Settling where he wanted the deadly shell to explode feet above the ground, devastating the area with high explosives and shrapnel, he calmly squeezed the trigger.

Toward the rear of Reaper 01, the 105 mm howitzer lurched in recoil and the airframe shuddered as the shell sped toward the Earth.

Deadman watched his screen intently. A split second later it flashed white, only briefly due to the sudden release of heat caused by the munition exploding. As the heat flash subsided from the screen Deadman could see the weapon had done exactly what it was meant to. Every vehicle within the weapon's deadly explosion radius was destroyed and smoldering. Smaller bits of heat reflective matter sprinkled his screen, he knew of course that would be a grisly scene of body parts. His training and experience had taught the seasoned operator to block out thoughts of the people who had just been killed, so he did.

Just then his headset came alive with the voice of his FCO.

"Good shot, SO. See those trucks just west of the impact area? I have movement around those vehicles."

Deadman quickly responded. "Copy. Vehicles and foot traffic to the west."

Chucky came back promptly over the radio. "Clear to fire."

Deadman selected the craft's 30 mm cannon. While it didn't quite have the punch or blast radius of the 105, Deadman knew the rate of fire and accuracy would more than make up for it. He confirmed the change to his FCO, "Copy. Select 30."

Once the reticle on his screen matched that of the weapon he desired, Deadman centered it over the next largest grouping of vehicles just west of his original shot. One second, he adjusted for the anticipated movement of the ground targets. The Taliban had always run like cockroaches who'd just had a light shone on them in these moments, but those bastards had some clue as to what was happening. The movement below the gunship right now was slow. They were probably still trying to figure what had hit them. Deciding the target didn't require much lead if any, he re-centered the reticle and squeezed the trigger three times.

While the report of the 105 was like a lumbering thunderclap from the heavens, the 30 mm cannon was more akin to a hammer smartly striking a wood plank. *BOP! BOP! BOP!*

Screens in front of the SO and FCO each reflected the same thorough devastation. Where Chevrolet, Ford, and Dodge pickups had once sat astride in the tree line below, now only smoldering wrecks, splintered trees, and body parts littered the torn earth.

Chucky raised his SO again. "Good shot, Deadman. Another line of vehicles bunched up door to door; just south of the last shots. You see them?"

"Yeah, I see them," Deadman answered.

"30 again?" asked Chucky.

Deadman nodded. "Yeah, sounds good."

He moved the targeting reticle over the next assembly of vehicles to the south as his FCO had indicated. With a small adjustment of his control stick, his targeting reticle was once again centered where he desired the ordnance to land. He pulled the trigger two more times. *BOP! BOP!* As before, two rounds left the aircraft and intercepted the desired targets below with awful and thorough effect.

Chucky scanned the screens at his control panel in the hopes that their work was done. His hopes were dashed when he observed a dozen white-hot signatures running by foot north and east. He relayed the discovery to Deadman who dispatched the runners with one well-placed 30 mm round. Chucky scanned the field below once again only to discover the fading white signatures of severed body parts and glowing fires. The officer was about to update his pilot with an 'all clear' when he caught a flash of movement toward the edge of his screen. He squinted and decided what he saw was a smaller, fast moving vehicle, maybe a dirt bike, leaving the firing area toward the town. He quickly brought up communication with his SO.

"Deadman, you see that mobile?! Looks like a motorcycle; small, fast, and leaving the AO (Area of Operations)."

Deadman found them on the screen. "Copy. Mobiles fleeing the area toward town."

Chucky checked his monitor again.

"Say again, SO. *Mobiles?* As in plural? I only see the one!" As the words left his mouth, he wished he could take them back. At that moment Chucky caught what his SO had seen. Yes, a person was fleeing by motorcycle. What he hadn't seen, however, was a second subject entering the town just ahead of the motorcycle.

Engaging the fleeing hostiles at this point he knew pushed the edge of their ROEs (Rules Of Engagement). Nevertheless, he contacted Chavez.

"FCO to pilot, two strays trying to make the town. Permission to engage with laser weapon?!"

Seeing on his screen what his FCO had been following the pilot returned, "Engage all hostiles *outside* of the town. The subject in town *off limits*. That's a *negative,* Chucky."

Frustrated at having missed the smaller runners he raised Deadman.,

"FCO to SO; engage stray heading for the town. Clearance granted to use laser."

"Copy. Engaging with laser." Without another word, Deadman selected the experimental weapon with a quick adjustment at his workstation. A smaller reticle appeared on his targeting monitor. He deftly centered the reticle on the motorcyclist's back. As he squeezed the trigger, the daring rider suddenly crumpled with his bike. Death below was instant, as if the hand of God himself had pushed a needle through the man's heart. Deadman keyed his comms with an eerie finality. "Target eliminated."

Deadman's cold report had a chilling effect on the crew, especially considering what they had just executed. Not one soul aboard Reaper 01 felt celebratory about the success of this particular mission.

Chucky called the cockpit. "FCO to pilot. AO is clear, targets eliminated."

Chavez responded, "Copy. AO clear. Mission accomplished. Reaper 01, return to base."

CHAPTER 16

Reuters Press Release

Report from Fredericksburg, Virginia.

2:00 A.M. 1 May 2021

At around 11:30 PM Eastern Time, a large militia thought to be bound for Washington D.C. was the subject of a pre-emptive strike carried out by the U.S. Military. Reports from sources indicate but have not confirmed, that hundreds were killed in the attack. Among the dead, were women and children thought to be used as human shields by the extremists. At this late hour, authorities are still on the scene.

CHAPTER 17

Patriots USA Headquarters
San Diego, CA

Sunrise crested over the horizon as Henry O'Brien watched a squad of private security contractors neatly file from the backdoor of an urban training building at Patriots USA headquarters. The distinct fragrance of recently discharged weapons lingered. Combined with the salty ocean breeze from the Pacific and his morning coffee, it gave Henry a sense of familiar satisfaction. Though his Marine Corps career was cut short at 12 years of service after sustaining separation level injuries while deployed to Iraq, Henry still found joy in some of the simpler things he had come to love about life as a Marine.

Henry's moment of joy was dampened somewhat when his boss, Graham Pinchot, interrupted with all the grace of a velvet sledgehammer. In his composed yet direct way, Graham hammered straight to the bedrock of the matter.

"Gunny, what the hell happened in there?"

Henry stopped trying to correct his co-workers long ago about his Marine Corps rank; they all knew he never quite made Gunny. Still, once one of the men gave him the name it had stuck as his call sign within the organization. Henry finished the mouthful of coffee he was savoring when Graham walked in.

"Are you talking about the guys not properly checking corners in the shoot room, boss?"

Graham nodded and said, "Yeah, that's exactly what I'm talking about. Why? What else did you see? On second thought never mind. Listen, I didn't schedule this NVG (Night Vision Goggle) training so that these guys could half-ass it all night."

Henry thought a moment about his observations while watching the team clear the buildings in the dark for the past few hours.

"I think most of the guys did what they were supposed to. We're not far off. I just saw the two guys miss corners; Carl and John. You want me to pull them aside for a quick, remedial session and run it again?"

Graham shook his head. "No, Gunny. Now that the sun is coming up, there's no point. Have the men stow the NVGs for the day; we'll reschedule for another night. Go ahead with your coaching though. Once that's done, have all the men in training room 1 by 0800 for a staff meeting."

Henry nodded at his boss. He had a great deal of respect for the man. Graham, like Henry, had once been a Jarhead himself. After 8 years as an infantry officer in Iraq and Afghanistan, Graham made a career move to the Navy, he wanted to be a SEAL. He went on to distinguish himself in the teams, so well in fact that the Navy promoted him straight out of the field to command a desk at the Pentagon. His new adventures in shuffling paper only served to frustrate and bore the man. Graham

Pinchot was a fighter, and he hated being sidelined. So, he resigned his commission and started a company to get back in the fight as a contractor.

Once the boss safely strode far enough away, Henry smiled to himself and thought, *the man left the SEALs but the SEALs never left him.* Henry knew the men were tired, they had trained all night. He also knew they would find no sympathy from the boss. That man had known fatigue like few others in the company probably ever would. Graham wasn't scared to hold his employees to higher standards and push them to realize their inner collective greatness as a team.

Henry chugged down the remainder of his coffee and motioned over to Carl and John. "Hey guys, come on over here a minute." He raised the hand not wielding an empty coffee cup toward the rest of the Patriots USA assault squad and said, "Everyone else stow your gear then get over to training room 1 by 0800. Boss wants to have a meeting before you head home to your wives."

As the squad trudged away to peel off all their gear, Gunny turned his attention to assault squad's two newest members. "Alright you two, if you don't want to get shit-canned back to security squad, listen up."

CHAPTER 18

CIA Headquarters
Langley, VA

Jennifer Miller's desk was covered in reports and memorandums. Her eyes ached as she tried to parse out all the noise and nonsense that was clouding a bigger picture she desperately wanted to understand.

She picked up the brief report that had been emailed to her from the field agent dispatched to Fredericksburg. Her eyes burned from being up all night reading reports, and it took some effort to focus on the words.

Our thorough search has yet to turn up any actual assault weapons of the type we had expected. So far, all that has been turned up and positively identified from the rubble has been Civil War-era firearms. Repeat, no contemporary weapons have been recovered.

Jennifer frowned and set the report aside. *Best leave this one alone until they finish the search,* she thought.

Next, she scrutinized a report from signals intelligence.

Lots of chatter on social networking sites regarding organizing local militias. Also, we are seeing a 915% spike in texts with keywords: President, revolution, civil war, take it back, militia, and fight back. There are of course hundreds of other keywords we monitor popping up on our matrix, this list is not exhaustive, just the highest results. Internet searches for those same keywords are also in line with the spikes we see in social media and texts. Phone intelligence is overwhelming; too many threat assessments to quantify at this time.

The analyst set the report down and rubbed her temples. *There is just too much information here, how am I ever going to coalesce this mess into something we can use?*

She thought about the vast network of satellites looking down on America with a renewed critical eye. *We could launch hundreds of additional satellites into geosynchronous orbit and it still may not be enough to identify every person who poses a threat.*

Jennifer reached for the bottle of eye drops, tilted her head back, and filled each eye with the sweet fluid. She wiped the excess fluid running down her cheeks with a tissue. Closing her eyes she thought, *what if I could get drones over these people to supplement the satellite assets?*

She shook her head. She knew, even if the President circumvented the courts and even if they could keep a drone over every state every hour of every day, there would still be real threats that could sneak through the cracks. Jennifer dismissed the notion out of hand.

So, what possible solution could I bring to my bosses and by extension the President himself to mitigate the threat and restore order, she thought. *What do these people need to be successful? What can the government deny them to cut the head off this snake before it poisons us all?*

Agent Miller pulled out a legal pad and across the top wrote, 'WHAT THEY NEED TO SUCCEED', in bold letters.

The first asset she came up with was communication. She reasoned, if they can't communicate with each other it will be very hard to organize into any force capable of threatening the Capitol. She scribbled down, *disrupt communication*.

Thoughtfully she glanced up at the muted T.V. screen in her office to see CNN talking heads in blocks over a headline. 'Is Martial Law Coming?' Below that, a continuous scroll of headlines crawled from one end of the screen to the other.

She looked down at her legal pad and wrote in all capital letters, CONTROL THE MESSAGE. Jennifer reasoned the government may just kill any opposition before it starts if the people can be made to *believe* everything the government was doing was in *their* best interest.

Satisfied that she had something useful to bring her superiors along with a mountain of pending threat assessments, Jennifer Miller opened up a blank memorandum template on her desktop and started typing.

CHAPTER 19

Patriots USA Headquarters
San Diego, CA

Training Room 1

Henry entered the company's training room ten minutes before the time Graham had set for the meeting to begin. Around the room sat the assault squad. Many of the men were occupied on their cell phones while others talked quietly. Facing the room was a modest lectern, its only adornment was the Patriots USA company logo. Just behind and slightly to the side of the pulpit stood the boss in muted conversation with his top two officers; Spurgeon Gorlick, the company CFO, and Thomas Sullivan who led operations and company contracts. Each were highly decorated Army veterans.

Spurgeon Gorlick, or 'Spurgo' as the men called him while out on maneuvers, had a resume that read like an Army history book. Spurgo had been fighting America's battles all over the world since 1990. Like Henry, Spurgo had also fought in Iraq, although his first trip there had been for Desert Storm. 1993 found the young soldier fighting again, this time in Somalia. Later in the decade Spurgo found himself in Bosnia with 10th

Mountain. Then, September 11th happened within a year of his completion of Ranger school. He was among the first U.S. boots on the ground for Operation Enduring Freedom where the Rangers were integral in the fall of the Taliban. While he had been stateside for Operation Anaconda, the Army got Spurgo back in the action for Iraqi Freedom where his unit took on Saddam Hussein's vaunted Republican Guard.

Thomas Sullivan's fighting history was significantly more shrouded than his counterparts up at the podium. Henry knew he had been Army Special Forces, beyond that 'Tommy' wasn't keen on discussing details. Graham had once told Gunny that Tommy was Task Force 11 and left it at that. After doing a little research, the only information Gunny was able to dig up on Tommy and Task Force 11 was that they were tasked with hunting HVTs (High Value Targets) in Afghanistan and elsewhere. Everything else about the men and their missions was shrouded in secrecy.

Gunny considered the three men leading Patriots USA to be some of the greatest warriors America had ever seen. He was proud to follow them. Typically, when they stood together in conversation like this it meant a fight was in their future; he thoughtfully considered where they might be going. Hanging on the wall behind the three men was a giant flat-screen television. Graham used the monitor to review recorded training videos, share information and intelligence about upcoming contracts and as a projector for power points he'd made. This morning however the screen was filled with CNN talking heads on mute. A cursory glance at the broadcast told the Marine everything he needed to know. They were debating violence from the previous 48 hours at the Capitol and sensationalizing the idea that the President may declare martial law as a result of it.

Gunny was about to take his accustomed seat near the front of the room when from the corner of his eye he caught the words flash on the television:

BREAKING NEWS!!! DOMESTIC TERRORISM CELL IN FREDERICKSBURG VIRGINIA STOPPED BY GOVERNMENT BEFORE INCITING ADDITIONAL VIOLENCE IN THE CAPITOL. PRESIDENT TO DECLARE MARTIAL LAW.

Gunny looked at the screen mouth agape. One by one, men around the room fell silent in disbelief. He heard one man wonder out loud, "Domestic terrorism cell? Who exactly?"

As if in answer he heard another voice say, "*Domestic terror* means our own people."

A third man spoke up, "So wait, the government killed our people for terrorism? How do they know the difference between a disgruntled American who wants some changes and an actual threat of terrorism?"

The first man to speak asked another question, "Martial law? How is *that* going to work?"

John, the young addition to the assault squad with who Gunny had just conducted remedial training, looked at him. "Gunny, they say the people were 'stopped', you think that means by force?"

Gunny looked at the young man and told him honestly, "I don't know."

Graham injected himself into the conversation.

"Yes, by force." He then addressed the room as a whole. "Alright guys, have a seat. Let's get started." The boss glanced at Tommy and the T.V. before saying, "Go ahead and shut that crap off, please."

One by one the men of the Patriots USA assault squad silenced their phones and slid them into pockets. The training room turned silent, Gunny thought he could hear his own heart trying to beat right out of his chest. Graham Pinchot gripped the lectern with his powerful hands, set his jaw, and then addressed the room.

"Alright guys, I know you've been up all night, thanks for sticking around. Rather than wasting your time, I'll get straight to the point. Late last night a large gathering of innocent American citizens was senselessly slaughtered. I am referring to the event you all just saw on CNN which is being spun as a defensive measure against a so-called domestic terrorism cell. That information is ludicrously false. The people they are referring to as 'terrorists' were not the shadowy degenerates our government would have us believe they were at all. Like every person in this room, those people were patriots. That was a gathering of Civil War enthusiasts, nothing more. They were all there to commemorate and re-enact the Battle of Chancellorsville. This wasn't an interdiction at all; it was a slaughter."

Every person present looked at their boss in shock. For a long moment, nobody spoke. Finally, one brave soul spoke up to ask the critical question, "Are you positive boss?"

"Quite. My father is a Civil War enthusiast who does this re-enactment every year," Graham answered quietly. "He called me last night from *that* campground to tell me how much fun they were having roasting hot dogs and preparing their uniforms. He told me..." Graham paused a moment before continuing. "He told me my son was having a great time riding his dirt bike and promised he would have him call before they turned in for the night. I never heard back from either of them." A long, deafening silence hung on the air like dense fog before

Graham spoke again in his calm and certain way. "Here's what I'm going to do, guys. I'm going to call in the other teams. I'm going to see about getting more information and exploring what we can assemble in terms of assets. Once the whole team is here, we'll talk about what happens next."

CHAPTER 20

Patriots USA Headquarters
San Diego, CA

Outside of Training Room 1

Graham pulled the smartphone from his left front pocket and called his secretary. "Jenny, Graham. Listen, here's what I need you to do. Send out notifications to the security squad letting them know I am activating them. Next, get Tommy on the phone, tell him I said to proceed with assets procurement. I'll also need you to activate the scout squad. With the scouts, I'll need you to include the following directions:

"While en route to report, conduct passive recon of government buildings and military base gates with focus on accessibility. Plainclothes only. No item of clothing which identifies them as Patriots staff or military permitted. Additionally, all scouts attach body cams. Use of handheld cameras or cell phones for surveillance purposes is not authorized. All weapons MUST be concealed."

Graham paused a moment as he noticed Henry walking up to him and then wrapped up his phone conversation. "Yes, please keep trying his phone; I have to go." With that, he touched the 'end call' button and slipped the phone into his pocket.

Graham took a breath, closed his eyes, and opened them slowly before locking onto his old friend.

"Hey Gunny, you call your wife yet?"

"Yeah, boss," Henry answered. "Shelby's good, just scared is all. She's worried about things getting out of control and there being issues with interruptions to medication supplies because of the transplant. She's worried about where you're taking us."

"Well, Gunny, we're going to talk about that here shortly with the entire leadership element. Before I can do that, we need a little more information. I dispatched the scout squad to get a feel for how deep the panic is running. Are we talking military lockdowns, National Guards activated nationwide, or is federal law enforcement being used to enforce this martial law and prosecution of raids? We need more information before just jumping into a fight."

Henry considered the boss for a moment.

"You want to fight the government? Graham, isn't that biting the hand that feeds us?" Henry asked. "Look I'll support you in front of the guys, but this feels like you are making decisions that affect all the men simply because you haven't heard from your dad or your son. Isn't it possible that they weren't even at the scene in Fredericksburg and those people are who the feds claimed they were? Isn't it possible that what happened in D.C., was an out-of-control protest gone wrong? Graham, obviously this is all very tragic and I hate that we are watching it unfold from 30,000 feet, but are you seriously wanting to get us into a fight we are unlikely to survive over partial intelligence and phone calls that haven't been returned. Boss, I think you need to slow down and think about what you are saying and what that means for all of us."

"Gunny, obviously I agree that the information we are operating on right now is incomplete. We need a better understanding. We'll see what kind of info the scout squad comes up with. I'm going to place a call to my friend, Bobby, over at Coronado; maybe I can get some insight there. Are you still in contact with General King over at Camp Pendleton?"

"Yeah, I still talk to the general." Henry grinned slightly. "What are you hoping to learn from him?"

Graham responded, "I want to know what the Marines are being told along with my SEAL buddies. I want to know if the directives they're getting from the top match and how they feel about it. The sample size is small and will not be representative of all commanders everywhere, they are people with lofty agendas after all. I think what we will learn could be telling. Specifically, I want to get a sense for how far the government is willing to go to ensure compliance of the people."

Henry slowly nodded.

"Alright boss, I'll call him."

CHAPTER 21

CNN Special Report

"Hello, America, this is Megan Kincade with a special report. While it has been widely speculated over the past few
days, this development is still stunning in what it means for
America. President Tinsley has taken a very bold step to curb
the flow of extremism in the Capitol, surrounding areas, and
now the country at large. A formal proclamation of martial law
has been made which is to affect all 50 states. The following
measures have been taken as part of this proclamation:

Right to bear arms – suspended.

Right to freely assemble – suspended.

Free travel across state lines – suspended.

Due process – suspended.

Warrantless searches are authorized where the government
sees fit to preserve public safety.

Right to trial by jury – suspended.

A national curfew is in effect for 9 P.M. in each respective
time zone.

Additional provisions to be added as needed by executive
order as needed in the interest of public safety."

The senior anchor paused for dramatic effect to shuffle a few papers, glanced at her script then back to the camera and continued.

"While on the face these measures seem audacious and far-reaching, the statement released by the Oval Office assures that they are meant to be temporary and only in place for the protection of American citizens until the threat of domestic terrorism has been dealt with."

Megan glanced back down to her script before finishing, "As a precaution, National Guard units in every state are to be immediately activated to assist in keeping the peace. More on this after the break."

CHAPTER 22

Patriots USA Headquarters
San Diego, CA

As the sun neared its zenith in the Western sky, Graham watched members of the scout squad trickle through the gates of the Patriots USA complex one by one. Without exception, the initial reports were unremarkable. As Graham had expected, military installations such as March Air Force Base, Marine Corps Air Station Miramar, and the Naval Station at San Diego had been zipped tightly. Gates had been set up with barricades as they had following the events of September 11th and military police were conducting visual searches of every vehicle entering and leaving the posts, limited as they were.

Graham's phone call to Coronado had been more informative in regards to the national landscape at least. Through his friend, Graham had learned that the U.S.S. Abraham Lincoln and all the sister ships of her battle group were on station North and West of Hawaii. The Hawaiian Air National Guard and Alaskan Air National Guard were occupied flying increased patrols with their F-22 Raptors to ensure deterrence of foreign intervention. While his contact had less knowledge of what was happening out of Norfolk, he felt the situation there was likely in concert with what they were seeing at San Diego. Meanwhile, the U.S.S. Theodore Roosevelt was making ready to sail as well with all her cadre of sailors, Marines, escort ships, and air wings. The SEAL made clear to Graham, this movement was unscheduled and he wasn't privy to the reasons for such a rapid deployment.

To Graham, the CAPS (Combat Air Patrols) made at least some sense. He could wrap his mind around the logic of defending the country from surprises while vulnerable and distracted. This new government apparently didn't want a Pearl Harbor-style sneak attack to unify the country. As for putting the fleets to sea, the tactician in him couldn't make sense of it. *Were they simply protecting assets or was some other agenda at play here?*

Next, from one SEAL to another, Graham had inquired on the big ugly elephant in the room when he queried, "And what about the teams and other Special Forces elements?"

The response Graham received was at first, predictable and vanilla.

"We're obviously in a constant state of readiness, as you know, Graham. As of right now, we are not being ordered anywhere. Haven't heard much from those Delta guys out in Kentucky." Bobby then uttered a simple sentence that turned Graham cold. "I think that Fredericksburg thing was a Spectre."

Graham had correctly surmised, that when the government issued a press release saying that the "domestic terrorists" had been "stopped", what they really meant was, by force. Where he had erred however was in his assessment in just how far this new government would be willing to go in stopping their opposition. Graham had wrongly assumed the event at

Fredericksburg had been more like the raid on Waco, Texas. An assault by the feds which had simply gotten out of hand, a public relations nightmare spun into a terrorism interdiction.

A gunship?! The thought was chilling in its implications and changed the game completely.

If this President is willing to order military strikes on his own people....

Nobody is safe! Anyone who they see as a threat is in imminent danger, right now!

Graham quickly rebounded with a follow-up. "Why do you think it was an AC-130 that hit Fredericksburg?"

"Just a hunch, deductive reasoning, and some coincidences," Bobby responded. "First, if this were federal law enforcement somebody would have had loose lips over their guilt by now. Or, some Johnny Cop would be wanting to sell his story to Fox News or CNN. Also, what little footage they released on cable news, that devastation was too thorough. So, now we consider mainline bombers like a Buff (B-52) or a B-1. While the devastation matches, I would be inclined to rule them out as well. What few reports have come out of the nearby town, none of them mention jets in the air around that time. One guy's comment did get panned and lightly made fun of that I thought was interesting. That old guy said he remembered jumping out of C-130s in Vietnam and that he would never forget the droning sound those 4 turboprops made as long as he lived. He said he distinctly heard a C-130 circling over Virginia that night."

Graham thanked Bobby, promised to call him soon, and ended the call. As he did so, one of his senior scouts, Blake Jarrett whipped into the parking lot and seemed to vault from the driver's side door seemingly before the vehicle's inertia had fully settled. Blake was a talented scout, and a man Graham had leaned on for years to bluntly color in pictures of what was happening rather than what he thought the boss would want to hear. Some in the company thought Blake was a bit rough in his tendencies to forego corporate style communication for harsh, straightforward realities. The only opinion of Blake that Blake seemed to care about was Graham's. The boss, he knew, appreciated not having to parse words.

Graham had never seen his senior scout rushed or rattled. Never. As the scout ran up to him Graham could see the man's brow was heavy with perspiration and his eyes were wide. Graham felt his gut rise inside as if it already knew that whatever information Blake was running toward him with was life-changing.

Blake's feet beat to a stop in front of Graham.

"They're killing people out there!"

"Slow down, Blake. I need you to be specific and tell me what you saw."

Wiping his brow with a forearm the scout regrouped and provided the professional report he had been trained to deliver.

"Graham, the National Guard post in San Diego isn't far from where I live. So I decided to drive by there first. I had initially planned to just attach the body cam to my seat belt so that it would look out the driver window as I rolled by. I figured that would minimize my exposure. Only, I never had the chance." He paused to chug a water bottle Graham handed him. "I couldn't get close, the Guard had all the streets barricaded that bordered their post. So, I parked a few blocks away and proceeded on foot to see what was going on. That's when I noticed a large group of people had walked around the barricades and were walking toward the Guard checkpoint just outside their gate. A Humvee was sitting there with a manned .50 cal on top. A hasty watchtower had just been put up as well. Just behind the Hummer, manned by Guardsmen with M4s." He downed the rest of the water. "The crowd seemed to be mostly young adults, male and female. A few were holding signs; anti-violence messages. They were ordered to disperse by a scene commander. Rather than disperse, some of them just sat down; defiant, not violent. I didn't see a single act on the part of the crowd that would be considered threatening besides the fact they just wouldn't go away. This went on for a few minutes and then without warning the .50 cal opened up! Nobody charged the Guard position, they all just started running. Some got away I think, but a lot didn't. That gunner, along with the guys up on the watchtowers cut them down. They were shooting people in the back as they ran!"

"Blake, did you have your body cam on?!"

"Yeah, boss. I got it all." The scout tapped the seemingly inconsequential button on his jacket.

"Good, get it over Kennedy right away. See you in brief." With that Blake strode away to deliver the camera's horrific contents to the company's computer techies. Henry passed him with a nod as he approached Graham. "You talk to the general?" Graham asked.

"Yeah, I got through. He wouldn't talk over the phone though. He seems to think the NSA will tap his phone. He said he'll come over to the house in a few hours and fill me in. I thought you might want to be there for that."

"Yes, of course," he agreed quickly. "If the general has concerns about being monitored, that in itself tells us a lot. Get with logistics. Tell them to buy every single burner phone they can find. Blanket approval on the expenditure: I'll handle accounting. Listen, Henry, it's getting bad out there, real bad. Blake brought back some footage that I believe is going to be a game-changer. We have a lot to talk about. Briefing in 20 minutes, get all the men to TR-1."

Henry gave a half nod before walking away. Graham pulled out his smartphone and called his IT director, Kennedy Sloane.

"Kennedy? Graham. I need that footage from Blake's cam over in TR-1 ASAP." He ended the call and looked at his phone. The seasoned operator mused. *I wonder if they are already watching?*

CHAPTER 23

Patriots USA Headquarters
San Diego, CA

Training Room 1. 30 minutes after Blake Jarrett's arrival.

TR-1 was buzzing with chatter. The warm aroma of freshly brewed coffee did little to ease the cold tension permeating the room. No one in attendance feared a confrontation, especially considering the luxury of vast resources and technical support they typically enjoyed. The chilling prospect of internal conflict was a different matter, the certainty of uncertainty was perhaps what unsettled the men most. Who would they fight? What would become of their family and friends? Furthermore, if they did fight and they survived it, what would their new world look like?

As the din seemed to be reaching a natural crescendo, Graham entered the room with his IT guru Kennedy and Henry O'Brien in tow. He didn't have to ask for silence.

"We have a lot to talk about and not a lot of time. Before we begin, I am going to ask that you turn off all electronic devices. Off, not silenced. Nobody records this meeting." He paused and watched men throughout the room turn off devices and slide them into go bags and pockets. Satisfied he opened his briefing.

"As you know, a few days ago a massacre occurred at the Capitol. This was sold to the country, through the media, as a burgeoning insurgency carried out by pro-gun extremists. Some went as far as to label the actions domestic terrorism. They claim this so-called terrorist group, which they have yet to name or provide evidence of, set out to incite violence that night and kick start a revolution of sorts. Further, this narrative of terrorist insurgency was used as justification to carry out a pre-emptive strike upon a reported 'second wave' threatening the Capitol. Political differences aside, these are the 'facts' as reported by mainstream media to this point. The threat was supposedly severe enough, that the new administration has deemed it necessary to declare martial law which all but negates any protections provided by The Constitution."

Graham paused a moment to take the temperature of the room. The men were all rapt. He thought he could hear his own heart pounding in his chest.

"Before I lay out what I know about these so-called 'terrorists' in Virginia and D.C. and bring you up to speed on what we're doing, there is a video you need to see. This video was taken by our own Blake Jarrett an hour ago at the California National Guard Post in San Diego. The crowd you'll see are American citizens; young men and women. Your neighbors. Your fellow parishioners. Perhaps your nieces and nephews, hell for a handful of us sons and daughters. I want you to pay close attention to the crowd's behaviors. I want you to keep a critical eye out for weapons of any kind. I want you to decide for yourselves what threat you may logically perceive from these people."

With the preface completed, Graham turned to Kennedy and nodded.

As Blake's raw bodycam footage played on the big screen some of the men slowly shook their heads while others wrung their hands in silence. As the massacre unfolded some of the men, battle-hardened warriors who had all seen death, openly wept while others stewed in rage. As the camera panned away from the carnage and the echo of the final shots ebbed, Graham turned the screen off and faced his men once again.

"A moment ago, I alluded to what I know. Last night, I spoke with my father by phone before he turned in for the night; from Fredericksburg, Virginia." The Velvet Hammer paused for effect and then continued, "My dad has been active in Civil War reenactments for years, he especially had interests in the Virginia battles such as Bull Run and Chancellorsville. This year he took my son to experience the history and culture. Anyone want to venture a guess where the reenactment folks were gathering for the Chancellorsville event this year?"

A voice near the back of the room offered, "Damn. Sorry, boss."

Graham nodded and gathered his emotions.

"There was not a single terrorist or insurgent in that group. My dad was *strategizing* how to find my son who was out riding his dirt bike when our call ended. I have yet to hear from either of them. No plots or strategies were afoot to usurp the government. All those old fellas were roasting hot dogs and polishing boots. Listen, men, I don't expect all of you to agree with me; this may not be the fight you want or need. That said, I need every single one of you. This isn't about left or right. This isn't about this politician or that. I'm not concerned with who you vote for, that's your business. I cannot stand up here in front of you in good conscience and tell you all it's going to be ok. What I can tell you is this, our government is operating in a very dangerous way at this moment. This is no gray area: ordering the murder of American citizens in Fredericksburg and San Diego for simple defiance is not a political issue. It is a moral issue. This is a question of right or wrong and where you stand. Will we be the men that sit on the sidelines and watch history happen and complain about it when our kids are forced to face the aftermath? Or, will you stand and fight with me?"

Another man in the room responded, "Boss, I don't think anyone here is going to run from a fight. What you're talking about is taking on the U.S government though. We are just one small group of people, you know as well as us, platoon strength. That's *IF* every single man is on board. How can you possibly think we can stand against the government, let alone win?"

Graham pursed his lips and assured the doubtful in the group, "We won't be doing this alone, men. I have irons in the fire. I sent Tommy out this morning to secure some assets using his connections. We won't enjoy traditional air support so I have him working on that and any other equipment he can get his hands on. Furthermore, he sent a few of his lieutenants out to recruit some extra hands. Contacts in the veteran community will be where they start, I would think. Those guys will in turn know people who will want to help and those people will know other people. Now, this National Guard issue complicates things a little. We can't assume freedom of movement with those guys in our rear, they'll have to be dealt with. I am hoping that cooler heads will prevail among their ranks and that maybe someone in that command structure has some sense about what the oath means." Graham glanced around the room and then continued. "Questions?"

The room was eerily quiet. Graham then dismissed the men.

"Alright guys, meet back here at 0600. Go home and get your affairs in order; tell your loved ones communication is going to be inconsistent and difficult for a while. We jump into this fight. You can bet the government is going to work to disrupt our comms or at the very least, monitor it." Holding up his smartphone he said, "Don't count on having these. If I don't see you back, I wish you luck. Those who do show up, be ready for anything. Now get out of here."

As the room emptied, he turned to Kennedy.

"What do you need from me, Graham? Do I need to pack my bags too?" she asked.

"No, once we're on the move, I think you would just be in danger," he admitted. "Today and tonight, however, I need you to get a lot done. I need a laptop with heavy encryption. Also, I'd like for you to get into the contingency plans program and print everything. I especially need hard copies of everything having to do with communications interruptions, resource acquisitions in hostile territory, and for the love of God absolutely everything we have in unit sustainability.'

Kennedy typed notes into her iPad.

"Anything else boss?"

"Yeah, backup everything you have to paper and keep the files offsite." Kennedy chuckled at her elder and his reliance on paper documents. Graham frowned. "I wasn't joking, K. Once we're into a fight you can bet the government's snoops are going to be peaking into what we're doing and working to crash it, get it done. Fast, please."

With that, he turned and walked toward the door where Henry was waiting for him.

"Nice speech in there, Graham," Henry grinned. "You do realize those guys are right? We're going to need a lot of help, and I don't think out-of-shape vets with Chevy pickups and hunting rifles are going to cut it. We'll need some bigger guns."

Graham's frown softened a little.

"I know, Gunny. Hopefully, the general has some good news. Let's get to that meeting."

CHAPTER 24

Henry O'Brien's vehicle
En route to the O'Brien home

Henry's H2 Humvee easily accelerated past 65 miles per hour as he merged onto Interstate 5 Northbound from San Diego toward his home in Carlsbad. What he observed was surreal. The traffic volume he had become accustomed to navigating was absent. The principal arterial between his work and his home was largely devoid of other drivers. Henry set the cruise control to 71 miles per hour as he listened to his boss take a phone call on the disposable phone he had just activated. Surmising it was Tommy, he intently listened for whatever information he could glean from the side of the conversation that he could hear.

Graham listened for a few long moments before he spoke.

"Forty-one? That's it?" Henry watched as Graham's disappointment manifested. He slowly closed his eyes and reopened them as he listened. "That's a lower number than I had hoped for, but it's a start. Anyone with special skills?"

The next break in Graham's conversation was a little longer. Henry glanced away from the road briefly, just long enough to catch a glimpse of a military Humvee crossing the overpass ahead. When Graham spoke again, Henry discerned that they had indeed recruited at least a handful of men with special skills.

"Well, those guys with hand radio experience could certainly become useful. Tell me again how that realtor is going to be of any use?" Another brief pause as the boss nodded and listened. "I see, and he's *that* good with his video drone?" Henry noticed Graham's eyebrows raise a little. "I'm sorry; *she*. High-resolution imagery, you said she's comfortable risking that expensive a drone to help us?"

Henry changed lanes to go around a line of RVs. Next to him, Graham was taking a measure of other assets Tommy had brought into the fold.

"A construction company owner? That could be good. Does he volunteer his equipment?" Graham shook his head quickly and cut off whatever Tommy had been saying. "No, not the tools, Tommy; *equipment*. I'm talking bulldozers and backhoes." Now the boss was nodding. "Yes, exactly what I was thinking. In these first hours, it will behoove us to contour the engagement zones to our advantage to make our force seem more imposing. That may involve roadblocks and kill boxes. Hence the need for that equipment. What else did you come up with? Any tech? No? What about air?"

Henry moved his H2 to the right as a vehicle approached him at high speed. A flash of trepidation quickly turned to relief as he saw the glossy, black Ford Mustang GT blow by him.

Next to him Graham inclined his head slightly and said, "So a Beechcraft 18 and one single engine Huey. Do they at least come with pilots?" Tommy affirmed that pilots were indeed part of the package deal. "And how do you foresee.... You've already mounted a .50 cal to the door of the Beech 18?! That may be the most special forces thing I've ever heard you say, Tommy, and that's saying something. You have a gunner in mind?"

Henry turned to look at his boss as Graham chuckled a little. "Yeah, you're right. Marshall will get a kick out of that. Let's see him put that 'Air Assault' talk where his mouth is." Graham then redirected, "Hey, I meant to ask before; any of these other guys you wrangled up actually have marksmanship skills?" Graham listened a moment "No I wasn't expecting *snipers*; any of these folks have hunting or tracking experience? I don't care if it is with daddy's hunting rifle or compound bows, can these people hunt and kill? Are they willing to pull that trigger?"

The conversation seemed to be nearing its natural end as Henry took the off-ramp toward his home.

"Ok, Tommy, good start. See about making contact with local law enforcement friends. I don't think those guys will just walk away and leave their communities high and dry. They will have their fingers on the pulse of the local neighborhoods, though. There are people in these communities who are about to have their livelihoods destroyed by this martial law. Hell, even the gangs have a lot to lose. You can bet these cops will know who we can tap into to find a common cause. We'd be foolish to forsake that resource. Also, get me whatever you can in manpower for the non-combat skills we'll need once we're on the move. We'll need people in those off radar skill sets like electricians and mechanics. Get back to me in a few hours."

With that, Graham pressed the end call button and set the phone face down on his lap.

"Well, Gunny," he shrugged. "It's not exactly a QRF (Quick Reaction Force), but I feel like we may be able to cobble something together. I would have thought more people would be mad enough to do something about it. How do I get these people off the sidelines and into the fight? How do I make them see the threat and feel strongly enough to do something about it?"

Henry steered into his neighborhood.

"Graham, right now the media is controlling the message, and therefore the people. They are coloring the government as good shepherds and freedom-minded thinkers as the wolves at the door. You need to flip the script. There are others out there. We just need to find a way to reach them." As he neared his driveway, Henry cocked his head in confusion. "Wait, that's not the general's car."

His brief apprehension was assuaged as the Marine remembered the strange vehicle parked in front of his home was that of the general's wife. She had been so proud to show it off when Henry had brought his wife to dinner at General King's residence. Henry pulled the H2 into the garage and closed the door.

CHAPTER 25

The O'Brien Home
Carlsbad, CA

Henry could smell the fragrant aroma of freshly brewed coffee as he entered the house. Graham trailed him through the
garage door. From an adjacent room, Henry could make out the
voices of his wife, Shelby, and General Antoine King coming
from the living room. Henry and Graham walked into the room
to find the general sitting in a plush armchair opposite Shelby,
each cradling a stoneware cup. In place of the utility uniform
Henry was accustomed to seeing him in, the general instead
wore Marine Corps issue running shorts with an olive drab t-
shirt and well-worn running shoes.

General King stood as the two men from Patriots USA
walked into the room and greeted Henry with a warm embrace.
"Good to see you, Henry."

"Good to see you, too." He turned and walked over to his
wife, leaning over to kiss her. Henry then motioned to Graham
and said, "General, this is Graham Pinchot, CEO of Patriots
USA."

The two greeted each other with a firm handshake. Graham said, "Nice to finally meet you, sir. I've heard a lot of good things."

"Likewise."

"Would you gentlemen like some coffee? There's a fresh pot in the kitchen," Shelby offered. "There's also an assortment of muffins on the counter if you need a bite. Blueberry, apple cinnamon, and chocolate chip I think."

All three men nodded. Shelby walked to the kitchen and returned moments later with a platter of muffins in one hand and tray of coffee cups in the other. Henry dutifully helped his wife set the trays down for their guests. Each in turn selected a muffin to go with their coffee.

Henry took a bite of his blueberry muffin and chased it with a swig of coffee as Shelby took a seat next to him.

"General, the PT outfit and driving your wife's car? Seems like an odd time to be getting your running in."

"An abundance of precaution, Henry." The general gave him a knowing look. "My Marines on the gates over at Pendleton are without a doubt loyal to me. I could come and go at will, and if I were to ask it of them, they would have the discretion to keep my movements confidential. Unfortunately, there are more eyes and ears to worry about. The Commandant indicated to me when we spoke by phone this morning that bases are being closely watched. By who? That conclusion is ambiguous at this point. The CIA? Secret Service? FBI? Satellites or drones? Maybe none of them, or all the above. Until further notice, I must assume, *all Americans* should assume, that we are being watched. Gone are the days of reliance on moles and informants. With recent advances in signals intelligence and the multi-spectral imaging capabilities our government has in place high above us, no secret is safe. Hell, even our phones should be assumed to be spying on us. That's why I left my phone at home and drove a different vehicle than usual. I don't want anyone to know I'm here."

Graham dispensed with small talk and cut straight to the point, "Do you know about that business at the Guard post earlier today, general?"

"It's worse than you know," he affirmed grimly.

"How could it be worse?" asked Henry.

"Do you think these atrocities are isolated to Southern California?" Before they could answer he explained. "Congress has consolidated the leadership of all the state's Guard units under the President. He's declared martial law. Do you have any notion as to what that *actually* means for Americans?"

"General, I would think it means a lot of things," Shelby answered. "What I found most troubling in that decree of his, though, was the suspension of due process. Couldn't they just execute citizens for sedition by labeling it treason at this point?"

"Exactly, Shelby; it's that simple," he said. They want to force the people into submission using any means at their disposal. It will be a true barometer of will power for people when they are forced to see a loved one hung in front of their City Hall."

"Why the National Guard then? Why doesn't he just order your Marines and the Army out into our towns to force this submission?" Graham asked.

"It's a good question, Graham. I'm not privy to the President's strategy. I'm operating on word from the Commandant at this moment and the rest is reasoned speculation," he admitted. "I don't think this President has ruled out mainline military assets. I suspect that he may be concerned with the possibility of mutiny. When the Civil War was in its opening hours, Abraham Lincoln offered the leadership of the Union Army to Robert E. Lee. Did you know that? Lee considered the offer. Ultimately he felt that his native Virginia would come into the fight on the side of the Confederacy and he couldn't stomach fighting the men of his home state. Every kid who ever carried a history book knows that brother fought brother in that war, what they don't teach at the public school level was the fact that many officers chose their loyalties. This President Tinsley is no idiot. By ordering us to essentially stand down and shelter in place, perhaps he hopes the public views this as restraint. I believe he's afraid that America's fighters will make their own decisions about the validity of orders when they are told to assault their home towns and take the lives of their neighbors."

Something was nagging at Henry. "So why is the National Guard different? Why are they safer for him to use?"

The general was matter of fact. "He's counting on governors to know who they have in charge with their general and field grade officers."

"Well, any chance he's counting wrong?" Shelby wondered out loud.

"I think there's a very good chance, Shelby. The generals in place are likely handpicked, but that second tier under them is another matter. I think one may be able to draw out those dissenters if someone can bloody their lips a little," he said. "Even the best of battle plans cannot survive first contact. The Guard has a lot of brave men and women in their ranks who are simply following orders. Given the chance to go home rather than murdering their fellow citizens, I would imagine most of them would do just that. Hell, one might even be able to recruit some of them to follow a different leadership group altogether."

"You mentioned word from the Commandant. What is it exactly he's asked you to do?" asked Graham.

"You're wondering if I'm going to pose a threat to you, Graham?" The general let the discomfort hang in the air for just a moment. "My official guidance is in line with that of all commanders across the country. By order of the President of the United States, I am to hold my Marines in place and maintain a high state of readiness. I am not to engage the public in any way unless ordered to do so, or only so far as needed to defend my post and the assets within it. That is the official order; from the top." He paused a moment to savor the last of his coffee and smiled. "I did, however, receive a call from the Commandant a few hours ago that I intend to treat as my actual directive."

"Well, what did he say?" Henry prodded.

"The Commandant said, 'Remember your oath and do the right thing, Antoine.'"

"I suppose I could be excited about you doing the 'right thing' sir if it were to align with what I have in mind," Graham admitted.

Sensing a bit of himself in Graham, the general set his cup down.

"I can't make any moves here locally against the Guard or anyone just yet, too many eyes and ears. If it is in your plans to move east though, there is a play I can make."

Henry raised an eyebrow. "What kind of play?"

"I have no intentions to take up arms against Americans for dissenting against a tyrannical government and exercising their Constitutional rights," General King said. "Rather than burn these communities to the ground I intend to build bridges. A week ago, I sent a QRF element, a small fire support element, a motor transport detachment, a scout sniper squad, and some air assets out to 29 Palms to support a training evolution. If you are moving east, I'm prepared to detach them to your command."

"Thank you, General, I'd love to have them!" Graham said, shocked.

Henry pressed for clarification. "Air assets sir? Fast movers?"

General King stood to leave.

"No, Henry, the fixed wings are out of Miramar. I don't have that command. Two Cobras and two Ospreys to move my guys. Maybe you can make a few more friends along the way. I wish I could do more, guys. What's happening is wrong and I will not stay on the sidelines, I promise. There is a time and place, trust me. I do want to help, and these Marines are some of my most talented fighters. They will feel like many more times their numbers if pressed to fight, you have my word. Now, I need to get back. Best of luck to you, watch your backs as you move. Godspeed and Semper Fidelis."

Henry mused to himself, *Always Faithful indeed, old friend.*

CHAPTER 26

NSA Headquarters
Fort Meade, MD

Annie Nguyen slumped into her ergonomic office chair, leaned her head back, and rubbed her temples. Just five minutes ago she had locked the computer screen to fetch a scone and hot cup of coffee. The unread email tally before she had activated screen lock was 547 and that had been after spending the first hour of her day checking and answering messages. Upon returning to her desk the messages had jumped to 652. A vast majority of which indicated attachments that needed to be reviewed. *Intelligence reports.*

Taking a deep breath to reset her perspective the talented technician leaned forward once more and clicked on the oldest message first. It read:

A group of citizens has organized on the Montana - Wyoming border. They are armed with rifles and handguns, some wear body armor. Look to be heading south. Destination, undetermined.

She mused, "Colorado maybe?" Then she moved on to the next report.

Angry mobs occupying a large area of Seattle's Capitol Hill. Intercepted cell phone intelligence suggests discord and potential violent reprisals over increased numbers of arrests.

Annie scoffed, "What else is new? Moving on."

Texas is in a full state of emergency as large chunks of Austin have become virtual war zones between pro-government control advocates and those who oppose gun control measures.

"Well, that certainly warrants some extra attention." Annie opened an email to her boss and attached the Texas report along with a request for additional satellite reconnaissance of the area.

She double-clicked the next report titled 'Oklahoma', and read the report.

Oklahomans have well established militias covering all surface-level ingress routes with roadblocks and checkpoints. Pockets of violence in the areas of Oklahoma City, Tulsa, and Norman are isolated and quickly controlled. Overwhelming chatter on cell networks and social media regarding organizing resistance.

Concerned she printed the report and set it on her stack labeled 'Top Priorities.'

Annie glanced back over to her email box which now displayed 702 unread messages. Exasperated she uttered a near animalistic growl in frustration. The newest report was titled 'San Diego.' She took a moment to consider how she might more effectively sort and prioritize the mountain of reports stacking up on her when another email popped up on her screen. This one was odd as it was from outside of NSA. While not unheard of to receive messages from counterparts at the CIA, they were rare enough to stick out. This one especially had a quality that seemed to reach from the screen and grab her attention. The name looked familiar:

Miller, Jennifer

Subject: Insurrection disruption strategy

Clicking on the email she read just two brief words within the message window, *See attached.*

Annie recalled out loud to herself, "Wait, you're Ms. Miller I met at the command center in D.C. after the protest. What are you sending me Ms. Miller?" She double-clicked the attachment which populated her screen with a memorandum on CIA letterhead. The memo contained two bullet points.

Bullet point number one said, *Disrupt Communication.*

Intrigued Annie read on.

Given the parameters and wide latitude given to leaders under wartime and martial law, I propose taking executive action to commandeer communication companies' assets to streamline the government's ability to communicate via designated government cell phones and devices. In the process disable civilian sector devices. Doing so will make it significantly more difficult to coordinate and form militias and groups capable of posing a threat to government interests. Additionally, I recommend crashing social media networks outright. What intelligence value we lose in the process will be greatly mitigated when those who wish to organize run out of tools to accomplish the task.

Annie thought the idea was both devious and brilliant. This plan would certainly minimize the activity of those who were truly committed to action and fast. Once the people feel cut off and alone, their fighting spirits would certainly be broken she reasoned. Any threats that remained would be isolated and easy to track. She relished the thought of once again having a more manageable workload.

Scrolling down she read the second topic, *Control the Message*.

This topic was a little bit outside of her expertise. In this phase of Miller's plan, the government would inundate the media with both misinformation and reports that colored all actions they took as for the benefit of the masses. It was outright propaganda, that much was crystal clear. While obvious after having read it, Annie still thought it clever in both its simplicity of implementation and risk-reward payoff. Picking up her phone Annie dialed the extension for her boss.

"Sir, have you read this Miller Memo from CIA?"

"Yes, I have," the NSA director answered.

"It's extreme, but also kind of brilliant. Has the President seen this?"

Director Anthony Flynn assured her. "Yes, Annie, he's read the memo. Wheels are in motion even as we speak."

CHAPTER 27

Office of Speaker Madison Regan
Washington D.C.

Speaker Madison Regan was troubled as she re-read an intelligence after-action report out of Fredericksburg, Virginia. *No weapons recovered. Numerous body parts recovered thought to be that of women and children.* A phrase uttered in the White House situation room by Senate Minority Leader Susan Brady haunted the Speaker now. *Couldn't this be a simple Civil War reunion?*

Speaker Regan pressed a button on her phone and waited. After a few seconds, her secretary answered.

"Yes, Madam Speaker?"

"Are they here yet?"

"They called just a moment ago, ma'am. They're running just a few minutes behind. Should I send them in upon arrival?"

"Yes, please do. Thank you," the speaker replied before she hung up.

Madison glanced at the bottle of vodka on her bar and considered pouring herself a glass. After pondering her beverage dilemma for a moment, she elected to forego the alcohol. She wanted a clear head for this meeting. Afterward, though, she knew that would be another matter. What was about to be discussed would merit a stiff drink.

She stood up and walked over to a small, fully stocked refrigerator and retrieved a cold diet soda and chilled glass. Moving to the bar, she put some ice in the glass and then poured the beverage over it. The cold drink was refreshing on her parched lips. Returning to her opulent desk she looked down at the Fredericksburg report.

Damn; not a single shred of evidence to support this action. You have put me in an impossible position, Mr. President.

Speaker Regan slumped into the chair at her desk weighed down by all the responsibility she felt for what was happening in the country she loved. *We have to stop the bleeding before this gets out of control.*

She had just closed her eyes to reflect when her office door opened. Senate Majority Leader, Crosby Moffitt, and Minority Leader, Susan Brady, walked in.

"Thanks for coming, Crosby. Susan, thank you for agreeing to this meeting." Madison gestured to the bar. "Please help yourselves."

Her guests strode to the bar. Senator Brady poured a bottle of water over ice while Senator Moffitt indulged in a small glass of top-shelf whiskey over ice. With refreshments in hand, Speaker Regan motioned them toward a small round table in her office anteroom where they could sit in a more casual setting. Speaker Regan opened the parley.

"Have you had an opportunity to review the Fredericksburg report?"

Senator Moffitt pursed his lips and slowly nodded. "Yeah, it looks bad."

"Looks bad?!" Senator Brady was decidedly more visceral. "I would say it looks downright criminal! Madam Speaker, I hope you didn't invite me to this meeting in hopes of bringing me around to justifying this obvious atrocity!"

Speaker Regan held up both hands.

"Please, Susan, I asked you here because I believe we are on a dangerous path. Getting this country turned around before it consumes itself will take a bilateral cooperative front."

"What are we talking about here? Are we going to paint this as an unfortunate friendly fire incident that missed the intended target?" asked Senator Moffitt with a raised eyebrow. "We could give the media and people that aircrew. It's not as if friendly fire from a gunship crew is unprecedented. I seem to recall a congressional briefing after Operation Anaconda; a gunship mistook some friendly Afghani trucks with Army Special Forces as Taliban."

Senator Brady was visibly disgusted. Before she could respond, the speaker shook her head and interjected.

"No, Crosby, I think that would be unwise. I was in the war room when the President ordered the strike. The area was watched for hours by NSA and CIA. We had the drone overhead for hours, the coordinates given to the crew were exactly where our people over at intelligence wanted them to hit." She ran a hand over the distressing Fredericksburg report. "At no time did those folks take any action which could have been mistaken as aggressive toward the Capitol; nor did they have any intention to do so it would seem."

Senator Brady considered her political rival thoughtfully. "So, Madison, you didn't invite us here to discuss press strategy. You want to talk about a political solution. Are we here to shelf the Amendment so that your people can weather this storm until it passes?"

"No, Senator, I'm not inclined to kick the can down the road. I still believe in the Amendment and will work tirelessly on all fronts to pass it."

Senator Moffitt inclined his head slightly. "What then?"

"Impeachment," she said quietly.

Aghast, Senator Moffitt pressed her. "Madam Speaker, you can't be serious! This is unprecedented. You're seeking the impeachment of a President from your *own* party? This is political suicide!"

"Crosby, I have far larger concerns than elections and opinion polls," she chastised. "You see suicide while I fear genocide. Will there be backlash and consequences in our careers for removing a newly seated president? Without a doubt. Consider if you will, the consequences of doing nothing. This President has already demonstrated he has no qualms in ordering the murder of innocent citizens based on poor intelligence to preserve an all but certain political outcome. Moreover, this business with martial law is a drastic and dangerous overreaction. What happens to your political ambitions when citizens in your district start getting imprisoned without facing a judge or worse yet, executed without trials? Who do you think they will blame? They may blame this president, but they'll start with you. Not only will you not be re-elected, you may not survive. This country as we know it, cannot survive. We remove Tinsley, seat Whitmore, then carry on with our business."

Shocked, Senator Brady listened in silence.

"But, the votes! How will you get enough votes?" Moffitt protested.

"I've already spoken with party leaders in the House; deals are in place. Crosby, Tinsley intends to take down vast sections of the public's telecommunications capabilities. He's going to crash social media. He's trying to simply crush opposition rather than seeking compromise. Unchecked, he will compel the public to revolt and burn it down. You want to preserve *your* political ambitions? We have to do something."

Moffitt dropped his head into his hands. "How is this happening?"

No sooner had the Senator asked, when a loud smash against the office door jerked their focus from the high stakes conversation. Another smash and the door exploded into the room. A dozen Secret Service agents stormed in and split into three groups of four. Each foursome made for the politicians. Before they could protest, they were forced face down into the expensive carpet and placed into restraints.

There were no Miranda rights. The would-be plotters were simply jerked up from the floor and hauled away.

CHAPTER 28

CNN News Desk

"Good evening, America, I'm Megan Kincade. Tonight, I bring you news from Washington. The U.S. Congress has issued this press release:

"Given recent events in and around the Capitol, the Congress will go into recess to ensure the safety of elected officials and support staff until it can be determined that there is no longer a threat from extremists in the public.

"The White House provided a press release yet declined to provide the press secretary for questions. President Tinsley insists that with the help of his advisors, he is doing everything in his power to bring about swift justice to those who are perpetrating the domestic terror threat against the United States. The President urges Americans to stay home and follow the guidance of their local officials, for their own safety."

Having dutifully read the statements as directed, Megan's lips pressed together in a thin line and she moved on to the next story.

CHAPTER 29

Patriots USA Headquarters
San Diego, CA

Graham Pinchot stood alone on the vehicle paddock at Patriots USA Headquarters. Even in their strained and exhausted states, his men resembled a beehive of activity everywhere he looked. Among the vehicles parked astride in his midst, were dozens of men loading the mission essentials. Hand-held radios, batteries, burner phones by the crate, food, and bottled water. Graham grinned in bemusement as one of Tommy's militia recruits carefully set her recreational drone on the seat she would be occupying. Another man laid an unstrung bow on the dashboard of a Chevy Silverado along with a quiver of arrows. He watched as another man he hadn't met yet was putting an old bolt action rifle in the back of a pickup. Next, he struggled to lift an ammo can into the bed. Judging the volunteer to be in his mid-40's, Graham approached him.

"What will you do if we make contact?"

"I'll fight my way back to it." The older man grinned and lifted his jacket to reveal a holstered handgun and three ammo pouches. Confidently the stranger explained, "Once I get to her, there's nothing I can't hit with it."

Graham nodded and moved on.

Beside the next pickup, a man in with a simple gray shirt that said, *ARMY*, across the front, labored to lift a five drawer toolbox. Graham offered a helping hand.

"Need help?"

"Yeah, that would be great. It's not normally this heavy, Tommy wouldn't let me bring my roller," the apparent Army veteran said. "Had to consolidate everything I could into this." He gestured to the other handle and Graham helped him lift it.

"What kind of mechanic are you?" asked Graham.

The man said, "Well, I mostly work on trucks now. In the Army, I worked on the power plant systems on Blackhawks."

Graham was impressed. "Excellent; welcome. I'm Graham."

"Name is Chad," he supplied, extending his hand.

Graham shook his hand and moved on. He pulled the phone from his pocket to check for messages; it showed *NO SERVICE*. "That's odd," he noted. He held a thumb down on the power button to restart the phone. A moment later, the phone restarted yet it still showed *NO SERVICE*.

Frustrated with the device, he shoved it back into his pocket. Graham walked over to one of his men loading ammunition into the back of a truck and asked him to pull out his cell phone. As the employee unlocked the screen, Graham's chest fluttered when the man said, "Curious, I usually get great service around here."

Anxiety mounting, Graham sought out Tommy. He found the senior company officer talking quietly with a man he didn't recognize near the paddock gate. As the boss approached the pair, Tommy observed Graham's demeanor and asked, "Everything ok?"

"You haven't noticed? Something is wrong with the cell towers."

"*What*?" Tommy replied.

"Yeah, no service."

Tommy pulled his phone out in disbelief only to find that he too, lacked cell phone service. He thought for a moment.

"Graham, this is bad. We have different carriers, boss. Do you know how unlikely it is that both of our networks go down at the same time? Not fucking likely."

Graham insisted, "The towers."

Tommy shook his head. "Graham, a single tower malfunctioning, while extremely uncommon, can happen. Usually, these failures can be attributed to weather-related or natural phenomena. Even then, the corresponding towers in the area that your phone uses to triangulate signals will pick up the slack. This may come with some temporary disruption in quality of service, but not a *complete* failure. This disruption is manmade."

"Wonderful, those burner phones…"

"Worthless."

"Damn it!" Graham rankled in frustration. He took a moment to regroup and said, "Well, we have the radios. Those will work fine for unit communication for the moment. Hopefully, we can figure out this network issue. I had already planned on ditching the personal phones in favor of the burners for tracking purposes. Still, we need the ability to stay connected outside of the unit."

Tommy wondered out loud, "Without a doubt, it's being watched, but I wonder if we could utilize the internet?"

Graham asked, "How do you mean Tommy?"

"Until we're able to sort out the cell towers, I'm wondering if we can communicate through the hard-wired fiber optics. Granted there may be some lag with it depending on how pervasive this cell issue is. Additionally, it's not truly fully hard wired, there is dependence on satellites for near real-time connectivity. Whoever is responsible for this tower issue wouldn't dare mess with the satellites in geosynchronous orbit, they're too valuable to the government to allow tampering. They are completely reliant on them for everything."

Graham gave a curt nod. "I think it's worth looking into, let's get into the office and see what Kennedy can come up with."

CHAPTER 30

Patriots USA Headquarters
San Diego, CA

Kennedy's eyes burned with fatigue as she frantically worked the keyboard. Across her desk, four high-resolution monitors had a dozen windows open. A debug program was running in one of the windows as she was desperately trying to troubleshoot the company's sudden communication issues. She had just finished refreshing a social networking window when her boss walked in with his entourage.

Graham and his men entered with a purpose. Their faces reflected her own exasperation. Graham wasted no time as he hammered straight to the point.

"Something is going on with the cell phones, K."

"For starters," she scoffed.

"What do you mean?" Tommy asked.

"Outgoing emails are extremely laggy, internet-based messenger apps are showing offline, and every social networking program I try to load is completely wrecked. Nothing is loading!"

"Hey slow down, K." Graham placed a hand on her shoulder. "Is it an internet issue?"

Kennedy shook her head. "I checked that, we have a strong signal."

Tommy cursed under his breath "That's not doing us a damn bit of good if we can't use it to communicate."

The room fell silent as Kennedy and the men thought through the conundrum. A long moment passed before one of the men spoke up. Dakota 'Einstein' Grant, a Navy Corpsman and junky of all vintage technology, turned Patriots USA medical officer asked the room at large, "Anyone here besides me own one of those Gateway Astro PCs back in the 90's?"

Tommy shot his Naval counterpart a stink eye. "Damn it, Einstein! This is no time for you to geek out on us; we're dealing with some serious shit here."

"Tommy, let him talk, please," Graham said.

Einstein explained, "Well, the Astro was a computer inside a monitor, one unit. I think Gateway was trying to be cutting edge in space-saving at the time. It was a piece of junk really, but it was all I could afford in my college years."

Graham interrupted. "Einstein, get to the point."

"*Anyway.* Back then AOL chat rooms were all the rage in so-called social networking. They were packed full of desperate lonely wives, sad single overweight men, and various other social outcasts with a few normal people sprinkled in. Naturally, I avoided that mess in favor of a chat app that was a bit more obscure, one in fact developed by Israeli techs. Even in its day, few people even knew of it."

"For the love of God; get to the part where this helps us already," Tommy grumbled.

Einstein smiled and answered him with yet another anec-
dote, "Well, the Israelis who developed it built in the best
security of the time. If it hasn't been crashed, then it is very
likely we can establish unmonitored communications. In fact,
I have an old buddy from the Navy who works up at Jim Creek
now. Just for the hell of it, we'll get online and chat using that
old app. It's called ICQ."

Kennedy's face transformed from frustration to excitement,
"Goodness Einstein, this could really be great! What is Jim
Creek?"

Einstein replied, "Jim Creek is a naval communications out-
post up north of Seattle. I'm thinking we could try using ICQ
to link up with my buddy and see what he can snoop up for us
on the down low."

Graham smiled widely and chuckled. "If this nerd plan of
yours pays off we'll never hear the end of it. Get on it."

CHAPTER 31

Jim Creek Naval Radio Station
Arlington, WA

Edwin Daily feverishly worked the keyboard at his station. Communication had been flowing back and forth all day among the fleet dispatched throughout the Pacific. Edwin was accustomed to managing several lines of communication at the same time. This day, however, had been a challenge. When a break in the frenzy of messages finally presented itself, he unlocked the screen on his personal laptop to check emails. As Edwin worked on clearing the flood of unread messages, a ping alerted him to a chat request from ICQ. An old friend was waiting for his response.

Edwin maximized the window to read the incoming message from *Einstein_76* or as Edwin knew the user, Navy buddy Dakota Grant. *Hey man, this thing working?*

Clicking into the outgoing text window he shot a message back. *Yeah. Busy as hell though. What's going on?*

1300 miles away Einstein received a message from *Topshelftechie_01*. Einstein smiled as he typed. *Not much.*

Just major local cell network interruptions. Also, all the standard social network apps are junk. Had a hunch ICQ might be up, glad I was right. Got any intel through your fleet counterparts about what's going on down here?

Topshelftechie_01: *Cell phone issue isn't an isolated issue, it's down nationwide.*

Einstein_76: *Wonderful, what's the endgame in that?*

Topshelftechie_01: *I imagine there is a threat they hope to mitigate. Think about losing comms with a ship. If we can't talk to our ships, how likely are we to coordinate movement?*

Einstein_76: *So you think they're scared of the people?*

Topshelftechie_01: *I think there is some concern. Here locally they have the Guard out doing patrols and threat assessments of local militia types. Seems like they're going after people who are known to organize and have military tactics training. Something to think about in your situation. There have been shots fired up here in Washington.*

Einstein_76: *Shots fired?! The Guard isn't out keeping the peace? They're actually doing strike missions?!*

Topshelftechie_01: *Not just here. I've heard of reports from other spots across the nation as well. You need to be careful.*

Einstein_76: *Ok man! Thanks for the heads up. Do me a favor and keep an ear to the ground. I'll be in touch.*

CHAPTER 32

Patriots USA Headquarters
San Diego, CA

Graham cursed under his breath as the two-man scout team gave their report. He had dispatched the duo to discern local National Guard movements following the report Einstein had provided from his friend at the Naval Radio Station. Graham had been hopeful that he and his men could exfiltrate the area undetected at night and make it to 29 Palms where meaningful force multipliers awaited them. The last thing he wanted was a firefight with the Guard. It seemed the local commander had other thoughts.

"Looks like we'll have to address this issue, Graham," Tommy said as the scouts left. "Why not take the initiative and dictate the engagement to maximize our strengths?"

"Obviously, if there's going to be an engagement it would behoove us to control it," Graham answered. "My only concern at this point is for those junior enlisted soldiers. Those men and women are following orders. I'd like to avoid if at all possible, a massacre for either side. Our goal, ultimately, is to break contact. Our mission, our focus, needs to stay on the source of these draconian orders."

Henry interjected, "Maybe it doesn't have to be a bloodbath."

"Go on, Gunny."

"As Tommy said, we'll need to dictate the engagement. You and Tommy will know best how to influence the movement of our opposition into an ambush. Do your Special Forces thing and get their convoy into a position advantageous to our guys. Only, instead of opening up on the entire convoy, we target key vehicles to create a kill box. Once their movement is paralyzed, we target senior officers, they'll be the ones ensuring these unlawful orders are being followed. After they've been removed, maybe the junior enlisted can simply be convinced to go home."

"I like the upside of this plan," Graham begrudgingly conceded. "However, I'm not crazy about the idea of targeting officers, Gunny. What's your plan look like if after we take out these field grade officers, the junior officers and enlisted fight harder to avenge them out of anger? Or, with leadership decapitated their 'fight' mechanism kicks in instead of 'flight' simply out of fear? Then, not only is it unavoidable to fire on them, now we risk the massacre of our men? What happens if a call goes out for QRF?"

Tommy offered his thoughts. "Graham, there's not going to be a plan we could implement quickly enough to overwhelmingly tilt the odds in our favor. At this point, we need to look at risk aversion. We set up this ambush. I'll position our better marksmen throughout the kill box in concealed positions to minimize exposure while maximizing visibility on the vehicle occupants. I'll have the construction company owner bulldoze roadblocks using shit like dumpsters and parked cars to cutoff flanking and egress routes for the convoy. I'll get that converted Beechcraft circling overhead to give us the edge, at least psychologically, of close air support being on our side. I doubt they are patrolling with air assets. I secured a set of spike strips from one of my sheriff buddies, we'll slide those out for the lead vehicle. Then the snipers can hit the command vehicle. You get on a megaphone to de-escalate and convert the soldiers. Throw that oath at them and hope they see it our way."

Graham closed his eyes as he rubbed his forehead. "What if we just move out right now? We're not weighed down by up-armored humvees and three tons. We can outrun them."

"Boss, we might outrun them. What if we don't though?" Tomy asked. "What if we roll out right now and run straight into a patrol? Now we are engaging on their terms. We hope to break contact, but at that point, they will view us as a threat. They will pursue and likely call for a QRF to flank us. Then we're truly fucked."

"He's right, Graham," Henry said. "We can't move with a constant threat in our rear. They'll have to be dealt with, better to make it happen in a way that enhances our strengths."

Graham reluctantly nodded.

"Alright guys, we'll set up the ambush. Gunny, I want you to embed with the assault squad in case this thing goes sideways. Tommy, get our best snipers to set up firing positions with intersecting fields of fire on either side of the kill box. Make it difficult for them to deduce where we're firing from. Confusion will slow them down; uncertainty is our ally. If they can be made to feel vulnerable and overwhelmed, that only increases our chances of them hearing what I have to say. Only field grade officers and radio operators are to be targeted unless they open up."

Tommy and Henry nodded. As they turned away, Graham said to himself, "The tree of liberty must be refreshed from time to time with the blood of patriots and tyrants." He looked at the ground in silent reflection.

"I'm sorry?" Henry clarified.

"It's Thomas Jefferson," Graham answered as he looked up. Tommy and Henry exchanged a look. Graham continued, "He was referring to the sacrifices made by the men who fought for our independence and the lives lost in Britain's efforts to preserve their dominion over us. For our fledgling nation to be born and grow, men had to die for their ideals."

"Yeah," Tommy murmured.

Graham went on. "We'll be labeled as traitors, as the Founding Fathers were before us. History will only remember us as traitors if we fail. That's not what bothers me, I'm not afraid to die for what I believe in. What bothers me most is that I just approved the deaths of fellow citizens to achieve our goals. I took my oath with the intent that my orders would shield America against her enemies. Al Qaeda, ISIS, communism, et cetera. I never imagined the line would be so gray."

Henry replied, "Boss..."

Graham cut him off as he turned away. "Go make it happen."

CHAPTER 33

California National Guard Combat Patrol
Just East of Downtown San Diego, CA

Captain Zefrem Rosencrans read the report on his laptop
and cross-checked their dispatch against the GPS. So far, the
patrol had been uneventful, quiet even. Eerily quiet. San Diego
felt like a long-lost ghost town. Devoid of traffic. They hadn't
come in contact with a moving vehicle, not even a kid on a bike,
since they had pulled into the patrol area.

Captain Rosencrans keyed his radio, "This is the right area,
Colonel. Intel report indicates a militia operating in this part of
town."

In the command vehicle just ahead of the captain, Colonel
Helms responded, "Copy that. We might have come upon them
unawares. Stick to the plan. Upon arrival at the compound, we
cover all routes of egress. The goal is to get them to come out
peacefully. All weapons to be confiscated as we briefed. Everyone gets detained pending threat assessment. Nobody gets
away."

Chagrined, the captain looked down at his rifle. The thought
of lining up the front sight post in his rear sight aperture on a

fleeing American repulsed him. His mind flashed to the scene at the National Guard post only days ago where the colonel had ordered his gunners to open up on the crowd. The moment was a surreal one for Zefrem. He had of course trained for countless scenarios as an infantry officer, none of that training prepared him for the atrocity he witnessed. In his sleep, he heard the screams of the terrified. He heard the cries of the stricken. He could still smell the awful confluence of bowels vacating themselves mixed with the tang of iron in the blood surrounding him. When he closed his eyes, Zefrem could still see the images of bodies collapsing in unnatural positions playing like a drive-in movie on the back of his eyelids.

The voice of Colonel Helms snapped the junior officer back to reality. "Captain! Private drone at convoy twelve o'clock; we're being surveilled!"

Trepidation crept into the junior officer for just a moment, being watched was one thing. A convoy of this size drew attention. To be surveilled in this manner was a different matter, this development he knew, was a potential indication that their quarry was wise to the threat.

Captain Rosencrans was still calculating what this drone meant for their assault plan when ahead of him the convoy sped up then diverted from their planned route. The realization was startling, Colonel Helms had made the very risky decision to chase the drone to its source as it fled. For all the colonel knew, this drone might only lead them to the doorstep of a teenager. Bottom line, Captain Rosencrans felt they were forfeiting the advantage of a well-organized plan for a half-baked goose chase. Colonel Helms was clearly making questionable decisions, and there was nothing Zefrem could do to stop it.

From the seat immediately to the captain's left, his vehicle's driver voiced his distress. "I don't like this, Cap. These streets are getting narrow and the buildings are getting taller. We're losing situational awareness."

The young NCO was right, he knew. With buildings to either flank, the convoy was now at a troubling disadvantage. In the midst of that realization, the captain caught a detail that was incongruous to the flanks. At first, the observation simply struck him as odd, but with each passing block, the odd became terrifying. Each of the side streets they passed was blocked. Some were choked with dumpsters that had been set on fire while others had sedans parked over the sidewalks, perpendicular to the smaller streets. The convoy movement was being dictated to them!

Captain Rosencrans was just about to key his radio to raise the colonel when the column's momentum came to a sudden and violent stop. Zefrem's anxiety began to swell as he quickly tried to discern what was happening. He looked out the side window to his right, while there was no apparent movement Zefrem had the uneasy sensation they were being watched.

On the radio, Zefrem heard the colonel query the lead vehicle. "What the hell is going on up there?" The captain glanced out the front windshield in time to see the colonel open his door and step out. Zefrem watched as Colonel Helms gestured toward the column front and leaned over to bark orders to someone still in the vehicle.

Suddenly a shot rang out! A cloud of pink mist blew out from the right side of the colonel's head and he collapsed in a heap. No sooner had the echo from the report ebbed, when a barrage of gunfire tore into the colonel's vehicle. The radio operator sitting in the back seat of the embattled humvee tried in vain to flee from the murderous fire, only to be cut down feet away from where he had just been sitting. Only then did the assault cease.

A long silence fell over the dreadful scene in front of Captain Rosencrans. With the company executive officer left behind at the post, Zefrem came to the startling realization that he was now in command of the convoy. Zefrem was trying to quickly piece together a withdrawal strategy when he heard a voice boom out.

"Attention to the men and women in the vehicles. This is Commander Pinchot, United States Navy. Make no moves of aggression. Ensure your firearms are on safe and place them on the floor boards. Those of you on .50 cal turrets, put your hands behind your back in a parade rest posture. You are flanked on both sides; your situation is dire. Circling above you is a gunship. You are to follow these orders precisely if you would like to go home today. We have no desire to conduct further violence."

There was a pause. Captain Rosencrans clicked the transmit button on his radio and quietly said, "Stand down."

Tension hung on the air like a dense layer of ocean fog on a coastal morning. The Guard Captain felt perspiration inside his gloves and chill of dangerous uncertainty. He nervously looked from side to side for any movement or indication that further danger was imminent. Seconds felt like minutes. Finally, slowly, armed men closed in on the convoy from either flank with weapons poised to eliminate any threat his men might offer.

Zefrem was transfixed on the men approaching his door. They were dressed in fatigues and full combat gear, they looked just like his own men. Each of the two men closest to him had full beards, tactical combat helmets, dark sunglasses, and a single ear headset. The soldier to Zefrem's right reached for the door handle and opened the door.

In a direct and gruff voice, the man asked, "You in charge here, Captain?"

Captain Rosencrans numbly nodded.

The other soldier lowered his weapon slightly and said, "I'm going to need you to exit the vehicle." Keeping an eye on Rosencrans the soldier spoke again, "Fireteam 11 has a positive ID and control of opposition officer in charge." The man paused a moment, he appeared to be listening. He then said a single word, "Copy."

Captain Rosencrans found himself suddenly spun around and pressed against the side of the vehicle he had just departed. He was roughly patted down and then spun around once again. This time as he faced the soldiers, a new face stood before him.

Meeting his gaze was a clean-shaven man, he estimated to be around 6 feet tall. An M4 was slung over his back in a way that resembled how Johnny Cash might sling his guitar. The stranger didn't offer his hand.

"My name is Graham Pinchot, Commander, United States Navy SEAL. I am now in command of Patriots USA incorporated, a private military contractor and a growing cadre of patriotic American militia. Your outfit has committed war crimes under the guise of following orders. Those orders are not only illegal, they are immoral. You have a choice to make, Captain, and I hope you make the right one for yourself, your men, and your country."

Captain Rosencrans protested, "Now hold on a minute; war crimes?"

Pinchot held up a hand. "Save me the false indignation, Captain. I have video of your men outside the Guard post; believe me, the media will see it."

Zefrem's shoulders slumped. He practically choked on his response, "That order was given by Colonel Helms who was being directed by General O'Malley. I agree; it was awful. The President declared martial law..."

Pinchot cut him off again. "Enough, Captain. We'll get to the general, or more accurately the American people will. Here's what I need from you. I need you to turn these soldiers around and take them home. You are to tell your commanders that we got away. If you catch a case of hero syndrome and elect to pursue us as we head north for Edwards, we will annihilate you. Even now, you are in my kill box. You cannot outsmart me. Do not risk the lives of these young men and women over your pride. Take them home and stay there. Do we understand each other Captain?"

Captain Rosencrans dropped his head in shame. "Yes sir."

Pinchot spoke into his headset, "We're done here."

PART 2

CHAPTER 34

White House Situation Room

Marvin Miller strolled into the White House situation room fifteen minutes before the intelligence briefing was scheduled to start. He carried a thick folder labeled, *VERIFIED THREAT ASSESSMENTS,* under one arm and his laptop bag in the other. The Secretary of Defense, William Smithson, was chatting quietly off to one side with General Seth Adams, Chairman of Joint Chiefs. Marvin wished he could hear what they were talking about. He wondered if General Adams had his fingers on the pulse of his subordinates, and if mutiny was in the air, how complicit was the general? As for Smithson, Marvin felt better about his fidelity as a political appointee. Ultimately, he decided the internal debate was silly paranoia.

Marvin set the laptop bag on the floor next to his chair and unburdened his arms of reports. Glancing toward his right he noticed National Security Advisor, Savannah Lasser chatting with NSA director Anthony Flynn. Where the military-minded conversation had looked amiable, the discussion between Lasser and Flynn looked decidedly more urgent.

"Something wrong?" asked Marvin.

Savannah replied, "There's been an…incident out in Southern California."

An incident. Marvin felt his heart race. Anytime senior intelligence advisors were caught off guard by an *incident*, contentious and uncomfortable briefings were often close at hand.

"What happened, Savannah?" he pressed.

"We've prepared a brief for the President, Marvin," she said.

Marvin flashed, "Damn it, Savannah! This is no time to play games! I don't want to still be formulating a plan when the President asks for me to respond to this *incident*. So, what is it?"

Savannah relented. "Fine, calm down. A militia in San Diego ambushed a National Guard patrol. Four guardsmen were killed, including a colonel. An officer, Captain Rosencrans, was able to break contact and return to post with the majority of the convoy intact. He reports this militia is on their way to Edwards Air Force Base."

"Edwards? How does he know that, Savannah?"

Realization of an unprocessed enigma crossed Savannah's face just before she responded, "One of the militiamen told him."

Marvin pounced. "So, this militia sets up an ambush. They kill the Commanding Officer and a few others. Clearly, they achieved the element of surprise. Then, they just *stop* shooting and *tell* this captain where they're going next?! This is the report you are bringing to the President? Forgive me, Savannah, I didn't go to WestPoint so my understanding of military tactics isn't highly refined. That said, I wonder if they teach this unconventional strategy where you inform the opposition about your intended movements."

"While I concede there is a hole in the intel, there is at least a concern that we need to address," she snapped back. "If they are heading to Edwards, we should make eliminating these terrorists a top priority."

Marvin held an icy glare with Savannah until she shifted uncomfortably.

"*Obviously* there is a threat here that needs to be dealt with," he condescended. "I strongly advise you, however, to thoroughly vet this assessment before you present it to Tinsley. For starters, let's say they are going to Edwards. Forget for a moment that they disclosed voluntarily their objective, why Edwards? What's there that they want?"

Savannah looked down at her brief and then answered, "Edwards is a prominent test range. At this moment there are F-35s and B-1s out there conducting testing. Additionally, there is a cadre of Global Hawks."

"Does your intelligence suggest whether or not this militia has qualified F-35 and B-1 pilots in their ranks?" he pressed. Savannah scanned her brief. Marvin continued, "I'll go out on a limb and save you the trouble Savannah, they don't. Maybe a few have flown Cessnas, but there isn't a rogue group of qualified F-35 and B-1 pilots large enough to threaten us out there. I'll talk to Smithson and Adams about getting those Global Hawks temporarily relocated, just in case. Nellis should be secure enough. Now, did we get a name for this militia leader?"

Savannah flipped a page. "Yes. His name is Graham Pinchot."

Marvin nodded his head and wrote down the name, "Good. What do we know about this guy?"

"Captain Rosencrans reports that this guy, Pinchot, identified himself as a SEAL commander."

Marvin looked up from the notepad he'd been scribbling on, "You verify this yet?" Savannah shook her head. Marvin continued, "Get somebody on it. Find out everything we can about this guy. Is that his real name? Is he really a SEAL or simply posing as one? That would indicate some advanced training. If legitimate, is he still on active duty? Lots of SEALS out there; that's where they train them, Savannah. If he's not active, what does this guy do now? What are his connections? Finally, and I can't stress this enough; where is he actually going right now? I seriously doubt a Special Forces commander would disclose real movements. Honestly Savannah, the President counts on you to come prepared, I don't want to have you showing up for these briefings half-informed again. Find him. Yesterday."

A moment later the door opened again and everybody stood. President Tinsley confidently walked in and crossed the room to his chair positioned at the head of the table. "Everybody take a seat," he said. "Let's get started."

CHAPTER 35

CBS Affiliate
Riverside, CA

Gary Mullens nervously adjusted the knot in his tie and took a sip of ice water while the program director for CBS channel 7 Riverside went over a last-minute rundown of the evening's news. His heart raced in anticipation. Only a week prior, Gary had been doing the fluffy, bottom-of-the-hour pieces. A chance to read the news that mattered was a decided step forward in his career. *Let the next generation take over those special interest pieces, I'm finally getting my chance*, he mused. He would only have to wait another five minutes for the top of the hour and his long-awaited news desk debut.

An intern had only just taken away his glass of ice water and replaced it with a channel 7 logo coffee mug when the studio door flew open. A team of men in fatigues stormed in, rifles slung over their shoulders. A tall, well-groomed man held up a media storage device and said, "You guys are about to get an exclusive. On this flash drive is video evidence of a massacre perpetrated by the federal government on unarmed citizens who were simply participating in a peaceful protest." He handed the device to the program director. He then reached for a pocket, Gary thought, for a moment that he was about to brandish a weapon. Instead, he produced a recording device. "This is an audio confession from a National Guard Captain. In it he positively identifies General O'Malley as the man who issued the order to carry out the atrocity. The other responsible party, Colonel Aiden Helms is no longer a problem for the people of California."

Dumbfounded by the highly unusual and aggressive intrusion, the program director stammered, "We can't possibly..."

The soldier who appeared to be in charge angrily interrupted, "The President of the United States has declared martial law, he's suspended the rights guaranteed to you under the Constitution of the United States. Do you have any notion what that means for you?"

Gary Mullens asked, "How can we verify the authenticity of this video? How do we know this isn't some piece of propaganda and you aren't just using us?"

"In the sense that we are trying to influence how people think, then this absolutely is propaganda," the soldier responded. "However, where the government back in Washington is using cable news networks to spin half-truths or completely omit important facts to achieve public acceptance of their agenda, this video is unaltered primal truth. Don't you think the people should know that this government will kill anyone who dissents?"

The program director mumbled, "I just don't think..."

Cutting him off once again the soldier said, "Do you want to be remembered as the journalists that fought to preserve autonomy from big government control of the media or do you want to keep it safe and run your approved stories."

Gary rankled at the suggestion that his journalistic integrity could be dictated. "Let's see the video."

The soldier gave a curt nod and allowed the technicians to make copies of his audio and video. When the file transfer had been completed, he gathered his men. "Good we're done, let's get down to March Air Force Base ASAP."

With that, the men collected themselves and left the news station with the story of their lives.

CHAPTER 36

Eastbound Interstate 10
Near Whitewater, CA

Graham Pinchot called a halt to the convoy just a few miles short of a checkpoint. They had just been alerted by their only gunship, a Beech 18, as it passed overhead en route to 29 Palms. According to the pilot, all lanes were blocked by humvees functioning as barricades. While the blockade itself was troubling, the door gunners Graham had placed on the aircraft were accustomed to sizing up the opposition. It was their report that offered Graham hope.

According to the scouts, while the vehicles looked imposing, activity among the men at the checkpoint indicated they were something less entirely. Nobody occupied the Humvee turrets. There were no established fighting positions.

"Some of the men and women stood in circles, it looked like they were...bullshitting," the scout reported. "It's like they think the threat isn't imminent."

"Did these idiots seriously take my word at face value?" Graham wondered. He imagined a checkpoint somewhere to the north was bristling in anticipation for an assault on Edwards. Deciding to refocus on the obstacle facing his men, he called his leaders to meet at his vehicle. Once his key players assembled, they began organizing an assault plan. Graham looked to Tommy. "Can we call the gunship back to lay down some suppressive fire?"

Tommy shook his head. "Unfortunately, no. The pilot called bingo on fuel, they gotta get to Palms."

Graham frowned and then turned to Spurgeon Gorlick, "Alright, Spurgo, do you think we can just detour around them?"

Spurgo thought a moment and shrugged. "Anything's possible, boss. I guess my concern with trying to drive around them would be the unknown. We're not familiar with the surface streets and two-lane highways in this area. Maybe it works out and the rest of the trip is uneventful. The other maybe is, we run into a patrol in close quarters and they tear us apart. Or, maybe we get hit with an ambush."

Graham's frustration built as he realized that assaulting the checkpoint, while not desirable, was probably the course of action he was likely left with. They couldn't shelter in place and wait for the Beechcraft to return, doing so exposed them to attack while waiting. What troubled him more than the assault option was divulging his location. Graham didn't want anyone to get off a radio call that identified his men and their movements. Finally, he settled on a plan.

"Alright, let's send out three sniper teams, two men each to occupy high ground to their flank. Once they radio back that they are in position, we'll advance toward the opposition front, about 500 yards out. I'll call a halt. They'll see a column approaching, but we'll be just at the edge of effective firing range. We'll take potshots at them to draw their attention, the sniper teams can then engage from the flanks. Top priority on anyone who looks to be in charge and especially on radio men."

"In a vacuum, this plan sounds good, Graham. What happens if we take casualties or worse yet, what happens if instead of fighting in place, they advance? Or, worse still, what happens if they call in air support?" Tommy asked.

"Obviously those are both awful possibilities, Tommy. So, what are your thoughts? Want to just send out snipers and harass them while we maneuver around?"

"I think we need to get off this interstate," Tommy said. "We need to find a side road to follow and park out under some wind turbines until dark. Then move out."

As the trio exchanged ideas about how best to proceed while minimizing exposure, the distinct report of gunfire erupted from the direction of the checkpoint. Experience had taught the men that when small arms fire was incoming, there was a distinct snapping sound as the rounds flew by.

The small arms fire they were hearing wasn't directed at them. The question was, who?

"Commander; hard to make out details at this range," came a voice over the radio. "Looks to me like we have plainclothes fighters assaulting the checkpoint. Say again, fighters in plain clothes engaging checkpoint."

Tommy smirked. "I suppose this might just answer the question about whether or not those media geeks would air the footage we gave them."

Graham Pinchot smiled a tired smile, "Guess so."

Spurgo asked, "Should we help them?"

"We could use this diversion to get around them," Tommy pointed out.

Graham only took a moment to deliberate.   "Establish a flank and assault. We're not going to leave those patriots behind."

CHAPTER 37

Drone Control Trailer
Edwards Air Force Base, CA

Clark Gibson glanced to his side where camera operator Leon Hall was analyzing the video they had just captured. "Leon, that was a mess. What do you make of it?"

Leon squinted at the screen and ran the video through state-of-the-art filter software and multispectral imaging. He chewed on his lip for a moment. "Clark, it looks to me like this convoy of pickup trucks to the west had just stopped short, as if they didn't want to process through the checkpoint. Filters picked up a lot of small arms among them. A majority of them are wearing fatigues. This other group coming from the south? I don't know, I don't think they were with the convoy group."

Clark frowned. "Now hold on. Are you suggesting that these attacks are not coordinated? That convoy group just up and jumped on the bandwagon with the first group in assaulting that checkpoint?"

"Yeah, that's exactly how it looked," Leon said.

"I don't get it. Why this checkpoint in the middle of no-where?" Clark puzzled. Leon shrugged. "Why don't we run some facial recognition stuff and see what we come up with, I'm going to turn it north and see if we can't find this guy Pinchot heading for Edwards."

CHAPTER 38

**Marine Corps Air Ground Combat Center
Twenty Nine Palms, CA**

Afternoon heat gave way to evening winds as the Patriots USA column approached Marine Corps Air Ground Combat Center, Twenty Nine Palms, California. Graham lowered the windows of his truck to speak with the Marine checking identification. Unfolding his wallet to display his ID badge Graham greeted the sentry.

"Afternoon, Sergeant. Graham Pinchot; Private military contractor, Patriots USA."

Nodding, the sergeant examined the ID.

"Afternoon sir, we were alerted to be expecting you. General King himself called our CO; you have friends in high places. I count more trucks here than we were briefed on, sir."

Graham explained, "Yeah, we picked up some friends along the way."

Motioning toward a group of fellow Marines, the sergeant told Graham, "That's fine, sir. I will need to search all these vehicles before you enter; orders. Also, your men will need to properly clear and stow their firearms. You won't need them here, sir. Also orders."

Graham reluctantly agreed to the conditions of entry. In truth, the risk seemed minimal and the upside great for the imposition. Upon completing the screening process, the column was once again on the move. Henry had advised Graham that the airfield at Twenty Nine Palms was still a bit of a drive from the main gate.

The desert breeze wasn't nearly as refreshing as those coming off the Pacific, but still, Graham preferred to leave the windows down. Artillery reports reverberated from somewhere across the expanse of the Mojave. *Training?* Graham wondered. The arid desert air was already drying his nostrils and his mouth. The survivalist in him made a mental note; *we'll need to pack a lot of bottled water ... we can't assume it will be widely available.* Even now, in one of the few places on Earth he should have felt safe and protected, the responsibility he felt for the welfare of his men was heavy on his heart.

Just ahead of his truck, Henry led the way toward the airfield. He followed as Henry made a turn off the main road. Tumbleweeds rolled along next to his vehicle as they slowly approached the airstrip. Even over the noise of his engine and tire friction, Graham could hear off in the distance the distinct rumble of a helicopter approaching. A CH-53 Super Stallion slowly passed directly overhead as the column rounded the end of the runway, its rotor wash blew sand through his lowered windows. Graham chuckled as he tried in vain to quickly raise them.

Just ahead, Henry's vehicle crawled to a stop. A Marine in fatigues was speaking to him. With the noise of the nearby flight line, Graham had no hope to hear what they were discussing. The conversation was very short, as the Marine made a few hand gestures and pointed to some camouflage netting off to the left. Each driver in turn was directed to park their vehicles only far enough apart to get out. A detail of Marines then covered them all in netting.

The Marine who had greeted Henry approached Graham to introduce himself. "Welcome to Twenty Nine Palms, Commander. I work for General King. My name is Sergeant John Galt. The general sent me here to assist you in coordinating efforts with the detachment he sent."

Graham offered an appreciative handshake, "Thank you, Sergeant Galt, nice to meet you. Any chance I could arrange chow for my men and maybe somewhere they can rest for a bit?"

Sergeant Galt pointed toward a hangar and nodded, "Way ahead of you, sir. If your men will just head over to the hangar, we have some hot chow and a potable water tank they can fill bottles up from. It's not chow hall quality, but it's not MREs either."

Graham gratefully accepted the hospitality and directed his men toward the hangar. Once all the men had made their way toward refreshment and rest, Graham was left with only his two lieutenants and Henry. He asked their new host, "Sergeant, if it's not too much trouble, where might I find the officers assigned to this detachment?"

Sergeant Galt pointed at a Quonset hut sitting adjacent to the hangar. "They're all in there, sir."

Graham thanked the young NCO. With his small entourage in tow, he walked over to the door at the end of the building.

Just as he was reaching to knock on the door, he paused a moment to admire the artwork painted on it. A silhouette stencil of the Iwo Jima flag-raising made famous by Joe Rosenthal's iconic camera work during the battle had been painted on the upper half of the door. Just underneath the painting, someone had neatly written a Ronald Reagan quote, 'Some people wonder all their lives if they've made a difference. The Marines don't have that problem.' He thoughtfully pondered Reagan's words for a moment, *I hope what I'm doing right now will make a difference to someone*, he thought.

Graham knocked on the door.

From beyond the door, a voice answered, "Enter."

As Graham crossed the precipice, he allowed his eyes to adjust from desert sun to a dimly lit briefing room. Standing around a table in the middle of the Quonset hut were six officers in flight suits, to his surprise one of them was a woman. Another officer wearing captain's bars was dressed in fatigues. The senior officer among those in-flight suits seemed to be the tall slender man wearing the oak leaf of a major upon his lapel. He welcomed the newcomers.

"You must be General King's friends." His greeting was not a question so much as a statement of fact.

Graham nodded toward the major. Offering a hand, he introduced himself. "Graham Pinchot, United States Navy Commander. Now I run Patriots USA, a private military." Pointing to his companions in turn he introduced them as well, "These are my lieutenants; Spurgeon Gorlick, Army Ranger and Thomas Sullivan, Army Special Forces." Placing a hand on Henry's shoulder he finished, "And this is Henry O'Brien, USMC."

Smiling, the major shook each man's hand and offered his introductions.

"Major Harrison Holder, I'm a Cobra pilot. General King put me in command of the Marines he sent. There are three other Cobra pilots; Captains Quincy Jackson and Brent Avery plus First Lieutenant Clint Cooper. Captain Carolyn Michaels and First Lieutenant Scott Pietsch pilot the Osprey attached to this operation." Motioning toward the officer dressed in fatigues he continued, "And this is Captain Chad Davis, 1st Marine Division. He'll be your liaison in command over ground forces."

Everyone exchanged handshakes and greetings. When the pleasantries were finished, Captain Holder asked Graham, "So Commander, let's hear what you have in mind."

Graham knew that while they may follow his orders because a general had told them to, he would have to earn their respect. The plan he laid out before them in the moments to come would set the tone for how these warriors viewed him as a commander. If they did not agree with his plans, with his vision, it would be a simple thing to simply defer to a tyrant to save their own necks. Graham knew they had been sent ahead under orders, what he didn't know was how strongly they believed those orders to be legal and virtuous.

Positioning himself at the table directly across from Major Holder, Graham started, "Patriots USA isn't simply a company full of meatheads with guns. What makes our men special is how we structure and train. In essence, we divide them into three disciplines, each with thirty men. Assault squad trains in close-quarters urban combat, hostage situations, take downs of hardened structures, and HVTs. These men draw heavily from the ranks of men separating from active duty Special Forces such as SEALS, Green Berets, Rangers, and Raiders. They are world-class fighters."

Graham paused a moment for a drink of water, noticing as he did so that the officers offered no indication as yet to what they were thinking. He continued, "Security squad is equal in talent and ferocity to assault squad. In their training, I focus on defensive marksmanship and techniques. They are exceptionally adept at perimeter defense and movement tactics. Finally, there is the scout squad. These men are my eyes and ears. I'll use them to blend into the environment and provide me with all the information needed to make the most of the assets available. Every one of them are incredible marksmen, akin to Marine scout snipers. Hell, that's where I got most of them."

Major Holder slowly nodded his head and asked, "We were informed you had augmented your forces, who have you augmented them with?"

Graham acknowledged, "Yes, we have, and frankly I think the only scenario where we will end up successful will involve adding militia to our ranks. A lot of militia. I'm not talking about just enlisting every veteran or hunter we can find, although they should be people we look at. We'll need men and women with special skills. We'll need pilots, people with knowledge in medical skills in triage and treating combat injuries. We'll need people who know how to operate radios and set up communications networks. We'll need mechanics. We'll need people who work construction and have the equipment. We'll need electricians. We'll need people to manage logistics and people who are willing to help in keeping everyone fed. I think having a cadre of people who work law enforcement will be invaluable as well. They will have the best understanding of their embattled communities and those we can call on to find common cause in fighting a greater tyranny."

Major Holder crossed his arms. "What's your endgame here, commander? Where are you wanting to move this army you hope to build?"

"D.C."

A long moment passed before the Osprey pilot broke the silence. "And if you're successful in getting this army there, what then?"

Graham met her gaze. "We take it back."

"How are you going to move this force across the country?" she asked.

This conundrum was the weakest part of his plan. Finding the people would be child's play compared to moving them all. Vehicles would break down, and once they had grown to a size to make a difference, they would also become a slow-moving, easy target.

"Admittedly, moving across the country will be an imposing task fraught with countless dangers. I envision we start by moving a majority of the forces by personal vehicles, at least until we're able to acquire some aircraft capable of moving them faster. I'll send out scouts in advance to screen movements and provide early warning."

One of the other Cobra pilots spoke up for the first time. Captain Brent Avery was a stout, muscular officer who spoke with a matter-of-fact, dirt roads of Oklahoma drawl. "So, what's your plan to screen this tidal wave of movement from the threat above them?" To emphasize his point, he pointed a meaty finger toward the sky.

Graham offered, "I admit, that possibility has me concerned. What I've heard through my sources is that as of this moment, military assets are not in play. I hope that it stays that way."

Major Holder sounded less so. "Commander, once the shooting starts all bets are off."

Deep in his heart, Graham knew the major was right, he thought about the rumored airstrike his SEAL source had told him was responsible for the assault on Fredericksburg.

Captain Quincy Jackson added, "You know, the threat from above may not even have to be our military brothers and sisters. You have to consider CIA drone strikes."

Major Holder advised, "Graham, we'll have to work out strategies to defeat the eyes in the skies until you have an answer that evens the odds somewhat in terms of air superiority. Might have to consider some of the lessons we've learned through counter-insurgency conflicts, only this time you'll have to think and move like an insurgent."

Captain Carolyn Michaels interjected once more. "Actually, there may be one tool we can add to the bag that our enemies never enjoyed. When's the last time you guys were out at China Lake?"

CHAPTER 39

White House Situation Room

President Tinsley studied the report before him for a long moment in silence while NSA director, Anthony Flynn pulled up enlarged drone camera stills on the White House situation room monitor. Tinsley had assumed, before his first intelligence briefing at least, that imagery would be a combination of blurs and pixelation. It amazed him then and still did now, how crisp the resolution was on the Global Hawks.

Tinsley asked his Chief of Staff, "Who else has seen this footage, Marvin?"

Flynn offered a response before Marvin could review his notes, "Mr. President, this footage has only been viewed by a handful of senior analysts at CIA and NSA, just to verify authenticity. Oh, and the pilots."

Satisfied Tinsley flipped through a few more pages before finally looking up at the images displayed on the screen. "Good, Anthony. So, who am I looking at?"

Pulling a laser pointer from his pocket, Flynn put a red dot on the center of one man on screen.

"*This* is Graham Pinchot. Pinchot is prior service, Navy SEAL. He now operates a private military contracting business. At any given time, he has approximately 100 fighting men on staff. The government has used him in Afghanistan, Iraq, Syria, Libya, Somalia and countless other hot spots we prefer to not have American troops identified in. He's a world-class warrior who trains other world-class warriors."

Tinsley wondered aloud, "He works for us; so why are we talking about him?"

Marvin clarified, "Worked."

Flynn continued. "Mr. President, not only does he command the men of his company, he's been recruiting militia. This man is responsible for the ambush of a National Guard convoy in San Diego where four men were killed, including a colonel. The word we had following that engagement was that he was moving his militia north, to Edwards."

Confused the President opened his brief once more and said, "Edwards? Didn't I read something about that town outside of Palm Springs, Whitewater?"

The NSA director nodded his head, "Yes, exactly, Mr. President. He didn't set out for Edwards after all, and we think that information was a ploy to throw us off his trail."

Marvin creased his eyebrows in a sign of concern, "So this Whitewater checkpoint, that was this guy Pinchot?"

Flynn nodded his head and pointed to another photo. "In this image, we see plain-clothed insurgents assaulting the checkpoint from the south, while Pinchot's men are positioned to the west." Using a remote control, the NSA boss switched images on the screen and then continued, pointing toward a group of vehicles approaching from the east, "In this image, it is evident that Pinchot used the militia to draw attention away from his own movement so that he could circle behind our men to flank them from the rear."

President Tinsley considered the director's words for a moment. "Here's where I'm not clear, Anthony. If we thought he was heading to Edwards, how did this drone pilot manage to know where to look? Secondly, if his company relies on government contracts to operate, why is this guy now fighting us? Finally, and maybe I should have led with this; clearly this guy is both pissed and dangerous, so what does he want and where is he going?"

Flynn replied, "Signals intelligence intercepted outgoing messages from Pinchot's cell phone days ago, apparently he is connected to the Fredericksburg cell. As for the drone catching him on video, I'd like to tell you we knew where to look, in truth sir, the intercept was a happy accident. We were surveilling activity at the Palm Springs airport when the report went out for troops in contact. The drone wasn't armed, so there was nothing the pilots could have done, but it was fortuitous to have caught Pinchot at the scene."

The President acknowledged, "That is lucky, so where is he now?"

Miller and Tinsley each looked to Flynn expectantly, only to see a man searching for an answer. As the uncomfortable moment drew longer Flynn finally conceded. "I don't know, sir."

President Tinsley piqued an eyebrow. "You don't know?"

Marvin was aghast. "You had the drone right on top of him, what do you mean?! How do you not know?!"

"The pilots didn't know in real time who they were looking at," Flynn explained. "They were tasked, after collecting the footage, to return north for Edwards where the drone launched from. Their mission on the way back was to scan for signs of Pinchot's militia along the way. While in transit the co-pilot ran the Whitewater video through the facial recognition database. By the time it was discovered who they had and returned to the last known position, Pinchot and his men had dispersed."

President Tinsley closed his eyes and breathed deep. Eyes still closed, he asked hopefully, "Any intelligence at all indicating where he *might* be?"

Anthony Flynn explained, "This Pinchot guy is savvy enough to make tracking him challenging. When we took down the cell phone networks, he was smart enough to know that his smartphone only functioned as a tracking device. All the cell phones associated with him and his men are all still pinging San Diego cell phone towers."

"That's a hell of a non-answer, Anthony," Tinsley warned.

Clearly frustrated that he didn't have all the answers, the NSA director had to admit, "In short; no, sir. I don't know where he's going. I can only surmise that he will look to grow and he appears to be working north and east. Maybe NORAD?"

"NORAD", said Marvin flatly.

"Lots of Air Force and Space assets coordinated through Colorado," Flynn offered.

Disgusted the President nodded to a picture of Pinchot up on the big screen. "Find him, Anthony. I want him eliminated."

CHAPTER 40

Marine Corps Air Ground Combat Center
Airfield Tarmac
Twenty Nine Palms, CA

When Captain Michaels had first put forward the idea of flying north to Naval Air Weapons Station China Lake to acquire the cutting-edge, stealthy vehicle covering the Navy had been testing, Graham didn't know whether to laugh or believe her. As a Navy SEAL veteran, he had been aware of China Lake's existence in the abstract, which is to say he'd heard of the base. In Captain Michaels' briefing, he'd found himself enthralled by the obscure enormity of China Lake's history and purpose. The lesson reminded him of a family trip as a kid to the Grand Canyon. His dad had been driving so long that day, Graham had wondered what the fuss was all about. Staring out the window all he had seen as a small boy were bushes, rolling hills, and desert. Lots of desert. Even after Graham's dad had parked, the boy couldn't figure out why so many people were there or what the fuss was about. That was, until holding his mom's hand they walked down a trail, and all of the sudden the Canyon unfolded in front of his eyes in a stunning panorama.

Graham had thought at that moment that he was beholding Heaven on Earth. The view stopped his breath and tears streamed down his face. Only then did he understand just how grand his country was beyond the outskirts of his hometown.

In the case of China Lake, the beauty was not necessarily in the obvious panoramic sense. The magnitude of what happened there in regards to naval weapons testing was a revelation to the commander.

Captain Michaels explained that NAWS China Lake is the Navy's single largest landholding, representing 38% of their land property worldwide. A vast majority of naval weapons research, development, and testing. In fact, 85%, happens at China Lake. The main site and primary ranges collectively totaled more acreage than the state of Rhode Island. Weapons developed and tested there included: the AIM-9 Sidewinder, AGM-45 Shrike, and Tomahawk cruise missiles. Even tech that didn't seem to have weapon applications such as the glow sticks used by on deck naval personnel, had been developed at China Lake.

It was this latter category, tech with non-offensive applications in testing and development that Graham and his men had an interest in. Enough interest to risk a movement north for.

Stealthy vehicle netting?

"Sounds like something out of a sci-fi movie", Graham said.

Captain Michaels countered, "Stealth fighters, drones, and laser weapons all were thought to be sci-fi at one point. Yet, the F-117 revolutionized how we prosecute air campaigns, that tech was developed in the '70s and is now decommissioned. Drone strikes sent terrorists in the Middle East into hiding. Laser weapons have been successfully tested on naval vessels and are now rumored to be in the testing phase on airborne gun-ships. Why then is the possibility of stealthy concealment netting such a farfetched concept? You say sci-fi. I say not only is it possible, but evolution is also inevitable."

Graham knew the captain was right. He also knew that any hope of safely moving his men and the militia they recruited across the country would hinge on beating the government's state-of-the-art surveillance assets. Their survival could very well depend on how well Graham was able to conceal move-ments. Stealthy concealment netting alone wouldn't be enough, many tactics would need to be considered and utilized along the way. When not maneuvering, however, he could think of no better method of shielding his people than making them ap-pear invisible.

The only conundrum left to Graham once he had been con-vinced that the personnel at China Lake would be agreeable to helping out their fellow countrymen, was how to get there. In-itially, he had considered taking a handful of trucks three and half hours across land. It had been Cobra pilot, Captain Brent Avery who again warned of the threat from above.

"China Lake and Edwards share airspace commander. I think it ill-advised to test the eyes of the drones flying out of Edwards so close to their home. That's a lot of exposure."

Once again, Graham realized the short-sightedness of his plan. While driving there himself offered a certain degree of control, it also likely meant certain death.

Captain Michaels put forth a plan that sounded more prom-ising. "We'll load up a small contingent of fighters into the Osprey, in case we end up off script and in a fight somewhere between here and there. One of the Cobras can fly escort. I know where they store the gear. I was there on a temporary assignment a few months ago. We'll transit and land under cover of darkness. I'll work out the details with the Marine Captain stationed there. He's been covering all kinds of Marine gear out there while drones and satellites look down and offer feedback. Regarding this tech, he's the subject matter expert and a true American."

Mission briefing for the flight north had taken place hours before dusk. Immediately afterward the ground crew responsible for maintaining the Osprey had towed it to the hangar and backed the aircraft in, presumably for maintenance. While they did conduct an in-depth pre-flight, Graham had subsequently come to appreciate the subtle genius of a simple flight line move. With the aircraft's loading ramp concealed from air surveillance, Graham and his handpicked team were able to freely move about the aircraft in preparation for their mission.

Graham had known from the moment the mission had been conceived that he would personally assume the risk of leading the small detail. He also knew that despite Tommy and Spurgo lobbying hard to fly with him, they would be needed to spearhead other efforts for success in future movements. Graham rolled out a map of southern California and Arizona for the duo on top of a desk in the maintenance control center. Placing the tip of his right finger on top of their current location he traced the roads back south to the town of Twenty Nine Palms and then west around Joshua Tree. The commander's finger then followed highways south toward Palm Springs before turning east for Indio. Just south of Indio where highways 86 and 111 began to diverge, Graham tapped his finger to emphasize the location.

Glancing up at Tommy, he laid out a mission. "Take scout squad and all the radio operators you'll need, minus two for the rear, and set out south. Break them up into small groups, no more than two vehicles at a time. We don't want to attract attention as we pass by Palm Springs and Indio. Once clear of the larger population centers, split the vehicles evenly between highways 86 and 111 going around this large water feature, Salton Sea. Establish observation posts as best you can. Obviously in places that offer the best concealment possible while still achieving situational awareness. The main force will follow, I need eyes on the routes we plan to take to screen their movements. Nothing that looks like a uniform, blend in."

Tommy studied the map for a long moment. "So you're thinking down through El Centro and east through Yuma?"

Graham moved a finger over Phoenix, Arizona on the map. "Correct, until we can do some recon around any given population center to ascertain how security is oriented, I don't want us just plunging headlong toward any more checkpoints blind. So that rules out taking Interstate 10 east."

Tommy asked, "You don't want to take a more northern route? If we take Interstate 40 east, it's wide open from here to Flagstaff. After Flagstaff, it's clear sailing until Albuquerque."

Graham grinned and pointed to a spot on the east side of Tucson, "That's true, but I've got my eyes on this place."

Tommy looked at him blankly. "What's there?"

"The Boneyard," Graham answered.

"The Boneyard", Tommy said flatly. "Why *the Boneyard*?"

"The Boneyard is a collection of perfectly good aircraft that have been cast away and forgotten," Graham said. "They also have parts there to bring grounded aircraft up to mission standards. Furthermore, there are A-10s stationed there which are fully mission capable right *now*, and the Air Force *trains* pilots there. Can you think of a better place we can go to cobble together some airpower?"

Tommy had to concede the creative genius of the idea. "Boss, I have to admit, this is definitely some outside-the-box crazy fox shit. I like it. Are you at all concerned about resistance? You think they'll just open the gates?"

"I'm not sure how hospitable the command there will be. I'm going to send Gunny ahead as part of your movement, only he's going to Yuma. We'll see if he can't make some friends there to help us out. If we are unable to gain entry through diplomacy, we'll take it by force."

Tommy was taken aback by the audacity of his commander's stance. "You *really* want to get in a fight with the active-duty military?"

"We'll have to make a stand somewhere. Without an air presence, we're doomed." Graham left no room for further discussion on the matter as he turned to Spurgeon Gorlick. "Spurgo, I'll need you to make the men and vehicles ready for the move south. We'll need vehicle elements for the east route, 111 and the west route 86. Each convoy will need a radio operator."

Gorlick brusquely nodded in approval. "Anything else boss?"

"Actually, yes. See if Einstein can find an internet connection to check in with his buddy up at Jim Creek. I'd like to get a feel for what's going on elsewhere."

CHAPTER 41

Jim Creek Naval Radio Station
Arlington, WA

Edwin Daily retrieved the club wrap he had packed for lunch from the staff refrigerator and, after a few tries, convinced the soda machine to take his wrinkly dollar for a Diet Coke. Returning to his workstation, Edwin set his lunch down and fetched a laptop from his backpack. Once unfolded, the screen took a split second to illuminate with a password prompt. He deftly entered the password and bit into his lunch.

Daily took another bite and looked at the screen. A notification for a chat request through ICQ was pending. The message was from Einstein_76. Daily had been concerned for Grant. Navy intel indicated militias were in clashes with Guard units all over the country, and he'd not heard from his old friend in days. He opened the chat window.

Topshelftechie_01: *Hey buddy, everything ok with you?*

A few minutes went by as he waited for a response. Daily finished his wrap and started drinking his soda.

Einstein_76: *Been in a few brief firefights. We haven't lost anyone yet, good planning and surprise. Been a few minor injuries, nothing serious. I'm good.*

Topshelftechie_01: *That's good. Where you at now?*

Einstein_76: *Sorry brother, can't' say.*

Topshelftechie_01: *Can you tell me if you're still in San Diego?*

Einstein_76: *I'm in California, can't give specifics.*

Topshelftechie_01: *Fair enough, just glad you're alright. It's getting crazy out there.*

Einstein_76: *What's going on?*

Topshelftechie_01: *Cable news networks are airing clips every night of anarchy in virtually every city. It's really weird man. There's no rhyme or reason. In one area you might have a group of people protesting the government's policies peacefully only to be confronted by those who support their agenda and things turn violent. Meanwhile, somewhere else pro-government rallies are being disrupted by Guard units or other elements and things turn violent. Cities are on fire. There have been massive increases in crime, especially looting. People are getting desperate for things like food and medicine. Haven't seen any clips on the news, but I read a darknet blog where the writer reports that looters were being hung. Like with a noose! Went back later and that blog had been taken down, he hasn't posted since.*

Einstein_76: *Holy shit!*

Topshelftechie_01: *I know right?*

Einstein_76: *You need to be careful.*

Topshelftechie_01: *I appreciate that. Listen, I run my stuff through so many filters, it'll be hard for them to track me down. Been doing this a while now.*

Einstein_76: *Just worry about you man.*

Topshelftechie_01: *I know.*

Einstein_76: *Why is the Guard breaking up pro-government rallies?*

Topshelftechie_01: *First, the martial law decree forbids public gatherings. The real reason though, citizen on citizen violence. There's been so much of that going on, it's keeping them busy full time just to maintain some semblance of order. Unchecked, they are worried about the population centers turning into full-fledged war zones. Word through our comms monitoring is they have undergone a complete paradigm shift in mission. They simply don't have the manpower to go root out militias.*

Einstein_76: *Well, that's good right?*

Topshelftechie_01: *Maybe.*

Einstein_76: *What do you mean maybe?*

Topshelftechie_01: *What if the President invokes the Insurrection Act?*

Einstein_76: *I can't imagine that every single general will willingly wage war on the American people.*

Topshelftechie_01: *I don't think so either.*

Einstein_76: *They would be forced to pick sides.*

Topshelftechie_01: *Just like the Civil War.*

Einstein_76: *That's terrifying.*

Topshelftechie_01: *You need to watch your ass.*

Einstein_76: *I will buddy, you be careful too.*

CHAPTER 42

CNN Evening News

Megan Kincade made a mental adjustment, forcing a poker face on as the program director was counting her out of the commercial break. Megan had been reporting on dramatic events her whole career with the media giant, CNN. She had covered; elections, natural disasters, military conflicts around the world, high-profile homicides, financial crises, political controversies, and more. None of that made her nervous. She was a recognizable face to a large segment of American viewers, and Megan had always prided herself on bringing them hard-hitting, honest journalism. This was a dangerous time in America, and she knew it. Reports received by CNN, unverified, had been laden with troubling news of late. Deep inside she felt anxiety. Anxiety over violence on the streets of America. Anxiety over network pressure to lob softball questions at administration officials. And currently, anxiety over the video interview she was about to conduct.

Megan reviewed the notes she had prepared when the segment had been formalized. The subject of her interview, Marvin Miller, the President's Chief of Staff, had an unsettling aspect about him. Megan felt as she had leading up to her interview with a Sheikh who had been detained at Guantanamo Bay for supporting Al Qaeda. Marvin Miller felt, dangerous.

"30 seconds, Megan," the program director said.

The program director in front of her counted down with his fingers and the "On Air" light switched. Looking into the camera, Megan forced her on-screen smile.

"Welcome back, everyone. As promised, we are excited to bring you an exclusive interview with White House Chief of Staff, Marvin Miller, tonight. Mr. Miller joins us by video from the White House amid an unprecedented time in American history. Welcome to the show, Mr. Miller."

A satellite image of Miller appeared on a monitor. Megan thought Miller's body language conveyed a certain arrogance. Worse yet, his smile felt, diabolical. Megan forced her body to restrain a shudder.

"Hello, Megan. Thank you for having me."

Megan began with a question about the ongoing civil unrest.

"Mr. Miller, we're seeing video from all over the country which appears to show citizens and government soldiers engaged in various levels of violence against each other. We've seen peaceful protestors being treated in a manner commensurate with that of the violent protestors. What can you tell us about the President's mindset regarding the handling of civil unrest?"

Marvin Miller shifted slightly in his chair before answering.

"Megan, that's a good question. I believe the President would remind the public about the dangers of recency bias. This is to say; relying too heavily on the natural cognitive function of believing what is happening currently will continue to happen, is foolish and doomed to failure. Take for example the events of only a few months ago up in Minnesota. Jake Thornton was a perfectly stable American citizen until he wasn't. A person who seemed harmless was, in fact, a ruthless killer. *And* ridiculously easy access to dangerous firearms cost many innocent Americans their lives. Only days ago, Megan, so-called peaceful protesters gathered on the grounds adjacent to many congressional offices. In that situation too, everyone was harmless until they weren't. We cannot simply assume that a protest will remain peaceful or that a seemingly stable American will continue to remain stable. To put the physiological phenomenon into lay terms; imagine a basketball player who has hit five straight 3 point shots. The sixth time that player goes to take a 3 point shot, every person watching assumes the shot will be successful. In truth, it is a statistical anomaly; eventually, that player will miss the shot. The President believes, and in my view justifiably so, that a peaceful protest is just *one* armed citizen away from a massacre."

Megan thought the statement to be one of the scariest she had ever heard. In her mind, the logic was inherently flawed. By his very own reasoning, the President was himself making decisions based on recency bias. Of late, protests had turned violent, yet that was not *always* the case nor would it necessarily continue to escalate. Megan decided not to confront the man on his assertions and continued the planned interview.

"I see, Mr. Miller. Are there any cases in these interactions with the public where the government is detaining citizens they deem to be dangerous?"

Miller's lips pressed into a thin flat line. Megan caught the subtle change in body language, realizing she had caught her guest with an unexpected question.

"While the President's martial law decree allows for these extreme measures, he categorically denies such measures are being taken." *Categorically denies, he's full of shit*, Megan thought.

On this point, Megan ventured as much opposition as she dared without risking an end to the interview.

"Mr. Miller, what then would you or the President have to say about reports coming into CNN, admittedly unverified as yet, that assert outright abductions for offenses ranging in severity from misdemeanors such as graffiti and petty theft, up to active resistance or sedition?"

Miller scoffed, "I would say, Megan, that the President has also heard these *ridiculous* conspiracy theories about some *government boogie man* haunting the streets of America. Naturally, we will not comment on fables."

Megan could smell a liar from a mile away. A career in covering politics had assisted in developing her deception radar, and this guy was triggering all her alarms. She decided to take a chance and veer off-script.

"Mr. Miller, our congressional correspondent, Christina Walker has been unable to make contact with leadership in the House and Senate for days now to no avail. What does the White House have to say about the troubling inaccessibility of our representatives to the media?"

She watched his body language as the man processed the question. Marvin Miller's torso seemed to stiffen as if he was consciously trying to override his natural physiological tendencies. Miller's chin, meanwhile, quickly inclined while he slowly moved his right hand over his lips. It looked as if he was trying to wipe the truth clean from his face.

"Megan, as you well know, the Capitol building and corresponding offices were scenes of a grisly assault at the hands of extremists and domestic terrorists just days ago. At this time, our colleagues over at intelligence are still processing active threat assessments. The Congress has been sequestered for their safety until the Capitol can be adequately secured."

Megan had just witnessed an astounding lie; she was sure of it. She was certain the network had reported on congressional deliberations following the riot, so why now go into self-preserving seclusion? It made no sense. What had happened, what was he hiding? Megan refused to let this floundering fish off the hook.

"You're saying the entire Congress is somewhere safe until Washington is secure?"

Miller squinted suspiciously. "That's right."

"Where, sir?"

"Obviously I can't say, Megan. If I did, they wouldn't be safe, now would they?"

Megan inclined her head slightly, "I suppose not, sir. I have just one more question."

Miller's shoulders seemed to noticeably relax. "Yes, Megan?"

Megan leaning forward, only slightly as if to indicate the pending answer had her on seat's edge, "If the ongoing violence escalates rather than dissipates, even with the peacekeeping presence of National Guard throughout the country, what steps is the President willing to take in response to that scenario?"

Marvin Miller's body language, for the first time since the interview's inception, was one of honesty.

"Megan, it is the position of President Ray Tinsley to have peace throughout the land. He will not, however, forsake the future peace to be gained through the elimination of privately owned firearms simply because Americans are temporarily unhappy with discourse. This President understands better than most that uncomfortable actions must be taken for the prosperity of life in America. Beyond that, I am not prepared to discuss options the President will consider to achieve his goals at this time."

Realizing that for one of the rare times in her career an interviewee had ended a segment before she was forced to break, Megan thanked her guest for his time and sent her viewers to the commercial.

CHAPTER 43

The Oval Office
Washington D.C.

The Oval Office was uncharacteristically crowded. Upon the Resolute Desk sat two briefings of vastly different sizes. The brief resting nearer the President's left hand had the words, *VERIFIED MILITIA THREATS*, in big bold letters on the cover. The brief's sheer volume dwarfed that of its more modest counterpart to the President's right. While slender in comparison, the second brief had the more imposing title; *Insurrection Act of 1807. History and potential implementation.*

Seated around the room were several of Tinsley's most trusted advisors. In the lounge chair to his left sat the Vice President while to the right Marvin Miller leaned against the wall. Others sitting in front of him, included William Smithson, General Seth Adams, Savannah Lasser, and Anthony Flynn.

Tinsley slowly closed his eyes as he ran the fingers of his left hand over the militia briefing and then re-opened them. Focusing on the room, he realized that everyone had stopped talking. Forgoing pleasantries he said, "I've spoken with the Attorney General. She has advised me that in order to invoke the Insurrection Act, I must first publish a proclamation ordering those in rebellion or causing unrest to disperse."

Nobody spoke.

The President continued, "Marvin, see that a dispersal declaration is drafted for my signature." Miller nodded. "Furthermore, a past precedent would suggest that I am clearly within my authority to invoke the act when a formal request has been submitted to that effect from a state's governor. In some states, we may be able to solicit the formal request, while others will stubbornly refuse. So, thoughts?"

Smithson ventured feedback first in the form of a question, "Where are you wanting to deploy the military to Mr. President?"

Tinsley flatly responded, "Everywhere resistance exists."

Smithson tentatively offered, "Mr. President, speaking strictly logistically, this would be a daunting challenge."

"While this command could be issued Mr. President, my concern would be how vigorously orders of this nature would be followed from the lowest enlisted soldier up through field grade officers and even generals," General Adams added. "We haven't put our warriors in this position since the Civil War. What happens when an officer is sent to their home state and ordered to fight their fellow citizens? Worse yet, what happens if they openly rebel?"

Waving a hand over the militia brief, Anthony Flynn pointed out, "Maybe our soldiers don't need to be dispersed throughout the country to deal with this crisis Mr. President."

Intrigued the President leaned his head back slightly, "What do you mean Anthony?"

Flynn opened his hands palm up as if his idea were an offering. "What if we put together airpower assets with NSA for real-time satellite positioning of these terrorists? Streamline it. Cut out the red tape, Department of Defense analysts, and the burdensome courts. All of which slow down the process so much that by the time we verify a threat, they've moved. Treat these people like we do elsewhere around the world."

President Tinsley slowly rubbed his hands together as he turned the words in his head. "I like it, he said. "How does this reduce my need for ground presence and uncertainty of loyalties at Defense? We're still using military assets I presume?"

"Mr. President, we could compartmentalize the info we provide the pilots. Tell them they are known and identified foreign fighters who have infiltrated our country to sow this discourse. Tell them they are terrorists like we did for the aircrew that neutralized Fredericksburg. Focus on the leaders in these strikes to break the resolve of those following them. They disperse, and we track them by satellite for as long as we need to in order to ensure no future sedition grows."

Nodding, the President asked, "And those who don't disperse?"

Lasser suggested, "We could continue to use the media as suggested in the Miller Report to manipulate the public."

"Explain."

Lasser continued, "Signals intelligence is overwhelmed with indicators that the public is terrified about what's going on. Feed their fear. We use the media to pin the blame on these rebels for everything they are frightened over. With enough despair, they will get desperate and organize to eliminate these terrorists for us. Our hands stay clean of American blood in the minds of the vast majority. Those who suspect or accuse your administration of wrongdoing, we identify and handle them as necessary via the authority of your martial law decree."

The President smiled. "I like it; make preparations."

"If I may?" Vice President Whitmore spoke for the first time since the meeting had begun.

"Of course, Adam."

"When you're ready why not go ahead with invoking the Insurrection Act?" Whitmore suggested, looking through the brief. "At the very least, even if you don't intend to use ground forces, it may be enough to compel some leadership to stay out of the fight. If there is an active order for deployment, they will remain in a state of readiness and perhaps will be less likely to stick their necks out in defiance."

"What about the governors who will scream that they did not request I do so."

Whitmore shrugged. "Mr. President, with all due respect, I'm not sure you need them to ask. You have declared martial law; this is a national emergency."

Tinsley nodded his head. "Good point Adam. I'll think on it."

CHAPTER 44

Home of Staff Sergeant Sean Patton
Just Outside Hurlburt Field, FL

Sean 'Deadman' Patton loved his job. He often reminisced, fondly, how as a boy, he marveled at airplanes that would pass overhead. They had always fascinated him. Some of the other boys he grew up with would poke fun at Sean. One time in little league baseball, the coach had put him in rightfield. During the third inning of a game, in which his team was losing 11-2, a fly ball was lofted toward Sean. He was, of course, focused on another flying object high above. A passenger jet was drawing a line across the sky with contrails that stretched as far as Sean could see. Meanwhile, despite shouting from his teammates, Sean was none the wiser that the ball was incoming. Naturally, the pop-up landed harmlessly at his feet. The opposing team scored two more runs and the game ended by mercy rule.

Sean loved airplanes, anything that flew really. He would harass his dad to take him to every airshow within a day's drive. While other boys would collect baseball cards to read the stats on the back and talk about the greatness of Tony Gywnn, Ken

Griffey Jr, and Greg Maddux, Sean studied aircraft identification books and theories of aerodynamics. Before long, at a glance, Sean could quickly discern at distance the difference between an F-18 and F-15. His dad would marvel at the skill while Sean would simply say, "That was an easy one dad. Hornet's vertical stabilizers angle away from each other while the Eagle is straight up and down. Also, look at the intakes. The F-18 is more circular, while the F-15 is sharper. OH and..."

Sean's dad would chuckle and say, "Okay, okay; you're right."

In high school, Sean studied hard and earned exceptional grades. His mom wanted Sean to go to college. Sean's eyes were elsewhere; the sky. He enlisted in the Air Force after graduating high school and found himself up close and personal with AC-130s after completing all his technical schools.

Sean Patton was living his dream.

Initially, the young airman found himself in the back of the gunship. Loading ammunition for fire control, the work was back-breaking and enormously gratifying. Eventually, Sean worked his way forward in the aircraft to sensor operator.

Sean earned the call sign, Deadman, on a sortie over Northern Afghanistan. Al Qaeda had encircled a combined team of Marines and Army Rangers near Bala Murghab. Sean directed his munitions onto the enemy so ferociously, so accurately, his FCO gave him the name inadvertently when the area had been cleared, "Nice shooting, they're all dead, man!" Another crew member mistook the context and said, "Nice job, Deadman!" The name just stuck.

At first, he didn't care for the moniker, but you don't pick your own call signs in aviation. Circumstances or colleagues pick them for you. The name grew on him and Sean embraced it as a badge of honor. An acknowledgment in the culmination of all the hard work he had put into being an exceptional aviator and warrior.

Deadman had never felt the remorse or guilt that other men and women reported after flying sorties that resulted in taking the lives of America's enemies. Deadman felt that each time he sent a round out the side of an AC-130, a corresponding American life was spared. In his mind, the equation was that simple.

Deadman retrieved a cold beer from the refrigerator and walked to his favorite chair. On his television Megan Kincade was narrating a CNN special timeline report, "America on Fire." He twisted the cap off, folded it in half between thumb and forefinger, and then dropped the cap into his beer. Once it rattled around the neck, Deadman would know when a refill was imminent.

He took a long pull from the bitter domestic beverage and played through the Fredericksburg sortie in his mind. Deadman reviewed mission performance in his head the way an elite professional quarterback might review film of opposing defenses. Like his athletic counterpart, the little things, especially off-script decisions and mistakes always stood out. A quarterback might bemoan an interception thrown directly to the opponent, while Deadman would endlessly stew over shots he took in danger close scenarios. His worst fear, like that of all aviators who flew combat sorties, was green smoke.

Friendly fire.

Firing on, and killing his fellow service members would be worse than death he thought. For the deceased on the ground, their problems were over. Forever. For Deadman, killing his own people would be just the beginning of a lifelong nightmare.

While a very scarce number of friendly fire casualties came at the hand of AC-130 aviators in Afghanistan and Iraq, they did happen. Most notably in Operation Anaconda. Thankfully for Deadman, those deaths lay at the feet of another man. His record was spotless.

Yet, as he sat in the recliner, a voice deep inside Deadman screamed to be heard. While the strike on Fredericksburg had been ordered from the highest levels, there was still something about the video on his screen in real-time that burned in eternal testimony on his retinas.

The way the vehicles were parked was...odd. No apparent defensive perimeter, fighting positions, or sentries.

Sensors showed *no weapons.*

Deadman threw back the remainder of his beverage and retrieved another. Sitting back down in his recliner, he listened to the television as Megan Kincade was outlining how a group of extremists managed to smuggle enough weapons through Capitol security to overrun all the checkpoints. Deadman mused, *Those idiots either weren't checking people or they are comically undertrained. One weapon? Sure, mistakes happen. Enough to breach checkpoints? Something doesn't wash here.*

Deadman felt his hand shaking as he lifted his phone. Unlocking the screen, he brought up the search engine and typed, *Fredericksburg.*

The initial search results listed dozens of the most recent news stories. All of which detailed, in various degrees of ridiculous misinformation, what actually happened the night his aircraft attacked the site. All of the mainstream outlets had run numerous articles about the destruction of a terrorist militia in Fredericksburg, none of which were able to even closely identify how the destruction had come about. Theories ranged from

Special Forces ground assault to a sabotaged ammunition dump exploding. The information was absurd.

Scrolling down he found an article from an internet blogger putting forth the possibility of a B-52 strike. *Interesting,* he thought. *Closer.*

Nobody had it right. The internet was totally full of shit.

Deadman changed the search criteria from *news* to *all* and began a new scroll.

On page two of his new search, an interesting result caught his eye; *Fredericksburg Civil War Reenactment.* He clicked it.

As he read the article detailing the annual Civil War reenactment in Fredericksburg, he came across the date. He blinked his eyes and looked again.

The day of the event had been scheduled for the day of his crew's sortie over Fredericksburg.

Deadman sprung from his chair and ran to his bathroom to vomit.

CHAPTER 45

Naval Air Weapons Station China Lake, CA

Graham Pinchot and his small security team shared jump seats on the Osprey with a fireteam of Marines as the aircraft approached China Lake. The flight from Twenty Nine Palms so far had been a thrilling one. Captain Michaels had insisted that as a precaution, she and the Cobra should fly nap of the Earth. Flying at nearly 250 miles per hour somehow felt faster the closer you got to the ground.

Wearing a headset the crew provided, Graham was able to keep up with how the mission was progressing. According to the pilot, they were only a few minutes away from the landing zone or LZ. The former SEAL had landed at many LZs throughout his career on several different aircraft models. Many of his insertions had come on Blackhawks, he'd been flown in on Chinook's a few times and even a Super Stallion once. This had been his first flight on an Osprey. It surprised Graham how quiet the aircraft was.

The transition from forward flight to hover was more seamless than Graham would have expected. Sensing the Osprey approaching the ground, Graham used the queue to switch his night vision goggles on. As he glanced toward the aircraft rear, China Lake was revealed in shades of green. In his headset, Graham heard the crew chief callout ground proximity markers. "Ten feet.... five feet..." Finally, he felt a slight bump as the Osprey came to rest safely on deck.

As Captain Michaels had briefed, the Marines disembarked first. There was no expectation of the LZ being hot, but the Marines were creatures of habit. Once they had cleared the ramp, Graham and his entourage followed. Behind him, the twin rotors atop the Osprey spun down to a stop and the LZ fell silent.

Too silent.

Goosebumps ran up Graham's neck to his highly tuned sixth sense. The only noise he could hear just off in the distance were the spinning rotor blades of the Cobra as it circled wide around the LZ, ready at a moment's notice to nose in and strike.

No machines running.

No China Lake personnel within earshot were apparent to welcome them.

No ambient noise from animals, not so much as a cricket.

Through his night-vision goggles, Graham could see warehouse buildings off to their flank. The lights of the building along with the moon and stars above were the only illumination at hand to assist his goggles in cutting the darkness.

Graham jumped as Captain Michaels walked up behind him and softly touched his shoulder. He gruffly asked her, "Where is this friend of yours, Captain?"

"With the cells crashed I couldn't exactly nail down the details" she explained. "Those Department of Defense servers can sometimes logjam email transmission speeds. He said he'd be here tonight."

One of the Marine riflemen was the first to notice a vehicle approaching from the direction opposite the buildings.

"Vehicle from the right."

Graham turned toward the direction the vehicle approached from. "Captain, is this your guy?"

Confusion weighed heavy in her voice. "Curious, I would have expected him to approach from that warehouse." She pointed to the left.

Graham keyed his short-range radio to raise the backup circling nearby. "Pinchot to Archer 02, advise, unknown vehicle approaching from western flank. Standby to vector in from the east." While Graham couldn't see the sentry circling off in the distance, he could discern a subtle change in pitch as the blades cut the air in an aggressive nose-down approach.

Thankfully, as the vehicle approached, whoever was behind its wheel left the headlights off which kept the newly arrived from being temporarily blinded while they removed night vision goggles. As the vehicle rolled to within about a hundred yards it became apparent the model was a Ford F-250. Meanwhile, the deadly backup approaching from the east became louder.

A tense moment sped to a crescendo as the Ford truck screeched to a stop a mere thirty yards away and Graham's friend above flared to a hover in a menacing show of force. The truck's passenger door opened slowly and an uncomfortable chuckle permeated the darkness.

"Got to say, Carolyn, standing opposite the business end of one of our own Vipers; that's a first for me. I can see how our enemies might get watery bowels."

Relieved, Captain Michaels cursed Captain McIntosh in frustration and gestured toward the warehouse where she had expected him to be. "Damn you, Franklin, you scared the hell out of us. Why weren't you over at your little hideout there?"

Franklin McIntosh grinned. "Well, that's because I brought you a little gift."

CHAPTER 46

Drone Control Trailer
Edwards Air Force Base, CA

Drone co-pilot, Leon Hall blinked in disbelief at the monitor in front of him, "You see that, Clark?"

Clark Gibson put the Global Hawk into a sweeping left-hand turn for a second look at the activity happening below their drone on the ground at China Lake. Centering the activity on his screen Clark prompted, "Run them through the facial recognition database."

Surveilling people from 10,000 feet in real-time could be an inexact science full of ambiguous deductions. It wasn't as if they could eavesdrop on conversations as they happened in crystal clear resolution, yet at least. Clark had read the briefings and participated in discussions within his drone community which detailed the research and development going into that technology. For now, he and Leon had to make do with the facial recognition software and multi-spectral imaging assets available to them.

Military aircraft operating in and around Naval Air Weapons Station China Lake at night was not at all unusual or even noteworthy. In fact, it was commonplace. What piqued Clark's interest, however, was watching what looked like a hot LZ insertion that did not include a weapons test element. China Lake was not where the Navy and Marines sent their warriors to conduct combat training. What was happening below simply didn't fit.

It looked like...*a meeting.*

Clark watched as the AH-1Z Viper pulled collective and banked away from the people grouped on the ground. "Get an ID on that tail designation, Leon?"

Leon shook his head, "Negative. The angle they turned out relative to our position, letters are obscured."

"How about that V-22?" Clark asked.

Leon zoomed to the markings painted on the vertical stabilizer of the Osprey. "Looks like a Pendleton bird."

Clark wondered aloud, "Any squadrons have detachments up here?"

"Last testing involving Ospreys ended months ago, Clark."

"So, these aircraft shouldn't be here," Clark concluded. Two of the personnel who had disembarked from the Osprey climbed into the pickup truck, leaving the rest of the party standing around the Osprey. The truck then pulled away toward the warehouse nearby. "What is going on down there?"

Leon abruptly grabbed Clark's attention, "Facial recognition just returned a positive ID on one of the men in that truck, and it's Graham Pinchot!"

Astonished, Clark wondered, "What's he doing here? Where are the rest of his militia?"

Leon worked his keyboard in a frenzy, "Uploading this to Langley."

CHAPTER 47

White House Situation Room
Washington, D.C.

President Tinsley studied the images on the screen. "We're sure this is Pinchot?"

"100% Mr. President. It's him," Savannah Lasser assured him.

Tinsley looked to his Secretary of Defense. "What do you have nearby in air assets, Bill?"

Smithson offered, "We could vector in a B-1 from Edwards, Mr. President."

"Do it." Said the President.

CHAPTER 48

Naval Air Weapons Station China Lake, CA

Captain McIntosh backed his truck up to the covered load-ing dock at the warehouse. It had at first struck Graham as odd that an isolated warehouse out in the middle of nowhere would have a covered vehicle dock. It was their host who explained to him that while it was cooler at night, loading and unloading vehicles during the day out in the Mojave could be very heat-intensive, back-breaking work, so the Navy added the cover along with giant fans to keep servicemen from suffering heat-related injuries.

Graham followed Marine Captain McIntosh into the build-ing along with a woman who accompanied their host to the covert rendezvous. He learned that her name was Charlotte Washington, but why was she here? Once inside, Captain McIntosh switched the lights on revealing a pallet of what they had come for; concealment netting.

On a nearby desk, a small FM radio emitted white noise. No talking. No music. Just white noise. Graham thought it was odd.

"What's the story with that crappy radio? is it broken or are you tuned in to one of those radios that listen for alien signals?"

Captain McIntosh replied, "Crappy radio, very funny. I use that radio in testing. On that particular frequency the pitch of that white noise spikes when a drone passes overhead. It's a handy little indicator we learned from Taliban detainees in Afghanistan. Can you believe an Afghani guy driving a shitty, beat-up Toyota figured that out before the U.S. military?"

"Interesting. So what about your testing requires you to monitor for drones?"

"I don't have to; just think it's cool."

"Guess we have different ideas of cool. So what can you tell me about the netting we're here for?" Graham asked.

The use of camouflage netting in wartime was by no means a recent development in human history, and it certainly wasn't new to Graham either. Historians had shown the use of concealment techniques dating back as far as the very first human civilizations. In fact, the idea of camouflaging oneself to avoid detection predated humans entirely. Natural adaptations in the history of evolution bore witness to the fact that animals had been exploiting the concepts of camouflage concealment throughout the history of the planet.

Graham thought as he looked over the pallets; *Looks like camo netting. What makes it different?*

As if reading Graham's mind, Captain McIntosh tapped the pallet with a smile.

"When I got word you were coming, I had my guys go ahead and put together a tidy little care package for you. There isn't enough of this stuff on the planet yet to adequately cover all your vehicles, we're only just wrapping up testing. Minus what I need to finish up my assignment, you're looking at all there is."

Graham asked their host, "Looks the same as any camo net-ting, I've ever seen, so what makes it special?"

"Have you ever seen the Harry Potter movies where they use that invisibility cloak?" McIntosh asked.

Graham raised an intrigued eyebrow, "Yeah?"

"Yeah, this isn't that shit." McIntosh laughed; Graham cocked his head in a look of confusion. Realizing the joke hadn't landed, McIntosh continued. "I'm sorry, been saving that joke for a while. Standard concealment netting works by visually disrupting outlines perceived by the persons observing it. Meandering lines of mottled camouflage patterns hide the outlines or contours our brains use to visually ID objects. It tricks your brain. Your brain wants to naturally connect the lines of camouflage with the environment around it, making objects under concealment appear invisible. Those proven pat-terns haven't been changed here, what has been changed is what we made it out of. You hear the word 'stealth' I'm sure one of your first thoughts might be the F-117, which itself used contour technology to break and disperse observation by radar. Later aircraft that are stealthy have somewhat more conven-tional shapes, which is to say they look more aerodynamic. So, how are they able to achieve this stealth?"

Graham answered, "Don't they use a special paint?"

McIntosh excitedly affirmed Graham's answer. "Yes, it's known as Radar Absorbing Material; or R.A.M."

Graham wasn't connecting with the captain's enthusiasm. "So, you sprayed this R.A.M. paint on this netting?"

"No, no of course not." Chuckling as he shook his head Cap-tain McIntosh enlightened Graham, "Painting this much netting would make it prohibitively heavy. Our engineers have isolated the elements within the R.A.M. which makes it so effective and found a way to convert it to a series of dyes we can use to color the netting. The real miracle though is far more exciting than avoiding detection by radar, we have developed at China Lake, a cutting edge microfiber that is exceedingly effective at concealing heat signatures. What the B-2 Stealth Bomber has meant for projected airpower around the world, this netting, in turn, changes the game for the future of troop movement. Once mass produced, even countries with satellite capabilities will have to be watching your specific movement in real-time to have any hope in knowing your whereabouts. Even then, if you can find a way to attach this netting to a Humvee and keep it from getting beat to hell at highway speeds, it might just take standing next to the highways to hear these vehicles rumbling by to know someone is coming."

"Are you the engineer?" Graham asked Charlotte, impressed.

"No, I'm a drone pilot," she supplied.

"I'm sorry, I don't understand the connection, Ms. Washington. Why are you here?"

Captain McIntosh held a hand up in a calming posture. "Graham, Ms. Washington has only marginally participated in the concealment testing, which is to say, she has flown over the test range to deploy her scanners to find objects under this netting. The sensors on her drone are by far the most sensitive and state-of-the-art currently being tested out on the Mojave. What makes her participation unique though is the command vehicle she operates from."

"How do you mean Captain?" Graham asked.

"Her command vehicle is everywhere and nowhere. It's a laptop she carries, so she's highly mobile, not bound to some windowless Conex box. Charlotte can pilot her drone from a Humvee or even aboard another aircraft."

Graham acknowledged, "That's amazing, but why are you *here* Charlotte? As in, *this meeting?*"

Charlotte fixed Graham with a confident look and said, "I strongly believe that tyranny doesn't belong in this country; Franklin tells me you are doing something about it. That's why I'm here, I want to help. Am I wasting my time commander?"

Satisfied, Graham was about to offer her a formal welcome to the team when the white noise droning from the FM radio drastically changed pitch. Thanks to his newly acquired knowledge about what the noise meant, Graham and his party sprung into action. Whatever was in the sky above, Charlotte wasn't piloting it. A laptop bag, presumably containing her gear, rested zipped up at her feet.

"Let's get this loaded right now!" Graham turned to Franklin, "Do you have a loose net we can drape over the truck? We're about to test your moving vehicle theory."

CHAPTER 49

White House Situation Room
Washington, D.C.

President Tinsley entered the situation room as his advisors were engrossed by live drone footage on the big screen. As far as the President could tell, the drone appeared to just be watching a patch of sand with a building on it. Secretary Smithson pointed out the warehouse to Tinsley.

"There's the building Pinchot went into, Mr. President."

"What happened to the Osprey, Bill?"

Smithson explained, "Mr. President, they lifted off a few minutes ago."

"So, he got away?!"

Savannah Lasser interjected. "Negative, Mr. President. There has been no movement coming out of that building; he's still there."

Calmed by the reassurance Tinsley wondered aloud about the departed military aircraft. "So, Pinchot rides in on that Osprey, from where we don't know. Then, they just up and leave him behind? Why?"

Smithson shrugged. "Tail designation tells us it's a Pendleton Osprey; though the commander out there is reporting no aircraft missing. We're still trying to figure it out, Mr. President. Our camera was trained on the building so that Pinchot wouldn't slip us twice. We didn't catch the circumstances of their pre-flight or departure besides catching the attack helicopter passing through the camera periphery a few times. It was the drone pilots who noticed the departing aircraft via their other sensors."

"We'll get to them later, then. How far out is the B-1?"

Surgically the SecDef replied, "They are commencing their run as we speak, sir."

"Good," Tinsley said. He stood with his arms crossed, focused on the screen.

"Munitions released," the SecDef coldly called out.

Time seemed slow. *How long does it take for a bomb to reach the ground anyway?* Tinsley wondered. Long seconds passed until finally, a brilliant flash illuminated the screen followed by a large plume of debris and smoke.

"We got him, sir," Smithson announced.

CHAPTER 50

Naval Air Weapons Station China Lake, CA
15 Minutes Before B-1B Lancer Strike

Captain McIntosh slowly nosed his Ford pickup past the edge of the loading dock canopy. Visibility from his driver's seat was exceedingly poor, it reminded him of trying to drive a vehicle with an icy windshield before it completely defrosted. The mad dash to manually throw as many netting bundles into the back of his pickup before covering it with one had combined with the sudden adrenaline infused urgency from Pinchot had left his chest thumping and his lungs gasping for air. McIntosh realized the drone's presence had necessitated their speedy departure, what he had yet to fully grasp was why they were in such imminent danger.

Frustrated with the agonizingly slow speed of the pickup, Graham asked, "Can we go any faster?"

"If we move too fast, the netting will ripple and that will break the continuity observed between the environment and us, we'll stick out."

Graham keyed his handheld radio. "We've got a drone above, I don't think it's armed, if it were, I imagine it would have struck by now. Could be an airstrike or there might be a QRF. We're in concealment, going to wait them out. Head to the FARP (Forward Air Refueling Point), we'll rendezvous with you there." Concluding his radio call Pinchot asked, "What was that FM frequency you had the radio set to?" He quickly adjusted the pickup's dial to the radio frequency McIntosh gave him and turned the volume up.

Seated behind McIntosh and Pinchot, Charlotte pulled out her drone control laptop. McIntosh studied her in his rearview mirror. "Are you launching, Charlotte?"

Focused on her screen and controls, Charlotte slowly nodded. "Given the visual range of drones, even if it's not essentially on top of us, they can still observe our movements. Your FM radio trick is a cute little tool, but it's not enough. If we're truly in danger, then we'll need to take away their eyes to slip the dragnet."

"You're going to try using *Medusa* on an airborne target?!" McIntosh grinned. "We've only talked about that!"

Confused, Graham interjected, "What the hell is *Medusa*?"

"You didn't really think we'd limit our drone test to mobile remote applications that look exclusively for hidden vehicles and people out, here did you?" Captain McIntosh glanced over at his passenger. "We develop and test *weapons*, Mr. Pinchot."

Having completed numerous deployments around the world and been a firsthand witness to countless drone strikes, Graham was aware that drone aircraft could be fitted with Hellfire missiles, a robust air-to-ground munition used by the U.S. military. *Air to ground.* To his knowledge, current drones had not yet been used in air to air combat. Incredulous, Graham asked, "You've put air to air missiles on a drone?"

Charlotte scoffed, "No. *Medusa* is far more elegant, far more lethal."

Graham thought he could hear each rock as the Ford slowly rolled over the Mojave sand. *More lethal than a missile*? Time felt as if it had been crawling along next to the pickup, he wondered how much space they had put between themselves and the warehouse.

A radio call crackled across Graham's handheld. "Archer 02 plus one, Oscar Mike, good luck."

A long moment passed before McIntosh broke the silence. "So, Mr. Pinchot, why does a drone have you so spooked?"

"I've led ambushes on the National Guard a few times," Graham said.

McIntosh grimaced, "I can see how that might get someone's attention. Why?"

In the backseat, Charlotte quietly said, "I'm airborne."

Captain McIntosh nodded in acknowledgment and prodded Graham. "So? Why are you picking fights with the Guard? I figure you have good reasons, but still, I'd like to know why you have drones up there looking for you."

Graham sighed, "Back in San Diego, the Commanding Officer there had led a massacre on a crowd of unarmed protestors, most of which were younger men and women. I have body cam footage. They weren't armed, just kids really. Out in Virginia, a military strike decimated a Civil War reenactment my son had gone to with my dad. Still haven't heard from them. "

As Captain McIntosh was framing his reply a large flash turned the night into day behind them and the vehicle rocked from the resulting shockwave. Sand, rocks, and debris were flung into the air before raining down.

Graham turned to check on Charlotte. "You alright?"

Charlotte's eyes were wide open and she quickly nodded several times, her expression reminded Graham of how some of his men looked the first time they had been close enough to an airstrike to feel the shockwave.

Captain McIntosh, seemingly shocked by the proximity of the explosion himself slowly said, "Someone bombed my office."

Graham said, "I'm glad you had that radio on, otherwise we'd all be dead by now. Any chance the shockwave compromised our cover?"

McIntosh admitted, "Possibly, it's still on us, I can't see out the windows. If it's not draped over the hood or back end, we may be thermally exposed."

Graham patted the Marine on his shoulder. Turning to Charlotte once more he asked, "Can you really take down the drone that found us?"

Charlotte thoughtfully pursed her lips together, still focused on her equipment and she replied, "I hope so."

Graham said, "I hope so too."

CHAPTER 51

Drone Control Trailer
Edwards Air Force Base, CA

With his state of the art Global Hawk orbiting high over China Lake, pilot Clark Gibson had a commanding view of the B-1B's objective below. Despite a veil of darkness cast over the target zone by the night, thermal imaging sensors and night vision technology revealed the scene below in high definition for Clark and co-pilot Leon Hall.

Clark checked in with his co-pilot. "Confirm time on target."

Leon Hall responded, "Aircraft on approach from the west; going to be a low altitude drop. They want to drop before anyone hears them coming."

Clark checked his sensors and monitor. With the bomber so close to weapons release this was no time for carelessness, he didn't want the target to slip through their fingers. The ambient light was optimal for night vision, the picture was crystal clear, with no anomalies. Thermal imaging had been most active when the Osprey and Cobra had departed the area, nothing around the warehouse below.

Leon called out, "Thirty seconds."

Clark focused his attention on the warehouse, hyper-aware of any sign of movement or indication of trouble. Nothing. The scene below was still, an image of tranquility moments before the explosive storm of a JDAM.

"Weapon released," Leon announced.

Somewhere below the Global Hawk, a B-1B Lancer streaked toward the warehouse, wings swept back for a supersonic low altitude bomb run. As the lone JDAM glided Earthward to its programmed coordinates, the bomber's pilot nudged the yolk back to gain altitude and turn out toward the north. A split second later the munition pierced the roof of the warehouse and detonated.

Clark and Leon had observed hundreds of explosions in their careers as drone pilots. At the moment of energy release, the sudden and explosive release of photons appeared as a flash on their screens when using night or thermal imaging. As a result, the effect was a brief moment of blindness as the light and energy dissipated. Upon reestablishment of visual acuity, thermal and visual light signatures were strongest around ground zero of the impact. This was of course due to burning buildings and rubble or secondary explosions.

What the two drone pilots were focused on, however, was not the burning warehouse. They were focused on picking up the telltale thermal signatures of little white-hot figures fleeing the chaos.

They were looking for survivors.

It was in this sweep that Clark's co-pilot detected an anomaly. An inconsistency that he had not expected to see. Leon squinted and blinked at the image on his screen. "Clark, there's something out there east of the warehouse. It's like a little red circle with a sliver of green around it. What is that? A glitch?"

"Is it debris flung from the blast?" Clark changed the filter on his monitor from night vision to thermal. As he spoke, the mystery object moved! The object appeared to be...rolling! "What is that?!"

Clark Gibson and Leon Hall began to feverishly work the cameras, zooming in close, trying to figure out what was moving out there. Neither of them had ever seen a phenomenon like this before. They had seen countless motor vehicles and humans scatter like cockroaches following an explosion, but never ... debris. Leon worked every diagnostic angle he could think of while Clark kept the drone oriented so that the camera wouldn't lose track of whatever it was.

Suddenly, as Clark leveled the drone following a minor course correction, all screens in the control trailer went black and the message feared by drone operators throughout the U.S. government appeared on his screen: *Signal Lost*.

CHAPTER 52

FARP Delta
Naval Air Weapons Station China Lake, CA

Captain Franklin McIntosh sped as fast as he dared in low visibility across the unpaved desert floor toward FARP Delta. The last thing McIntosh wanted was to get disoriented in the desert and drive headlong into an active refueling operation. As the vehicle drew nearer to the area where he expected to find the aircraft, Graham rolled down his window.

"What are you doing?" McIntosh asked.

"How many times have you pulled up to a hot FARP?"

"A few times, why?"

Graham craned his head toward the opening and fresh air. "The thing about conducting nighttime operations in my experience is, you learn to engage all your senses. A hot FARP will not be quiet. Besides the turning rotors, you should expect to hear a very loud and high-pitched whine coming from the refueling truck. Then there's the smell, jet fuel has a distinct odor. It's hard to miss." Graham stopped short with his attention piqued. "There, you hear it?"

McIntosh rolled his window down and focused. The sound was faint, but there. He thought it sounded like a whiny dump truck, only constant. The Marine thought it odd, years in the military and he'd never forced himself to appreciate the subtleties of operations happening under his nose. As he drew closer to the FARP, the odor of jet fuel became heavier. Then he saw them, two Marine Corps combat aircraft sitting about a hundred feet apart with their rotor blades turning and taking on fuel. Silhouettes moved around the back of the Osprey while only the apparent refueling personnel stood abreast of the slender attack helicopter.

Graham sprung from his seat as the truck came to a stop next to the fuel truck. Motioning toward a handful of personnel standing nearby, he asked, "Can I get a hand moving this gear to the Osprey?" Grabbing all the netting he could carry himself, Graham made for the idling aircraft.

The modest lighting provided by the refueling truck made the aircraft appear almost ghostly ahead of Graham. As he got closer, the rotor wash kicked up dust and sand causing him to squint and tilt his head to deflect the microprojectiles. He ascended the ramp and stowed his cargo. Picking up the headset provided to him by the Osprey's crew chief Graham raised the pilot. "Pinchot to Michaels."

Captain Michaels' welcoming voice answered. "Welcome back, Mr. Pinchot. We saw the flash from the explosion; were you able to get out with what we came for?"

Graham replied, "More or less. We loaded everything he had on the dock; wish it was more. Seems to work though, we covered the truck with it as we drove away."

"You covered the truck with the netting and drove?" she asked.

"Very slowly, yes." Graham said.

Carolyn Michaels was taken aback by the statement despite her extensive knowledge of the concealment material's capabilities. They had never tested it in motion. The repercussions were stunning. If true, she thought, virtually any moving object could be made stealthy.

Any object could potentially include those who may wish to track them. She asked Graham, "So Pinchot, how did you know an airstrike was coming and how did you know the netting would work while in motion?"

"As for the performance of the material over a moving vehicle, I didn't come up with the idea," he answered. "Your buddy Franklin theorized it could work if one could prevent it from rippling at speed. Hence the agonizing crawl in our getaway. Even then, I was worried the blast had blown it off the vehicle and exposed us. Discovering the drone observing us was a lucky coincidence I also have Franklin to be thankful for. He had explained how it was possible to be alerted to drone activity if you know what radio frequency to monitor. Turns out that was a very serendipitous nugget of info tonight, the chance conversation saved our lives."

"There's a drone on top of us?! Why didn't you lead with that?!" Carolyn fired back. "We need to get the hell out of here before they vector another airstrike on us! One well-placed JDAM and this whole FARP goes up!"

"Working on it." Graham watched as Franklin and Charlotte strapped in. Charlotte still had her drone control laptop out and was focused on piloting her aircraft. "As for the drone, it's been handled. We're clear for the moment. I agree though, let's get the hell out of here before anyone comes looking."

"What do you mean, *handled*, Pinchot?" Carolyn sharply demanded.

Leaning his head back in the cramped jump seat, Graham finally calmed his vitals after the literal and psychological shock of the attempt on his life. The obliteration of the warehouse was a symbolic representation of his former, normal life. Graham had lived through countless dangerous airstrikes in his life as a special forces operator. He'd never been the target before this night. His life had exploded into a new reality, and he knew the Marine pilot was right. Another airstrike could be imminent, he had no reasonable assurance that despite the destruction of the drone that another asset was not currently tracking him and everyone within his personal blast radius. Graham responded to the irate Osprey pilot, "Franklin's friend shot the drone down, but you're right. We need to get the hell out of here. Might want to stay low and fast on our way back to Palms, Captain."

CHAPTER 53

Marine Corps Air Ground Combat Center
Twenty Nine Palms, CA

The eastern Mojave sky burned orange as the early dawn light filtered through a morning haze of desert sand. Captain Michaels skillfully hugged a jagged range of mountains to her right with the Osprey while the Viper escort kept pace easily to her flank. Circling the end of the range, desert mountains gave way to a sea of sand and finally, the airfield they had departed from hours ago.

Dipping the nose of the attack helicopter, Captain Brent Avery sped ahead while the Osprey pilot transitioned her aircraft from fixed-wing orientation to its short runway settings. Manipulating the nacelles with deft precision, her thumb rotated the rotors until the aircraft looked more like a helicopter. Within minutes the Osprey gently settled onto the Twenty Nine Palms runway and taxied to the hangar where a Humvee awaited them. A distinct placard in the front window of the vehicle displayed three stars.

Graham descended the ramp rubbing his fatigued eyes in the morning light. After allowing a moment for his vision to adjust and refocus, Graham spotted the stars. Anxiety crept in as he looked around. Had a general found his operation and come to arrest him for treason? What happened to his men? With the jet engine noises fading, the flight line drew quiet and that unsettled him.

Turning back toward the Osprey he looked at Charlotte, engrossed in her laptop controlling her experimental drone. Graham asked her, "You have eyes above us right now?"

"No, I actually have the craft on approach right now. It will be safe on deck in a few minutes. Why?"

Graham's eyes darted around, trying to quickly diagnose the scene. Surely a general wouldn't direct an airstrike on top of themselves, so any potential threat would have to be an ambush. Where would they come from? The lack of situational awareness along with having only recently been targeted by the U.S. government had Graham seeing threats in the shadows. He walked slowly toward the open hangar door. A familiar voice echoed; Henry O'Brien.

Realizing that he was likely dealing with some fresh onset paranoia, Graham walked briskly toward his friend. A moment later he spotted Henry talking in a small group with a few of his team leaders, John Galt, and a man he had not seen before. As Graham drew closer Henry greeted his boss.

"Hey! Welcome back, Graham; how'd it go?"

Unsure about the stranger Graham carefully responded. "All things considered it went well, thanks. What's going on, Gunny?"

"Preparations are complete, Graham" O'Brien assured his boss. "I've personally made sure each vehicle is loaded with water, ammunition, and essential provisions for the next leg of our trip."

"Where's Gorlick?"

"Spurgo left just a little while ago to check the town and Palm Springs for shops where he could acquire communication gear, like walkie-talkies, and to stock up on batteries. He said he'd catch up as we moved out." Henry paused a moment to take a drink of his coffee. "There is also word from General King back at Pendleton."

"He radioed?"

"No, he sent a courier." Henry motioned toward the stranger. "Radios from Pendleton are being monitored apparently."

Of course, that would explain the Humvee outside, Graham mused.

Just then the stranger stepped forward to extend his hand in introduction.

"Lieutenant Colonel Dick Sharper, I'm on General King's staff. He ordered me to rendezvous with your outfit to ensure you are brought up to speed with what commanders back at the Pentagon are doing about organizations like Patriots USA. I'm also to offer you support and logistics. Henry says you plan to move on Davis-Monthan. If you would consider a stop at MCAS Yuma on the way we can offer bolstered air support as you strike east from there."

Relieved that the Humvee outside meant support rather than arrest Graham let down his guard. "The support means the world to me, Colonel, thank you. We would be grateful for whatever you and the general have to offer. If you would, what information do you have from the Pentagon?"

Sharper drew a map from his cargo pocket and laid it across a workbench just a few feet away. Using a toolbox to hold down one end of the tightly rolled map to the left he stretched it out and weighed the other end with a maintenance manual. Graham noticed colored pencil marks all over the landmass depicted on the map. It was the lower forty-eight states. Sharper put his right forefinger on some red marks in the state of Texas.

"Here." Sharper paused and made eye contact with Graham. "Reports of militias the size of divisions have assumed control of the state. They've set up checkpoints at all major interstate intersections to control rapid ground movement and isolated Austin. The Texas state capital is essentially encircled. Private aircraft have been used to conduct surveillance of National Guard movements which has allowed the organized militia to fade and blend before being forced to engage armored infantry."

Graham nodded his approval. "Smart, any idea what their end game might be down there?"

"What do you mean?" Sharper cocked his head

"Do we know if they are planning an offensive to break out of the hide and seek cycle? Or are they solely focused on simple survival until there is some resolution?" Graham accepted a cup of coffee from one of his men and took a long drink.

"We think they will try to bring Fort Hood into their fold before moving north for Whiteman."

Whiteman? That took Graham off guard. "You think the Texans are going straight for stealth bombers and nuclear strike capability?!"

Realizing in retrospect how his theory must have sounded, Sharper pumped the brakes with a hand gesture. "Actually, we don't believe they intend to use the B-2s at all. We believe the Texans want to secure them in place so that the nuclear deterrent will not be used against the populace."

220 · MATTHEW H. WHITTINGTON

"I see." Graham glanced over the map, he noticed a red "P" with an arrow pointed toward Twenty Nine Palms, yet no marks had been made to indicate his overnight China Lake raid. Graham wondered if General King had been informed of the sortie or not. Shifting gears, he asked, "What hit Fredericksburg?"

Sharper seemed uncomfortable with the question. Graham decided he either knew the answer and wouldn't say or he had his own unsettling suspicions. A long moment of no eye contact passed as Sharper pretended to study the map. Finally, the officer framed his response. "There's a tidal wave of intelligence from the Department of Defense, state guards, and private militias to sift through out there. None of it points to that Virginia situation. The Special Forces guys out in Kentucky have been very quiet, which isn't unusual. What did stick out was an experimental AC-130J weapons test reported canceled over North Carolina due to an in-flight instrumentation issue."

"You don't think the flight was cut short?" Graham thought to mention this conversation with his SEAL friend, Bobby, who had hypothesized this scenario during their last phone call.

"The destruction at Fredericksburg fits the profile," Sharper shrugged.

The thought of his father and son having fire raining down on them from the vaunted gunship, the terror they must have felt, made Graham sick to his stomach. He hoped that it was fast. Graham choked down his emotion.

"Anything else, Colonel?"

Sharper waved a hand over his map as if to reinforce the vastness of the United States. "Conflict and skirmishes are widespread. Most of the conflict decision makers seem to be concerned with is violence within the major cities. The inner-city situation is chaos. Governors have re-tasked National

Guard units nationwide to keep from losing control of population centers altogether. There are supply shortages; people murdering each other over life-saving medications such as insulin and transplant medications. When the cell phone networks went down, everyone panicked. It's scary out there, you will want to avoid metropolitans in your movements."

Graham glanced at Henry whose face was clouded in despair. He knew Henry and Shelby would have made preparations for emergencies to cope with supply chain disruptions. Just how long would any surplus last though and which would expire first? Her medication or the blossoming conflict? Graham shuddered at the truth that he knew. Tamping his personal feelings, Graham thanked Sharper and turned to his men.

"Let's roll out. Henry, I'd like for you to fly down to Yuma on the Beechcraft with the netting we brought back and get a jump on coordinating logistics. See if the commanders at Yuma will make room for our plane in a hangar and find an area to conceal our ground vehicles with the netting. We'll want to keep our assets as obscured from satellite surveillance as possible. Until we have a handle on additional air assets, that old bird is the only one we own outright. The rest of us will follow by ground."

Turning to the team leaders Graham laid out his movement orders.

"Two vehicle teams spaced ten minutes apart. One radio in each element. Get down to Yuma; by then O'Brien should have a concealment plan in place. If you run into trouble, do everything you can to break contact. Our objectives aren't here. Scout team has the routes screened; make radio contact only if it is necessary. I'll bring up the rear with McIntosh and the drone pilot. I think I can convince her to fly overwatch. Stay vigilant guys."

CHAPTER 54

Squadron Briefing Room
Hurlburt Field, Florida

Sean Patton waved at a group of maintenance personnel grouped around engine number one of the AC-130J parked on the hangar deck as he walked briskly for the door leading upstairs to the briefing room. Adorning the walls of the corridor were countless unit citations, recognition plaques, and photographs. Approaching his destination, the aroma of coffee and murmur of voices carried down the hall toward him.

Drawing near the briefing room threshold, Sean could finally distinguish the voices of his pilot and FCO. Captains Tony Boyton and Charles Masters respectively. As Sean stepped into the room, the two officers looked up and nodded before resuming their conversation.

Electing not to interrupt their business, Sean stepped to the front of the briefing room and powered up the big flat-screen used by aircrews to play intelligence videos and gun camera footage. He then used the computer attached to it and pulled up a search browser where he entered *Fredericksburg Civil War Re-enactment*. Sean changed the search criteria from *news* to *all* and clicked over to the second page just as he'd done the night before, and found the link for the current year's event. Double-clicking the hyperlink brought the re-enactment schedule into large, high definition resolution. Sean turned on a second, smaller monitor and used the computer to bring up his crew's sortie history, and selected the same date as that displayed on the larger screen's event schedule.

Glancing over at the officers still engrossed in conversation, apparently oblivious of what Sean had been doing, the Staff Sergeant casually walked over to the coffee pot and poured himself a tall cup of jet black. Sean loudly slurped his hot beverage and neither of his companions took notice. Finally, he walked over to the briefing lectern and stood there staring at the duo until they sensed the discomfort.

Agitated, Captain Boyton snapped, "For Christ's sake, Sean; what is it?!"

Sean took another drag of coffee before setting the styrofoam cup down. "I think we fucked up. Royally."

CHAPTER 55

NSA Headquarters
Fort Mead, MD

Conference Room 1

Upon entering Conference Room 1 at NSA headquarters in Fort Mead, it was apparent that the government's secretive intelligence-gathering arm worked on a budget that any other publicly funded entity could only dream about, save perhaps the Department of Defense. For starters, the primary screen used by the agency's director to conduct briefings in the room was not only massive, but the display also featured virtually unheard of 8K resolution and voice controls matched to Director Anthony Flynn. Barking orders in staccato clarity, Flynn could populate the screen with video, slide shows, and even the agency's state-of-the-art code-breaking software program. This allowed any staff he cared to gather the opportunity to workshop complex data analysis and hostile signals information. With a simple voice command, he was able to prompt the computer controlling the room to switch the windows from transparent to reflective, so that anyone passing by would not be able to observe the room like a fishbowl.

Each seat around the conference table featured a compact, high speed/high-resolution computer which analysts could use to remote access their office workstations where many kept up on projects and stored notes and briefs. Embedded in front of each place into the table itself was a smaller cup-sized circle which with the push of a button on the employee's armrest could be turned either hot or cold to keep their chosen beverage at an optimal temperature. The room itself was kept at a crisp temperature to preserve electronic assets, though the seats were custom made to be heated if a person so desired.

Director Flynn wanted his people comfortable at work, it was as if he never wanted them to rather be home. At this late morning hour, a vast majority of his talented analysts were at their assigned workstations throughout the complex; gathering, deciphering, and compiling data from around the country. The sheer volume of outstanding threats being assessed from within America's borders was overwhelming for even the most seasoned of his people. In fact, the director had only insisted on a single analyst for his teleconference with the CIA: Annie Nguyen.

On the big screen, a video conference prompt spun; the computer was waiting for the outgoing invite to be accepted. Using the idle moment to communicate with her boss, Annie sought clarity.

"Director, the limitations put on the public for communications may have slowed or stalled some of the threats. In reality, it seems to be having an effect closer to slowing than stopping and we lost something in the process. With so many people divorced from devices now, they are much more difficult to track. Our listening assets are being pushed past their limitations. We

can hear the chatter, yet with so much of it and no way to pinpoint using cell tower triangulation identifying where exactly
the threat is has become exceedingly difficult. What exactly are
we offering to the CIA in this briefing? I fear we will come out
of this meeting looking bad."

Flynn betrayed no indications of concern or uncertainty.
"Annie, I appreciate your concerns regarding our image and
reputation. Please keep in mind that I'm aware of our current
limitations and have a plan. I'm seeking a more seamless mar-
riage of assets and information between the two agencies. If
they are reticent to accommodate, I will work political back
channels until I get what we need."

"I see."

Annie glanced down at her small cup of Vanilla Chai tea
and absently stirred the drink. *Work political back channels until I get what I need?* There were definitely times that Annie
marveled at the bulldog within her boss, and then there were
times that his apparent savage resolve unsettled her. This fell
into the latter category.

Another moment passed before the enormous screen came
to life with the face of a woman. The stranger was well dressed
and professional in appearance, yet still featured a stressed and
sleep deprived aspect. Slowly batting her eyes as if trying to
absorb caffeine infused eye drops, she introduced herself.

"Good morning. Jennifer Miller; CIA. Sorry for the delay,
it's been a long night."

Director Flynn greeted her icily. "I'm sure it's been a long
night for many of us the community, Ms. Miller. We have
much to discuss. I had hoped to be meeting the director. If I
may be so bold, will he be joining us?"

Ignoring the thinly veiled condescension and contempt, Jennifer apologized once more, "I'm sorry, Director Flynn, he will not. We lost a drone over the Mojave last night under unusual circumstances. He is in meetings even as we speak trying to figure out what happened."

"You lost a drone," Flynn repeated flatly. "I had hoped to work out a plan to sync some of your drone and satellite assets to threat assessments we are trying to process."

"I understand, Director. If you could send over a written request, I will bring it to the appropriate people for priority analysis and the mission management team." Annie watched and cringed as Jennifer casually typed some apparent meeting notes into her computer.

In an attempt to assert a power role in the conversation, Flynn fired a curt response. "Ms. Miller. I need you to do better than *promising* to bring my written request to the *right people*. I need eyes to go with what we are hearing out there. I need, at minimum, an element of drones dedicated to NSA and our mission. I need it *yesterday*."

Jennifer in turn seemed to finally make a concerted effort to establish lucid and meaningful eye contact with the director. "Director Flynn, I understand your position and frustrations. Unfortunately, I am not in a position to give you exactly what you are looking for at this very moment. Drone mission tasking is not solely the province of even our director. There are many factors to be considered when prioritizing and managing our strained drone asset program, some of those factors are political and trickle down from the very top. What I *can* promise, what I *can* control is my word to you. I *will* bring your mission requests to the appropriate people, sir. Is there anything else I can do to help you today?"

"No, that will be all." Flynn pressed the button on his computer to end the call. He turned to Annie and voiced his concern. "This just will not do. By the time I get drones where we need them, these terrorists will have moved or their objectives will have evolved. Have we learned nothing from the insurgencies in Afghanistan and Iraq?"

Annie allowed the question to hang on the air for a long moment. "Director, could we do some prioritizing of our own and consider different methods which we have more unilateral control over to achieve our mission?"

"What do you mean, Annie?"

"Director, the people we are hoping to surveil have evolved their tactics to make detection more difficult," she offered nervously. "Maybe we need to evolve."

"Go on." Flynn's anger seemed to be ebbing.

"Why don't we arrange for some direct observation assets? Let's put people on the ground; put real eyes on what we are hearing. If we can offer better, more reliable, actionable intelligence than our counterparts, maybe then you'll get what you need, sir."

Annie took a sip of her lukewarm Vanilla Chai while her boss warmed to this idea.

CHAPTER 56

CNN News Room
Program Director's Meeting

Megan Kincade flipped through pages of notes on the yellow, college ruled legal pad in front of her as CNN program director Stephen White opened the meeting with his on-screen talent. Speaking with correspondents from around the country, Megan had compiled a wish list of human interest stories she had hoped to convince her program director to air. To her consternation, it became clear immediately the network had other thoughts.

"Pretty straightforward tonight, folks." The grizzled CNN veteran Stephen White motioned toward the large screen at the room's front where programming talking points were listed. "It's all about calming the people down and conveying the message that everything is under control. *Absolutely* no mention of rebellion or discourse; got it?"

Megan betrayed no indications of her personal thoughts on the journalistic gag order. Inside however, she recoiled at the censorship. *I'll read your damn teleprompter, White, but I don't appreciate being spoon fed this pie in the sky crap. Lots of stories out there, why are we ignoring them?*

One of Megan's colleagues pried. "Aren't you concerned about our credibility? Our viewers in the larger population centers know better, Stephen. All they have to do is step outside of their houses, they can't even get to the drug store without being stopped or turned around at armed checkpoints. It's unsettling."

Stephen shook his head. "No reports whatsoever that may be construed as inflammatory. This comes from the highest levels."

A doubtful voice from another colleague repeated, "Highest levels?"

Stephen shifted uncomfortably. "From outside our ownership group. The *highest levels.*"

Megan knew immediately what the program director was saying. *This is from the President of the United States. We are now a propaganda tool for the Oval Office.*

Megan Kincade felt sick to her stomach.

CHAPTER 57

**White House Situation Room
Washington, D.C.**

Outside of the White House, morning haze yielded to early afternoon sun while in the situation room, storm clouds seemed to be gathering. In the briefing's opening hour, tempers flared as CIA figureheads stumbled through theories about how a drone could have been shot down over United States soil. Only one thing had been conclusively agreed upon: it was not due to pilot or mechanical failure. Beyond that, there was no clear consensus among the agency leadership regarding the incident, and as a result, the uncertainty had not played well in front of President Tinsley. The bumbling exchange had culminated when the President's temper inevitably flashed.

"God damn it, you are the Central *Intelligence* Agency! How is it possible not one person at Langley can explain to me how this drone was lost?! Can we not, at least reasonably, assume the criminals they were tracking had a hand in it?! Find them; kill them! General Adams, once they are found I authorize an immediate airstrike. No drone. Sortie a manned flight."

General Adams somberly nodded and scribbled in the legal pad sitting in front of him.

Sitting next to the general, Director Flynn had the slightest hint of a grin on his face as he glanced over to Annie Nguyen seated at the room's periphery. A moment later Flynn was called upon to give his briefing by Marvin Miller.

"Despite our position being somewhat handicapped with virtually no cell phone interceptions to interpret for context, we are finding other ways to canvas key areas for threat assessments. Primarily, we are leaning on satellite and drone coverage when we can get it. Software updates to the newer drones can provide us with enhanced abilities to hone in on certain areas and listen to what is being said without putting agents at risk. These capabilities have led us to develop a better understanding of likely hot spots to focus on. For example, areas such as Seattle, Chicago, and San Francisco seem relatively stable right now.

"When you think about it, that's not surprising. You carried those counties easily in the last election, so they are the most likely to remain controllable and the drone monitoring substantiates that assumption. Meanwhile, other population centers are not certain. Take, for example, Houston Texas. While the popular vote within the city itself leaned your way, it was not by a wide margin.

"Drone eavesdropping has revealed a concerning trend. Initially, the city seemed stable and relatively peaceful. However, over the past days surrounding communities have migrated in which has caused some problems. Grocery stores, drug stores, and hardware stores began struggling to keep up with demand increases, shortages led to flared tempers. Flared tempers have led to conflict.

"Inevitably conflicts have turned violent. Community out-siders have organized and then moved in to seize vast chunks of the city. Houston is a veritable warzone and this scene seems to be playing out in other cities as well. At this current pace, suburbia and rural America threatens to overrun areas where your administration had previously found support and sanctu-ary. Where now we have relative peace, tomorrow or next week we may lose footing."

Once he felt the President had a good understanding of the threat swelling within the country, Flynn transitioned to a pitch for a mercenary force the President could put in the field with NSA. Flynn's own proxy military. The force would be well paid and could function with the advantage of shadows. Most importantly, they would not be constrained by the Geneva Con-vention or United States Constitution. Even as Flynn concluded his presentation he observed President Tinsley's body language transform. Where the President had been full of anger minutes earlier, Flynn thought he saw a smile start to form on Tinsley's face.

Flynn glanced at Annie with a smile of his own.

CHAPTER 58

Marine Corps Air Station
Yuma, AZ

Rolling slowly through the main gate at Marine Corps Air Station Yuma, Graham thought the installation looked more like a ghost town than a military airfield. The only traffic moving was his own. Military police assigned to the gate had been expecting them. Sending his Marine brother, Henry, ahead had been the wise move. The Marine's connections with officers and leadership throughout the Corps once again proved invaluable. Still, where Graham had expected the advanced notice offered by Henry to warm the reception, the opposite appeared just as likely. The MPs assigned to permit the caravan access seemed to offer, at best, tacit approval.

Shaking off the cool welcome on the hot Arizona day, Graham and the rest of his team slowly trickled toward the hangars. As Graham's element approached, a Marine motioned him toward a side road which in turn took the team between buildings and onto the flight line. Once there another Marine, this one in coveralls and a cranial, pointed toward the next hangar down the line. As Graham's vehicle approached the massive hangar doors, they ponderously opened to him.

Inside, the two Cobras General King had dispatched to assist Patriots USA were the first vehicles Graham recognized. They were hard to miss. As the doors opened wider Graham knew he had been guided to the right place beyond any doubt. His vehicles sat door to door, astride in rows, parked just far enough apart to allow occupants to slide out sideways. It was an impressive sight to be sure. More important to Graham, however, than the impressive sight of so many vehicles in one building was the realization that all of his men arrived here safely. The radio silence he ordered before departure, while tactically necessary, was agonizing. Relief fell upon Graham hard, and nearly overwhelmed him. The hardened SEAL ground his teeth and forced tears back down.

Graham, still battling to be in command of his own emotions, looked out his side window to see a familiar and welcoming face approaching him. He lowered the window for Henry. "Good job, Gunny, where's my plane? Where's the Osprey?"

Henry chuckled at his commander's gruff and direct demeanor. "You alright boss? Allergies?"

"Fuck off, Gunny. Where are my birds?"

"I'm happy to see you, too," Henry chuckled. "We couldn't get everything in one hangar. The Osprey is inside the next hangar down along with a half dozen others. We couldn't get that old Beechcraft to fit in anywhere so the Commanding Officer here offered a solution. There's a small private airfield just east of here where Civil Air Patrol does some training and local organizations like VFWs and Legions hold events. Dateland Auxiliary Field; a bunch of old aircraft there right now. The CO thought our bird might blend in there and we could collect them on the push to Davis-Monthan."

Graham's legs and hips were stiff as he stepped out of the vehicle and stretched. A young Marine Lance Corporal helped himself to the vacated driver's seat to park the vehicle for Graham. Looking around he didn't see any other familiar faces. "Where is everyone, Gunny?"

Anticipating that his boss would want to see his people, Henry readily responded. "I arranged to have everyone fed. They've been ferried over to the chow hall. Afterward, they are being offered access to the on-base commissary to stock up on hygiene and whatever else may be needed for personal effects."

"Gunny, if they swipe those debit cards the intelligence spooks will be on us in no time. You can bet they have a watch list on everyone attached to this company."

"I provided each man $200 cash for that very reason."

Graham raised an eyebrow. "You gave each of them *$200* for hygiene and personal effects?"

"You have to remember, Graham, every single one of them walked away from the life they knew to follow you on short notice." Henry's voice was even and sober. "Some of them have wives who wonder if it was for the last time, and for some, it probably will be. I'm one of them remember? We all did it for the principal, for the idea of what America should be. We all believe in this direction, but do not believe for one minute that despite those convictions some of them are fighting their internal conflicts. For many it would have been easier, safer, to sit out on the sidelines and if you think that none of them are harboring those doubts then you're a damn fool. So, yes, I fronted them more cash than they need for some deodorant, toothpaste, and packages of fresh socks and underwear. I guess you need to ask yourself, what is that level of dedication and loyalty worth to you?"

"Sorry, Gunny, you're right." A long moment passed before Graham ventured a reserved follow-up, "Anything else?"

"Actually, yes, there's more. General King reports that back in San Diego and Orange counties, militias sympathetic to the government's policies have organized and are harassing the communities. The general says there have been a handful of fierce firefights between these new militias and revolutionaries like us. Local law enforcement is overwhelmed by the skirmishes and there aren't enough organized Guard units to manage the crisis either. King is planning to strike out into the community to restore order. For that reason, he isn't able to help us as much as he'd intended. That said, he did send some reinforcements. Two more Vipers, three additional Ospreys, and a Huey. Aboard those Ospreys were a handful of Marine scout snipers, a squad of Raiders, and some communication assets. He's also talked with someone down at Miramar, the hope is we may get some help from them at some point. Make of that what you will, not sure what *some help* means."

The news buoyed Graham's spirits. "That's great! Did he say when to expect them?"

"They arrive here tonight," Henry grinned. "General King wanted the darkness to minimize their exposure."

Graham nodded. "Outstanding, get the men rested; we'll move out after ground crew does turnarounds, refueling, and arming."

CHAPTER 59

Dateland Auxiliary Field, AZ

To the west, a blazing Arizona sun gave way to water-painted skies over the desert. A north-westerly wind and shade of hangar number three provided a welcome respite from the heat as members from the local VFW set up for their monthly meeting. In reality, the event was closer to a social function than a parliamentary obligation. Just outside the hangar doors, a Gulf War veteran set up his propane grill and loaded it down with hamburgers, hot dogs, and corn wrapped in foil with buttery garlic marinade. Nearby a customized Beechcraft 18 was chocked. A handful of the veterans migrated toward the unconventional aircraft to admire and take pictures next to the side door where someone had mounted a machine gun.

Just off the tarmac inside the hangar, folding tables bordered neat rows of folding chairs. The tables were loaded with condiments and side dishes. Standard cookout fair was available in abundance. Stockpots of baked beans, bags of potato chips, and casserole dishes holding scores of special recipes represented a vast majority of the unhealthy choices available to the veterans who had gathered. Someone had brought a veggie platter which was slightly picked over.

Many of the chairs assembled in the hangar had been claimed, held mostly by notepads and even a few electronic devices. Despite the heat one Air Force veteran had claimed a spot with his bomber jacket. Sewn upon the back and sleeves were custom patches the airman had earned from deployments and special detachments. On the upper right breast, a unique patch had been sewn on featuring a stylized cartoonish A-10 Thunderbolt. Where the traditional mouth full of razor-sharp teeth was typically painted around the GAU-8/A Avenger cannon, alternate nose art was depicted on this patch. The nose art on this patch portrayed a more animated snarling quality and it seemed to be biting down on the massive cannon as if it were a fat cigar. Sewn on the left side, above where the wearer's heart would be when worn was a squadron patch. The black dragon extended a red-forked tongue over a field of yellow. Bordering and embroidery had been stitched in black while the banner below read, '*357ᵗʰ Fighter Squadron.*'

After an hour of socializing and eating, the meeting was finally called to order.

CHAPTER 60

**White House Situation Room
Washington, D.C.**

President Tinsley studied the still photo on the screen that CIA had provided from a drone overflight of southern Arizona. From 10,000 feet above the desert, easily distinguishable features such as roads and runways were easy to spot, even for eyes not trained to pick up subtle details. Adjacent to the runway, President Tinsley could see there were several aircraft parked on the tarmac although identifying models was beyond his skills. Also apparent were the handful of hangars and utility buildings peppered around what he now knew to be Dateland Auxiliary Field thanks to the computer generated text across the image's bottom margin. Tinsley squinted at the small hand-drawn circle to the left side of an aircraft fuselage.

"What am I looking at here, Savannah?"

"Our analysts claim that is a machine gun barrel, sir."

Tinsley stood up and walked over to stand up close to the screen, he then leaned in and squinted harder. "This isn't one of those restored bombers from World War II?"

Secretary of Defense William Smithson shook his head. "No, Mr. President, this is a Beechcraft 18. The same model was used by the San Diego cell that assaulted the National Guard. We believe this is the same aircraft, sir."

Tinsley nodded. "I see. And the people? Any positive ID's on the ground or have they moved on?"

Tinsley knew before a word was said that they didn't have the definitive answer he wanted. Finally, Savannah replied, "No visual confirmation on San Diego cell leadership, sir. We did, however, capture movement around the airplane; could be support staff like maintenance."

The President stepped back from the screen and turned to Savannah, "I don't see people in this picture."

Savannah responded, "The drone captured video of them walking into that hangar." She pointed at the largest hangar next to the Beechcraft.

"Are they still there?" His advisors nodded. Tinsley asked hopefully, "What about the other aircraft we saw at China Lake?"

Smithson offered a reply. "We don't believe the military aircraft are at this site, Mr. President."

"What leads you to that conclusion, Bill?"

"There's no intelligence to suggest their presence, sir," Smithson replied frankly.

"The hangars?" Tinsley offered.

Smithson shook his head. "No, Mr. President. To move an aircraft with skids such as the Viper we're looking for around the flight line you need special equipment. Ground crews utilize hydraulic wheels that can be attached to the skids to get them off the ground which attach to a tow bar. The tow bar is in turn attached to tow trucks. None of that equipment is evident at this airfield. Additionally, the hangars look too small for an Osprey, let alone an Osprey plus helicopters and the ground vehicles we expect them to still have."

President Tinsley fell silent for a moment as he pondered his counsel. He arrived at a conclusion.

"This aircraft…" He motioned back at the Beechcraft in the photo. "We're certain it is the same plane used back in San Diego?"

Savannah confidently affirmed the intelligence. "Mr. President, it matches exactly. Besides, not very many people out there have access to .50 caliber machine guns and this model of aircraft. It *has* to be them."

Tinsley had heard enough, "Very well. Even if the leadership or full complement of insurgents aren't there, they won't be far away. Let's hit this place now before they leave. Seeing their friends wiped out may just be enough to shake their resolve. Bill, what do we have in the area to carry out a quick strike?"

Smithson offered, "Mr. President, the drone has…"

President Tinsley cut off the secretary mid-sentence. "No drones. I want multiple JDAMS dropped on this place. Nobody walks away."

Smithson was struck by the President's resolve and ferocity. Reflecting on the potential repercussions that could ripple from this action and others the secretary considered, briefly, pressing his boss for a less audacious alternative. Perhaps, he thought, we could alert the local ATF office and instruct them to conduct a raid on the airfield. A door-mounted machine gun attached to a private aircraft certainly broke some federal laws. Before offering the alternative, he considered the congressional leaders who had plotted an impeachment hearing and wondered what had become of them. Finally, he acquiesced, "There are currently F-35s at Luke Air Force Base we could scramble, Mr. President. Should I route the order?"

With a steeled face Tinsley gave consent, "Make it happen, Bill."

William Smithson solemnly gave his acknowledgment. As President Tinsley left the room with his Chief of Staff the Secretary mused, *I wonder if Hermann Göring ever felt like I do right now?*

CHAPTER 61

Undisclosed Detention Facility

Madison Regan lay flat on her back in an orange jumpsuit and stared at the ceiling above her hard bunk. *Why are there pencils stuck in the vents? How did someone reach that high to put them there anyway?* She thought the ceiling must be at least 10 feet high. She vaguely recalled a congressional hearing in which correctional officials had testified about the square footage of cells. At the time she thought the number had seemed sufficient. Now as she reflected the realization had struck her that some clever person had manipulated the math. *I only considered the space between walls when hearing the numbers, I didn't even consider the height.*

Outside of her cell, the sound of a correctional officer making her rounds echoed down the corridor of her cell block. The *clip-clop* of steel toed boots mixed with the light clatter of keys bouncing to the woman's steps. The officer's cadence resonated as a harsh audible reminder every thirty minutes or so for just how far off the tracks her life had come. Sometimes Madison could hear the other women sobbing. Sometimes she could hear them screaming at the uniformed staff. Occasionally she

246 · MATTHEW H. WHITTINGTON

could hear a familiar voice offer some promise of future special treatment in the form of government funding in exchange for sneaking out letters only to be scoffed at.

All of those sounds and more were common, yet without rhythm.

The *clip-clop, clip-clop* of black steel toes carrying a chain full of heavy keys though, functioned like a clock. Madison could utilize their tireless consistent harmony as a pseudo time-keeper. Actual clocks weren't permitted, after all, she was forced to adapt.

Breakfast came around 6:30 in the morning. Eight instances of *clip-clop, clip-clop* later lunch would arrive. Another ten or so *clip-clops* passed before dinner arrived, this time delivered by different officers. After dinner trays were picked up, she and the others on her cell block had a long wait until lights out.

When the lights went out, the cell block transformed.

Weeks had passed, or had it been *months*? *How long has it been*? The Speaker remembered the intrusion into her office as if it were yesterday. The intruders placed her in hand restraints along with everyone else she'd been meeting with. Against her skin, the cold steel bit and pinched making any movement she attempted excruciatingly painful.

At no time had she been advised of her Miranda rights or even given verbal advisement about which laws she had broken. Madison remembered screaming at her abductors, "Don't you know who I am?! I'm the Speaker of the House!"

The protestation had seemed to have as much impact as a common criminal screaming their innocence. Madison may as well have screamed, *"I'm a mouse in the house!"* At least that may have caused one of the men to crack a smile she mused.

Realizing her mind was trailing the white rabbit through some kind of mental time warp, Madison re-focused on the sounds outside her cell. She stood up and walked to the slender window in her large steel cell door and peered down the range. Across the floor, tiny white objects glided from door to door like miniature apparitions.

What is going on out there?

Suddenly the large door used by the officers slid open and the clip-clop got progressively louder until it finally reached crescendo outside her door. A quick flick from the flashlight beam dilated her eyes and she recoiled at the sudden brightness. As suddenly as the flash came, it passed. The officer's walking rhythm was slower compared to that of her daytime counterparts, thanks Madison deduced, to the need to illuminate each cell with her obscenely bright flashlight.

As the officer walked further away, Madison looked out her window and down the cellblock. The frenetic movement of tiny apparitions had disappeared with the arrival of the officer. *Curious*, Madison thought. *Whatever is happening out there, is not to be seen by those who walk the halls freely.*

Finally, the officer seemed content, at least for the next 30 or so minutes and she departed the block. Once again Madison heard the scurrying throughout her corridor, it sounded like tiny mice playing tennis with sugar packets she thought. This went on for minutes. Or was it *hours*? Madison felt she truly had no reference. *Wait it can't be hours, the clip-clops haven't come back. Minutes, only minutes.*

Madison wondered if she was teetering on the brink of madness.

Then she wondered, *how does one know if they are going mad?*

The Speaker felt her mind being tugged by the vortex of another rabbit hole when she caught a sudden flash of white in her peripheral down by her feet. Her initial response compelled a quick step back in apprehension. At her feet, one of the white apparitions abruptly appeared. Madison forced her eyes to blink unnaturally to be sure this was a lucid moment.

A long moment passed as the once brilliant politician stared at the small inanimate white object; dumbstruck, as if it were a teleported delivery from an alien planet. Then a moment of realization came over her, *this is one of those things sliding across the halls.*

Caution finally gave way to curiosity. The Speaker stepped forward, leaned over at the waist, and picked the object up. Turning the object over in her hands she realized it was tightly folded paper. Taking care to avoid ripping the paper she carefully undid each fold until the small package had transformed into a simple, single sheet of paper.

A simple, single sheet of paper with a handwritten message.

We should assume the guards are listening and reporting everything we talk about. All communication going forward will be done this way. Read and destroy. Pass no messages during staff rounds.

This isn't about elections anymore, it's about the survival of our nation. Are you ready to talk?

-SB

Madison read the prison telegram as if it were a letter from beyond the grave. The resolve within the message struck her. Even in this dark forgotten place, someone has kept their wits enough to not only string together coherent thoughts but also plans.

No, not plans, Madison, she reflected. *This is something stronger, more resolute than a plan. This risky communication harkens back to the defiance of our very founders. This is ... revolutionary. This is ... hope.*

Before complying with the destruction of the message she re-read it again, and again. Looking at the initials she tried to clear the cobwebs from her mind to ascertain who '*SB*' might be. *So many women in the Senate and Congress, who is SB?* Forcing her mind to process information, Madison began a deductive reasoning process.

First, this must be someone with political savvy. Second, this reads like a person who I do not align with politically wrote it. This must be from someone in leadership, the initiative to reach out like this suggests as much.

Susan Brady! This message is from the Senate Minority Leader!

Madison tore the message into tiny pieces until her fingers were raw and dropped the pulpy remains into her toilet. Even as the fibers in the paper soaked in the toilet water, the range door opened and the familiar *clip-clop* grew louder. She quickly flushed the toilet and rushed back to her hard bed. Just as Madison's head touched the lumpy mattress, an intense flash of light illuminated the room and her body. She acted as though the intrusion mildly irritated her by rolling away from the light and the sentry moved on.

Madison rolled back to staring at her ceiling. Her mind raced with excitement as she formulated a response. Sleep would not come easily on this night, there was so much to discuss. Years of building walls to block opposing ideals and aisles to screen olive branches had fallen apart, dissolved by the toilet water. Flushed away was the hostility of political inter-ference, made anew was the hope of a co-existent future.

CHAPTER 62

F-35A Lightning 2
Skies over Arizona

Lieutenant Colonel Bradley Hamilton, call sign 'Hambone', pushed the Pratt and Whitney F135 power plant to full power and seconds later pulled back on the stick as his F-35A achieved sufficient velocity to generate the lift needed for take-off. Shortly after breaking contact with the Luke Air Force Base runway he retracted his landing gear and made the turn to vector for his objective. Through the visor of Hambone's $400,000 helmet, he could see the ground fall away as if the fuselage wasn't strapped to him at all thanks to the innovative imaging software of his fighter and helmet.

External wing pylons slung to each side of the fuselage held a cadre of JDAMs. While the F-35A was considered a Stealth weapons platform, this mission was deemed to have a low risk of air defenses. The lack of radar-detected threats to the airframe justified this particular armament configuration.

Streaking for the small airstrip at Dateland Auxiliary Field, Hambone reviewed his targeting objectives. Nagging at the colonel's obsessive mission preparation was a missing piece of the puzzle. He had been briefed that these terrorists had commandeered Marine Corps attack aircraft, though it wasn't thought to likely be present at this location. If the intelligence people were wrong however and the terrorists were capable of operating the aircraft, the AH-1Z did possess modest air to air abilities. So, he couldn't risk casually cruising through at the helicopter's standard operational altitudes. Hambone weighed his options between a high altitude weapons release or streaking in nap of the Earth.

High altitude munition releases had proved troublesome when piloting his original airframe, the F-16 Fighting Falcon. While flying the F-16 in Iraq and Afghanistan, Hambone routinely ran into frustrations concerning hitting ground targets, especially in "danger close" scenarios. Air Force regulations forbade munition releases when American fighting men and women were in close contact. Dropping the altitude would increase accuracy, yet in war zones, the enemy tended to fire back. As a result, Hambone was frequently required to drop his weapons off the center of his targets to minimize risk to friendlies or often not release at all. On numerous occasions, the soldier on the ground could only hope for a "show of force" which was far less intimidating than it sounded. Essentially, Hambone could only make low altitude, high-speed flybys of the enemy. The tactic worked to lower their heads, temporarily.

This was Arizona though, not Iraq. These targets were presumably Americans, extremists according to the briefing, but still Americans. Shoulder-fired anti-air weapons are not readily available here in the United States, and the veil of darkness offered Hambone an extra layer of security. Furthermore, operating at a higher altitude offered greater operational awareness.

A nap of the Earth approach virtually guaranteed destruction of the target, though it increased the unlikely chance of taking small arms fire. His first pass would catch the enemy off guard, that was certain. Should any survive his initial assault and manage to keep their wits about them, subsequent passes increased the chances of stray bullets damaging the airframe and possibly himself.

Hambone's deliberation was a brief one. The F-35A's state-of-the-art avionics and targeting equipment would make this mission a brief one. This would be a strike from 15,000 feet. Adding altitude offered far more upside in operational awareness while still almost certainly wiping out his objective. The approach would be from east to west. Hambone resolved to drop one JDAM on the hangar. He would drop an additional JDAM, this one set for an airburst, over the aircraft-laden tarmac. Should the unlikely happen and they miss or fall harmlessly and fail to arm, Hambone would re-attack. Conducting the mental preparedness at this stage of the mission allowed him to fly seamlessly as if from muscle memory later. The aviator imagined he would pull back on the stick for an Immelmann maneuver. He would pull up into a loop, upon reaching the apex the aircraft would be inverted. Then he would roll the ailerons to reverse the inversion and push the nose down into a high-angle attack. This follow up move would be devastating in its accuracy and almost impossible for any survivors to counter.

A few minutes after finalizing his mental preparations, Hambone reached the rally point and started his attack sequence.

***

Inside hangar three at Dateland Auxiliary Field, the din of conversation bounced off the walls. The meeting agenda had been exhausted and the conversation evolved into the socializing phase. An overall theme of debate over what was happening in the country dominated discussions. Spilling out past the hangar door, a group of Army Gulf War veterans walked about the tarmac. One attendee, who regularly participated in World War II re-enactments as a paratrooper, lingered around a venerable Douglas C-47 parked astride the modified Beechcraft.

Having just circled the old bird, he could see into the hangar where most of the local VFW remained in conversation. Bright lights from the building gave the tarmac a warm glow, making the aircraft silhouettes almost ethereal. Standing there with hands in pockets the veteran thought the beauty of this evening embodied so much that was right about America. Less than a football field away men and women who had signed contracts to defend freedom openly discussed their differences. The beauty was not lost on him, their actions had made these very discussions possible. He admired, from afar, how not one person among the group appeared demonstrative or hostile. Quite the opposite. There was a lot of nodding and open body language. The old veteran marveled and wished those engaging in strife throughout the nation he loved could see America as he did at this moment.

After a long moment of soaking in the scene, the veteran pulled a cellphone from his pocket to check the time. He decided it was getting late, that he had better get home to his wife. A violent *WHOOSH* cut the air and he looked up just as what had been a beautiful picture of Americana turned into a fiery hell. The energy released in the blast reached him almost as suddenly as the light of the explosion, and he was blown off his feet. His cell phone flew from his hand in the chaos and as he was blown back away from the percussive blast, he landed on his shoulder and head.

Dazed by the cataclysm he tried to stand up, yet the messages sent from his brain were disregarded by the remainder of his body. He couldn't feel anything, he couldn't hear anything. The world had gone mute and, in the attempt, to open his eyes the world seemed to spin around. *I have to MOVE!* He fought to restore command of his motor functions, yet only his eyes seemed to come back online. Forcing them open he consciously batted them in an attempt to recalibrate his focus.

Relieved to have his sight, the man was confused when a sudden flash turned the darkness into daylight.

***

Hambone rolled the ailerons to point the aircraft's right wing at the ground and nudged his stick back to turn north, allowing him a good look at the airfield he had just assaulted. The hangar he had targeted was fully engulfed and at a glance, he could count at least 6 aircraft strewn about the tarmac on fire as well.

Rolling the aircraft back 90 degrees Hambone leveled the aircraft and set a vector for Luke Air Force Base. Accessing the communication software, he entered a message, *MISSION ACCOMPLISHED. RTB.*

CHAPTER 63

Marine Corps Air Station
Yuma, AZ

News of the airstrike reached Graham Pinchot by way of a network of handheld radios established along Interstate 8. He had trusted overwatch of the airfield to one of his more seasoned scouts, Blake Jarrett. Blake was tasked with providing the Beechcraft aircrew with an early warning should anything appear out of place. Sadly, even Blake could not have provided sufficient warning for what had hit the hangar and flight line at Dateland. Blake Jarrett's relayed message was jarring, he had reported a local group was holding an event in the hangar. No firearms were present among the group. The men and women who had gathered came wielding coolers, no more. Whoever had assaulted the field did so unprovoked.

Graham felt he knew what had triggered the attack, the presence of his gunship. Some intelligence spook had found it. He felt sick to his stomach over the loss of life. How many had died tonight because the government wanted him dead? His mind raced in a mad search to find a coping mechanism to keep his temper and wits. The warrior woven into his fabric wanted to step out of the shadows and fight in the open.

To Graham the fighter, run and hide tactics felt alien.

For Graham the CEO, he felt a powerful obligation to stay vigilant for those who relied on his leadership.

Graham the Patriot wanted above all, vengeance.

Vengeance for his father and son. Now, Graham reflected as he clipped the radio hand mike back into the retaining clip, vengeance for the murdered at Dateland as well. *Those people are dead because of actions we .... I have taken.*

Raising his head to the men standing around him, Graham felt their steely resolve looking back at him. Spurgeon Gorlick, Thomas Sullivan, Henry O'Brien, and a handful of Marine officers from Camp Pendleton, 29 Palms, and Marine Corps Air Station Yuma all stood there hanging on words they expected Graham to say.

Sensing the anticipation hanging in the air Graham asked, "How long until they track us here?"

"Probably not long, boss," Sullivan replied. "I would imagine by now they already suspect we're in the vicinity of Dateland. The list of logistically appropriate concealment spots isn't long."

"Any thoughts about where the attack on Dateland originated from?" Henry asked. Like his boss, he felt his stomach turn with nausea. Re-routing the Beechcraft to Dateland had been his call. Keeping the aircraft at MCAS Yuma almost certainly would have doomed the entire company. The concealment netting acquired from China Lake wasn't wide enough for the wingspan and overlapping sections broke the camouflage illusion when the desert winds gusted. There hadn't been enough space in the hangars either. Henry knew as much, yet he still felt personally responsible for the loss of life.

"Had to be an airstrike." Graham had already turned the question in his head upon hearing the news. A ground-based incursion would have been seen coming in unless that is, the assault was indirect artillery fire. An airstrike made a lot more sense. The question nagging Graham was, *where did the flight come from?*

As if sensing the commander's deductive quandary, a Marine Colonel who Graham had not previously spoken to offered, "Could've been out of Luke."

"What makes you think this attack could have come from Luke, Colonel?" Graham asked.

The colonel shrugged. "If we're going to operate on what I believe is a sound assumption this was an airstrike, then it's a simple process of elimination."

"Please, go on."

Attention squarely on the Marine officer, he expounded, "First of all, we must first consider the human factor. Whoever ordered it didn't want this lead going cold. They would have wanted a short turnaround from the time their target was identified to the time it was eliminated. You can rule out this place off the top, it would have been easier to keep the aircraft here if our command had the intent to comply with such orders. Further, you would already all be dead or in custody if we were your enemy. That leaves Davis-Monthan and Luke Air Force Base." He paused to take a drink of water, the only sound in the room. "So next we consider what aircraft are available to sortie at each location. Out at Davis-Monthan, you have two active A-10 squadrons and a training squadron where the United States qualifies foreign pilots alongside our own on the F-16.

The order wasn't given to a trainee I promise you. So that leaves the A-10s. Your scouts would likely have observed the signatures of an A-10 assault, they are hard to mistake. Very low and loud. That leaves Luke."

Spurgo asked, "What's stationed at Luke, sir?"

The Colonel answered flatly, "F-35s"

Once again everyone fell silent. If the Marine Colonel's assumption was sound the reality was daunting. It meant the United States Air Force was now in on this fight, and it wasn't on their side. Worse still, they had sortied one of the most technologically advanced pieces of equipment on the planet. The aircraft's array of next-generation avionics and targeting capabilities made its presence overhead a large problem they would have to deal with. Even if he and the men made it to Davis-Monthan, whatever airpower they could cobble together would be easily outmatched and overwhelmed by the F-35s should the Air Force elect to deny the airspace. Yet, if they remained in place with analysis paralysis, the entirety of he and his men was almost certainly lost. Graham felt that if he failed to act, the future of a free America would die along with them.

"We need to move out," Graham sighed. "Sitting in any one place for too long is dangerous. If they track us here bunched up like this that will be the end for all of us."

Henry countered, "If we're spotted by big brother's eye in the sky, it'll be a desert turkey shoot, Graham."

Graham's face was a picture of exasperation, encumbered with the weight of the world and the lives of his men. "One well-placed JDAM and it's all over for us here, at least on the road we're spaced out and moving."

A long uncomfortable moment hung on the air. All in the room knew that remaining in place was a massive risk. The right decision tactically was to stay on the move. Still, the pro-spect of risking detection in the open and having precision munitions fall upon them inspired little motivation. Sensing the conundrum, the Marine Colonel spoke up once more.

"Maybe there's something I can do?" he offered. "I fly the Marine version of the F-35 here. I have a few friends in the community of F-35 drivers, including a good buddy over at Luke. We play golf quite a bit. There are some amazing courses in the Phoenix area. Maybe I could make contact and take his temperature about what's going on. I believe that if those guys know what got hit and how unreliable their information is it would sicken them. Nobody who takes that oath revels in the idea of murdering American citizens. Knowing the airstrike did so could be enough to give them pause on other sorties."

"Colonel, how are you going to make contact? Cell phone networks are crashed," Henry pointed out.

The officer's reply was simple. "I'm going to fly over and have the conversation in person."

Thomas Sullivan had a concern of his own and couldn't hold it in anymore. "What if the colonel is wrong and this wasn't the airstrike he thinks? What if this was a Predator strike and they're still up there waiting for us to move?"

Graham smiled half a smile. "I had considered that Tommy, and you're right; it could have been a drone strike and they could still be circling over the area on the lookout. We brought a surprise of our own to fly overwatch though. It's a little something else we picked up at China Lake." He glanced over toward Charlotte and grinned then continued, "All the same, keep the vehicles spread out. No closer than 500 yards. If an assault comes they won't catch us in a big group. Also, I need you all to write down a radio frequency. No rocking out on our way to Davis-Monthan, guys."

CHAPTER 64

The White House Oval Office Study
Washington, D.C.

The West Wing of the White House was built in 1902 by the order of then-President Theodore Roosevelt. At the time of construction, the executive's formal workspace was not actually oval. In 1909 the West Wing was expanded under Taft and the office was re-modeled into an oval shape to match other rooms throughout the Presidential residence. Taft's renovation served subsequent Presidents until a fire in 1929 led to the need for reconstruction of the West Wing. It was demolished in 1933 and re-built in 1934 to the space's current design.

A door on the west side of the iconic room opens to a small hallway. Immediately to the left upon entering the corridor is the President's study. President Ray Tinsley had wondered when assuming residence of the White House how many people thought he worked in the opulent Oval Office when actually the vast majority of his work time was spent in the more modest study.

Tinsley resisted the urge to look at the clock. The President felt as though the past days were one constant shuffle of his feet from one brief to the next. Had it been an hour ago or six since he had departed the situation room following the airstrike in Arizona? Seemingly his head had only just touched the pillow before a nudge had stirred him from shallow rest for another situation. Now, apparently, the entire state of Texas was in open revolt along with their northern neighbor Oklahoma.

Headaches weren't limited to the south-central region either. Even in states he had easily carried just the past November, law enforcement was overwhelmed with issues springing from his security policies. Supply channels were suffering disruption issues from gangs barricading streets upon delivery trucks entering their areas. Trickle-down consequences meant food and medication shortages for those who needed them most. Violence had exploded. Significant felony-level crimes were occurring faster than the police could process the evidence. Home robberies were leading to gunfights in suburban America and there was nothing anyone could do about it. The Wild West appeared to be making a comeback.

Making matters worse, military readiness was apparently on the decline. Instances of software and maintenance issues were on the rise with even the newest equipment in the arsenal. A new report from Luke Air Force Base sat on top of the large stack he had planned to review. At a glance, it appeared some glitch in targeting software had caused several airplanes to be grounded pending consultation from the contractor who had developed the aircraft's systems.

Yet another report detailed what was known about a drone lost over the Mojave, it appeared to have suffered a catastrophic failure from the outside. *Well, isn't that expert analysis helpful*, the President mused in frustration.

President Tinsley was considering a phone call to his National Security Advisor when he finally relented and glanced at the time, 3:11 A.M. Deciding to allow Savannah a little more sleep, Tinsley leaned back in his chair and closed his eyes to think. Reflection had turned into sleep. The President realized he had fallen asleep when a soft knock on the study door jarred him upright.

"Come in!" Tinsley's eyes moved to the door where his secretary stood.

"Apologies, Mr. President. Director Flynn from NSA is in the lobby. He's asking to be seen."

"Go ahead and show him in. Also, if you don't mind, swing by dining and have them bring some coffee."

"Of course, Mr. President."

Tinsley stood up and walked around the room to boost his alertness. He felt heavy with fatigue. The thought of appearing less than razor-sharp to a subordinate unsettled him enough that he would rather appear to be pacing anxiously than lethargic. A few minutes passed by before Anthony Flynn was led in.

"What brings you to the White House at this hour in person Anthony? Has something else gone horribly wrong?"

Flynn set a thick folder labeled '*Top Secret*' on a small table next to the President's desk and helped himself to a chair reserved for advisors. "Mr. President, I'm here at this hour because the intelligence community is failing you. My counterparts over at the CIA have been overly reliant on satellite and drone imagery. While these images have their place, they fail magnificently at giving you insight into the human behavior of those who are threatening this country."

Tinsley's interest piqued, he leaned forward slightly. "Go on."

"Take for instance this pesky San Diego cell. We have had drones identify the leader's whereabouts twice in the past week, yet he along with the majority of his followers are still at large. Can the CIA tell you where they are right now?"

President Tinsley had to admit the situation out in California and now Arizona had him frustrated. "If I had good intel about where they were located, I would have acted on it."

"My point exactly, sir." Flynn opened his palms as if in offering. "I believe the NSA can offer a solution that will provide you with reliable, actionable information."

"What's this solution, Anthony?" The president regarded him with optimistic skepticism.

"Hound dogs." Flynn smiled at the imagery he imagined would be conjured in the President's mind.

"Hound dogs?" Tinsley looked back at Flynn puzzled over the unexpected solution which had been brought to him at nearly four in the morning.

"Hound dogs, Mr. President. When one is hunting, they might bring a hound. The hound goes forth with snout and ears to the ground in search of quarry and then flushes them out. You need people on the ground to do that for you, sir. Someone who can expertly track humans and see things invisible to drones or satellites. The details, Mr. President. It's all in the details."

"I see." Tinsley leaned back. His secretary entered with a platter of snacks and a carafe of coffee. She poured a cup for each man and discreetly excused herself. "Are we talking about those mercenaries you suggested, Anthony? I'm not sure how much that idea panned out."

Flynn set his cup of coffee down. "The mercenaries that have been put in place out there will prove useful sir, you

266 · MATTHEW H. WHITTINGTON

should give that more time. They are meant to harass these nuisance rebellions and make it hard for them to move or operate. I have faith that tree will bear fruit. In this case, though, I am not talking about mercenaries. The people I speak of have advanced training in human intelligence and are far more valuable. What I suggest is a razor blade rather than a sledgehammer, far sharper and less obvious."

"I like it, Anthony, when can we put these people in the field?"

"Mr. President, I have already deployed agents to each region in the event you wanted them activated. Say the word and they are on the hunt."

Nodding Tinsley said, "Do it." Then he motioned with a hand toward the 'Top Secret' file sitting nearby, "Is this brief for the 'Hound' program?"

Flynn shook his head, "No, Mr. President. This is something else. I was consulted on this project because of the effect it would have on our ability to collect intelligence. Initially, I had great reservations about the possible application, but if at any time you feel it may be necessary to keep control of the people this option may be something to consider."

Intrigued the President pressed Flynn.

"Well, what is it, Anthony?" He reached for the file as the NSA director handed it to him.

Flynn asked, "What do you know about EMPs Mr. President?"

CHAPTER 65

Dateland Auxiliary Field, AZ

Smoke hung heavy on the desert wind like an oil slick on the ocean. Looking east, the horizon hinted at approaching sunrise, its glow splitting the darkness in hues of orange and amber. Pin-wheeling over the stricken airfield, Agent Carlos Gutierrez spotted a committee of vultures. *This is the place.*

Creeping slowly down the sandy road, he noticed a pack of cars and trucks still neatly grouped. As Gutierrez drew nearer it became evident energy from the blasts had smoked the vehicle windshields and debris had peppered them with damage. As he approached, Gutierrez thought it odd that such a large militia group would bunch their vehicles together so brazenly in the open. Gutierrez stopped his blacked-out SUV just short of the orphaned vehicles.

Next, he gathered his gear from the passenger seat and elected to continue the investigation on foot. Years spent cultivating human intelligence, first for the DEA and later CIA, he had acquired several valuable techniques. Chief among them was to not be overly reliant on electronic intelligence. There would always be details missed by computers that a human eye could spot. Human intelligence was the province of the CIA and DIA. Failure to be thorough in all aspects of the craft could, and had, lead to the loss of American lives.

Gutierrez had cut his teeth in human tracking along the United States' southern border. One of the ways agents tracking criminal activity along the border would locate their quarry was by using environmental observations. Vultures or crows in large numbers almost always meant death, sometimes for wildlife, but more often for humans. This technique in particular proved accurate this morning.

The Dateland airfield wasn't large; Gutierrez knew this by referencing satellite maps on his phone. Skeletons of buildings from decades past stood vigil nearby while the vultures who had come to feed lingered just outside the circle of destruction.

Approaching the smoldering carcass of the hangar, distinct odors became increasingly evident to him.

Burning jet fuel.

Burning rubber. *That would be the aircraft tires*, he reasoned.

And finally, the unmistakable stench of burning flesh.

Yes, this is definitely the place.

Gutierrez made a conscious effort to give the bombed structure, now backlit by a smoke-shrouded sun, a wide berth. Should what remained of the walls collapse as he walked by, he did not want to get trapped. Nobody besides the NSA director knew he was here.

Reflecting on the call from NSA Director Flynn as he slowly walked toward the flight line, Gutierrez recalled how odd the offer of this particular assignment had felt just a few days ago. NSA's turf was in the cyber realm. To his knowledge, they

employed no field agents. Yet, this man Flynn was now attempting to do just that.

Some kind of agency power play? A bureaucratic turf war?
Motivations aside it didn't matter he supposed. The offer was
too good. One million dollars to track and neutralize a man
named Graham Pinchot. *Dead or alive* as it were. He chuckled
and wondered if Pat Garrett had felt as he did right now while
tracking Billy the Kid across New Mexico.

Gutierrez reflected that unlike his tracking predecessors, he
was no gunfighter. Gutierrez would do his killing by proxy.
Director Flynn had made that point clear. His exact words
were, "Find Pinchot and call me. Do not let him out of sight
for even a minute, not until I bring fire down on him."

Gutierrez supposed that meant he'd be calling in an airstrike
even though he had absolutely no training to do so.

A few measured paces later, Gutierrez crested around the
burned-out structure. The scene of destruction that unfolded
before the agent stopped him cold and took his breath away.
Morning sunlight filtered through the thick smoke resulting in
a pall of hazy orange on the tarmac. He counted at least three
separate burning masses of what resembled aircraft fuselages.
Much of the debris strewn across the landscape lacked discern-
able shape. He guessed some of the black formless piles were
human remains, though he didn't care enough to pry.

His objective would not be among the dead. This place was
simply a starting reference point in the hunt. Someone associated with his mark was known to have been here, and Gutierrez
hoped to find a clue in the carnage that would illuminate his
next step.

A hopeful sentiment now shrouded in doubt considering the
apparent complete destruction.

Pressing forward he took an initial step toward the sea of ashes, only the first step felt funny. What should have been the sound of his boots crunching the Arizona sand instead felt soft and awkward. Gutierrez pulled his foot back and looked down. Distracted by the overwhelming site of the airfield just a moment ago, he hadn't thought to look at the ground in his immediate space. What had been obscured in the chaos before now drew into sharp acuity. His first step into the carnage had been onto a partially charred hand.

Gutierrez recoiled at the realization, and after collecting himself once more the agent stepped gingerly around it. From that step forward he slowly moved about the tarmac, careful to watch every step.

One clue, I just need one solid clue.

Approaching the first smoldering remains of what he presumed was an aircraft, Gutierrez spotted a hat. The hat was distinct, recognizable. Not a simple generic ball cap, rather what his eye caught was the glint of a VFW pin on a singed garrison cover.

Interesting. He considered the incongruous find. *The intelligence brief they emailed made no mention of local VFWs.* Gutierrez considered the headwear as he crouched down for a closer inspection. Carefully, reverently even, he picked it up as if he were trying to hold an injured bird. Turning it in his hands he noticed blackened embroidery indicating that the owner had belonged to the Arizona chapter. *Curious.* He gently set the cover back on the ground where the blast had placed it and pulled out his cell phone to re-read his brief. Upon further review, he confirmed that intelligence indicated the recruited had come from California, not Arizona.

Gutierrez navigated what bare concrete his feet could find as if he were carefully avoiding landmines until he arrived at what had been a Beechcraft. At a glance, he observed it was impossible to determine what color the aircraft had been and identification numbers were hours ago scoured from its skin. Circling to the port side cargo door he spotted the unconventional item that had led to the destruction surrounding him.

It was blackened.

It was significantly scorched and heavily damaged.

It was indeed a door-mounted .50 caliber machine gun.

Gutierrez stared at the flame-scorched barrel. *Thanks to you, this place was destroyed and people died. Yet, not the one I'm looking for. Where did he go?* His question, admittedly, was a rhetorical one. Still, this ballistic carcass was the morning's first solid yardstick. *The intelligence geeks got at least this much right; I'm standing next to Pinchot's plane.*

Gutierrez turned to face the devastated hangar and decided to have a look. Maybe a search of the militia's shelter would turn up something to indicate where the rest of them scurried off to. Taking care to be thorough in his canvas, Gutierrez snapped pictures of the destroyed Beechcraft from a few angles for the file. He could review the stills later at leisure should the need arise. The habit reminded him of how DEA would process crime scenes along with counterparts in other agencies. A small insignificant detail present now could prove useful later.

Satisfied, Gutierrez stepped away from the aircraft that had dealt the destruction to Dateland and walked slowly around the other wrecks smoldering all around him. With each passing deliberate circuit of the remaining wrecks, he couldn't help but grow angry with his target. For Graham Pinchot, he harbored no trace of compassion. The man was in active rebellion against the country he loved. Pinchot was raising a militia to undo what had been built.

Gutierrez reasoned *He's a criminal. He's a traitor.* The one million dollars offered was a strong incentive, yet deep down Gutierrez thought he might have undertaken this hunt for free. A threat to his country was personal.

Still, not all those persuaded to follow Graham were necessarily forsaken. Gutierrez imagined that a portion of them had been brainwashed and convinced to follow the traitor through a fork-tongued, impassioned plea. Offered the chance to reflect and lay down their weapons, Gutierrez imagined that some, maybe a good number, could be compelled to do so. He stepped over a tattered leather boot that was not empty. The grisly scene brought melancholy on him.

Not all of these people deserved this fate. What must it have felt like in that last moment? Did they know the gates of hell fell upon them? Or was it instant?

Closer to the hangar, what had been a Douglas C-47 laid on the ground as if the landing gear had folded upon landing and it slid belly down into the inferno. Gutierrez poked around the old plane's remains only to find nothing of use.

Turning toward the hangar once more, he was finally able to appreciate the extent of the destruction without his perspective being distracted by the carnage and death that was Dateland's tarmac. What had been a shelter for B-25s in the 1940s was now mostly rubble. What had been the hangar doors now framed the hellscape.

With the sun now fully above the eastern horizon, light washed away what remained of darkness and haze to reveal in full magnitude hangar three's fate. Gutierrez thought it curious that the lack of recognizable evidence to inspect struck him.

What had been living, according to his brief, dozens at least simply vanished. He pulled the camera out and centered the debris field in the hangar door frame for a picture.

Walking once more to the hangar, Gutierrez came upon a folding chair that had somehow escaped destruction laying on its side. Underneath the chair laid what appeared to be a jacket. The jacket was olive drab with several patches sewn onto it. A bomber jacket.

I wonder if the owner was sitting out here when the strike happened and the blast from the bombs just blew it over.

Reaching casually for the chair, and without much thought, Gutierrez picked the chair up and set it back upright, facing the decimated airfield. Then he picked up the jacket, shook it out, and draped it reverently over the chair.

Whatever your owner did to end up here, the life was not without merit.

Finally, Gutierrez walked through the arching precipice of hangar doors into the debris field. Steel and concrete had crushed whatever remains might have been useful long ago when the rafters yielded to the heat and flames. That is if any of them even survived the initial blast. Standing there staring at the overwhelming rubble, Gutierrez doubted that even if he were to pull the mess apart there would be a silver bullet of intelligence that could have survived the onslaught.

His lips creased as if admitting defeat and he slowly turned to face the flight line once more.

Why is that Beechcraft here, Pinchot? Why Dateland?

The agent turned the intelligence reports in his head and tried to make sense of what this place had meant tactically to the Navy SEAL. *Such an obscure hole of land, did you think to hide here?* Frustrated over the information he did not have and failed to deduce; Agent Gutierrez absently walked toward the chair he had propped up.

Gutierrez found himself with a hand on the jacket's shoulder, almost protectively as if its wearer were sitting there now. Of course, that wasn't the case, Gutierrez looked down at the orphaned jacket sadly. The tradition of patches on jackets such as these had always interested him. They served as a quasi-resume in garment form. Presumably, the owner had been attached to, flown with or had affiliation with whatever unit or airframe had been depicted on the patch. Gutierrez mused over Hollywood frauds who wore collections of patches in movies that would never be on one jacket together.

This jacket was different. This jacket was authentic, Gutierrez thought as he ran a hand over the shoulder as if to smooth out wrinkles that weren't there. Whoever wore this actually….

Gutierrez blinked. He couldn't believe that he had missed it before. The patches!

This jacket's owner had two patches that now stood out like lighthouse beacons in the fog, piercing the confusion and chaos with stark clarity. They seemed to be calling out, *this is the way forward.*

Upon the jacket's chest two distinct patches had been sewn. One featured a black dragon on a field of yellow, the other was a fearsomely animated A-10 biting down on an oversized nose cannon. Only one place in the state of Arizona housed the venerable A-10, Davis-Monthan Air Force Base just east of Tucson.

Where else would a band of criminal outcasts go to liberate their own air support besides the storied Boneyard?!

Admittedly, Gutierrez knew this was really just a hunch. Still, it was all Dateland had to offer him.

CHAPTER 66

Casa Grande, AZ

The men of Patriots USA had encountered no problems or interference throughout the silent, nocturnal streak across Arizona once the decision had been made to mobilize. A fact not lost on Graham. He had expected some challenges. Drones overhead. National Guard patrols or checkpoints. Vehicle breakdowns. Possibly even gangs up from Mexico looking to exploit the chaos running rackets like road pirates. All of those contingencies and more had been briefed.

None of the scenarios Graham had briefed the men on played out. So far, the trip had been quiet. Too quiet.

Naturally even as the unease took up residence in Graham's gut the first hint of trouble surfaced as his vehicle passed a sign for exit 172, Thornton Road in Casa Grande. Graham's driver seemed to sense the danger at nearly the same moment as he slowed the vehicle down. Just ahead, several hundred yards the eastbound lanes were blockaded.

Graham's driver performed his next task without as much as a hint or direction. He pulled the vehicle to a stop perpendicular to the roadway, driver side toward the threat hence providing a layer of protection for his commander. Graham appreciated the initiative from his man, nodding as he piled out of the vehicle weapon in hand. Once confident his cover was secure, Graham alerted the convoy spaced out behind him to the threat. He quickly retrieved a reference card from his pocket where he had written down call signs everyone had settled on. Graham felt silly using the call-signs on the radios, but his men had insisted on the added layer of security. In case anyone was listening, they didn't want to make things too easy for the spooks. As an avid Eric Clapton enthusiast, Graham had gone with the call sign, 'Slowhand.'

"Slowhand to Hawkeye, do you have eyes on the roadblock to our east?"

Several vehicles back, Charlotte was well protected by some of the best riflemen Patriots USA had employed. As soon as the threat ahead had been identified, the vehicle she rode in had pulled to the side of the road, well out of rifle range from the potential threat ahead. She of course had her custom drone laptop out and had been flying it around Dateland Auxiliary Field which caused her to fly catch up to the group. It was for this reason she had not been able to identify the potential threat ahead of time. Charlotte reminded Graham of that fact, "I'll be in range in just a few minutes, Slowhand, going as fast as possible to catch up."

"Copy." Glancing at the man in his security detail with the TAC-50 he asked, "Can you get down low and put that scope on the road ahead? I'd like to know more about how they're set up, how they're armed."

No questions asked, the man dropped down into the prone position. Using the vehicle for cover he employed the tires for his concealment purposes, just in case someone was looking back at them. A fact almost certainly guaranteed to be true. In the likely event that someone was observing them, and they were armed, a sighted long-range rifle could be construed as an imminent threat. Graham and company weren't trying to instigate a gunfight, at least not here. A gruff report was proffered just a moment later.

"It's completely blocked, I'm estimating a hasty count of at least four dozen. All armed with small arms. None are uniformed.'

Not uniformed, well at least that likely ruled out the military, so no heavy guns or support equipment. That was good news. Still, Graham grimaced. At this range and in this climate of social conflict, it was impossible to ascertain what the motivations might be for these people ahead. Were they sympathetic to his viewpoints or were they of an obstructive nature? Were they simply attempting to curb criminal activity and movement? If that were so, would they deem the activity of his group criminal? None of these questions could be answered without talking to the folks blocking his way. Approaching close enough for a parley, however, presented an enormous risk as well.

Graham, deep in deliberation with his inner tactician, hardly noticed when Henry walked up behind him, weapon in hand.

"What happened to our scouts, Graham? How did they miss this?"

Where *were* the scouts?! The company was coming up on a major road intersection, just ahead Interstate 8 would be joined by Interstate 10, they should have come through here, and they should have given a warning! Graham was still wondering why his scouts had been silent when a shot rang out and a high-velocity round snapped over his head.

The arrival of incoming rounds made Graham forget, at least temporarily, about the disposition of his advanced scouts. The situation was less than ideal. While the drivers of Pinchot's caravan had the sense to park tactically once stopped, they were stalled in the middle of an interstate in Arizona. Graham directed his men to setup fields of fire. So far, the incoming fire was ineffective. Graham thought those blocking his way must be amateurs, and for that much at least he was thankful.

"Stay in cover, keep your discipline! When you take shots, make them count. Gunny, where are the Snakes?"

O'Brien knew of course he was referring to the four aircraft element of AH-1Zs. Vipers. Henry picked up his radio at Graham's urging and keyed up to raise their only air assets.

"Gunny to Archer 01, Gunny to Archer 01! Troops in contact on Interstate 8 just west of interchange! Request immediate fire, objective is a blockade of the interstate!"

To their rear, Graham and Henry finally caught the sound of their muscle racing for the fight. Pitching forward to gain speed, the Vipers four main rotor blades feverishly cut the air. Gunny craned his head in their direction in time to see the morning sun glinting off one of the windscreens as the fearsome helicopter rapidly approached.

Even as the Vipers gained ground, the incoming fire felt to be closing in as well. At least a half dozen rounds peppered Graham's vehicle only to be answered by as many outgoing rounds from his men. The SEAL hoped that his compulsive firearms training days with the men were paying dividends and that with each slow trigger pull, a corresponding threat disappeared on the other end.

Graham's radio crackled as he heard another exchange between his air and Henry. The incoming transmission indicated hope for a swift end to their current engagement, "Archers 01 and 02 vectoring in from the west. Heads down, guys."

No sooner had the warning passed Graham's ears before he heard a savage WHOOSH! From just over their heads two of the Vipers were almost on top of them when the volley of 2.75 inch rockets rushed from their pods toward the blockade. Before those in cover on the ground could stretch for a look at their effect, a host of the blockade's vehicle muscle erupted in explosions and flames. The agitators who had to this point been torturing Graham and his men, at least those lucky enough to survive the barrage cowered or ran.

Not yet satisfied with their work, the snakes broke right into a turn for a lineup on a follow-up run. As the first two Viper pilots were executing a minimum radius turn, the second pair fell upon what remained of the blockade from the north flank. A sharp whir preceded a duo of 20 mm bursts into what remained of the resistance.

Graham's adrenaline coursed and he lost track of real-time. How much time had passed from the first call for fire support until this moment? A minute? He doubted it had even been that long. Their answer in the face of aggression had been sudden and savage.

Archers 01 and 02 streaked overhead once more for what had been their target, only to have their rockets remain in reserve for lack of threats. Only then did Graham notice the pilots seem to relent their fury, the Viper's noses picked up slightly to slow their airspeed. Graham now thought the circling hunters looked more like prowling wolves than striking snakes.

Pinchot was about to take a deep breath to slow his heart once more and take stock of his men. Even as the SEAL flicked the selector switch on his combat rifle to safe, the man standing directly next to him fell in a heap from head trauma before the sound of gunshots reached his ears. In the confusion of the gunfight, the opposition had moved to flank the men of Patriots USA. Pinchot, himself a world-class warrior, had underestimated the enemy as common street thugs without tactical sense or marksmanship skills. He had let himself get caught up in the incredible show of force from the Vipers and ignored the significance of his missing scouts. Worse yet, Graham had committed the cardinal sin of letting his situational awareness go missing.

The time allotted for Graham to mull his miscues was short. All it took was a split second for the threat's origination point to be identified. Even with his natural training kicking in, the SEAL just wasn't fast enough. As he raised the weapon to return fire, two rounds of 5.56 mm entered the front of his torso and tore out large chunks in his back upon exit. Graham felt nothing, the weapon which had been a fixture in his hands like a ballistic prosthetic fell silent to the ground while its operator crumpled to the ground with it.

In his final moments, Graham Pinchot didn't see, he couldn't hear the fury of the counter-attack his men prosecuted upon their assailants. Graham had no awareness that Archer 02 emptied its rocket pods into the threat at danger close range, while Archer 01 pulled into a hover above the fallen as if to assume the role of a guardian angel, spitting 20 mm into any resistance that dared move. Graham had no sense that the men he assembled and had worked long hours to train came out of the gunfight victorious.

What Graham Pinchot did see was light; spectacular light. Graham thought a smile might have curled his lips when the face of his father smiled back at him through the brilliance. A melancholy recognition fell upon him when the man who raised him was not accompanied by his son.

Dad, I don't understand, where is my son?

The disappointment lasted only a moment though. As quickly as the light flashed for Graham Pinchot, the regression to darkness happened equally as fast.

CHAPTER 67

Casa Grande, AZ

Henry crouched in what modest cover was available while a maelstrom of lead flew about him. Hovering just over the besieged men of Patriots USA, Captain Brent 'Merle' Avery unleashed hell into the flank. What warheads remained in the helicopter's rocket pods had just ripped their attackers to shreds. The blasts had been alarmingly close; so close that the time between the whoosh of departure off the racks and detonation was imperceptible.

Head still ringing from successive concussive blasts, Henry saw the 20 mm cannon spinning above him before he was able to hear it. Gathering his senses, O'Brien pushed himself to rally a counter assault. Utilizing hand signals, he indicated to a fire team nearby that he wanted them to counter flank their agitators while the Viper had them suppressed.

As the men sprinted with weapons at the ready to execute their maneuver, Henry glanced back to where he had last seen his boss. Henry could have sworn Graham was standing there just a moment ago, yet now it appeared the boss had moved.

Had the SEAL led men to close with the hostile firing positions on his own?

Henry decided he didn't have time to work out his confusion amid the chaos. Overhead, the Viper's cannon spun to a stop. O'Brien sighted his rifle in toward where the enemy fire had originated to provide suppressive follow-up fire should his flankers require it. They did not. Their sweep of the firing position was savagely fast and efficient. Only then did the frenetic gunfight finally draw to an end.

O'Brien had only just replaced his partially spent magazine with a full one and moved his weapon's selector switch to safe when he heard the frantic call, "Medic!" More jarring than the actual call was the direction it originated from. The call for help came from where he had just looked for Graham moments ago. *Graham had been standing there with a few other men. Was it one of the riflemen that had fallen?* Henry felt ashamed when he found himself hoping it had been. There was no best-case scenario.

Even as Henry ran toward the man calling for help, anxiety worked to paralyze his legs. A sentiment seemingly validated when one of his men ran by him with a triage bag in hand. So fast, Henry felt as though his boots may have become sodden with concrete.

The Marine's boots were, of course, concrete free, and the fear that seized him into a temporary state of shock passed as he came upon his fallen comrades. Henry had just set his weapon down to assist the medic when he saw Graham.

O'Brien knew the horrific truth at once. A hurried medevac would not be needed, Graham was gone and so too were the lives of the men who stood with him in his final moments. In the spot where they had fallen on Interstate 8, the highway soaked in their life's blood. The medic who had so quickly brushed past Henry in the rush to provide aid confirmed as much with each check for a pulse.

Henry knew all three men. One of them had a wife back in San Diego, with a little girl who had only recently taken her first steps. The other man had been a recruit of his own from the Marine Corps. He was not married, at least not yet. The young man did however have a little boy with a woman who he had hoped to marry soon.

Entangled with them was one of his best friends, or at least his body. Henry hoped that his soul had finally found peace. He hoped that there was life in Heaven after death. Henry hoped that the slain loved ones Graham cherished and fought for were there to greet him. Still, his hopeful thoughts did little to assuage the grief that overcame him next. Trying to picture Graham embracing his father, son, and fellow warriors was more than he could handle.

Burdened with the weight of anguish and grief Henry sank to one knee. Then he slumped into a seated position among his fallen friends. Initially, the Marine fought to keep his bearing and despair in check. He quietly wept. Yet, the longer he fought to contain his emotional devastation, the stronger his anger and sorrow fought to escape. Finally, overcome with raw and primal emotion Henry gave in and openly sobbed.

To any observer who may have come upon Henry O'Brien at that moment, they might have thought the man lost a heart-wrenching battle. To a real warrior like O'Brien, there were no revels in victory, just the horrific reality of survival. His best friend had been killed by a fellow American, and deep down Henry knew it had all just begun.

PART 3

CHAPTER 68

The Oval Office
Washington, D.C.

High-pressure summits, negotiations, and political parleys have been commonplace within the walls of the Oval Office since its construction. Perhaps no place on Earth, at least certainly within the United States, boasted a home field advantage like that of the President's formal workspace. Countless messages to the nation and world had been made from the Resolute Desk. Décor was unique from one administration to the next. Presidential prerogative dictated how the furniture would be arranged, which paintings would adorn the walls, and what style of throws or runners world leaders would traverse across during their visits to America's seat of power.

Ray Tinsley's predecessor had a distinct taste. One might flatteringly categorize it as simple elegance. The floors were clean and sharp to look at save the runners placed under a pair of matching half couches facing each other. Guests who sat on the cream-colored microfiber often remarked at the comfort.

Their simple classic colors only worked, in contrast, to show-case the beautiful runners underneath, themselves a gift from Egypt's leader.

Meanwhile, artist renditions of former Presidents hung on the walls in paintings, all with watchful eyes to stand for eternity in testimony for what happened in this very room. Theodore Roosevelt. John F. Kennedy. Abraham Lincoln. Ronald Reagan. Thomas Jefferson. Those were the statesmen America's previous lead executive had chosen to watch over him. Tinsley himself had desired a shakeup of the artwork, though his tumultuous opening months had left little time to set a high priority on interior decorating.

Tinsley looked around at the room and those gazes caught his attention, he felt as though their eyes were following him around the Oval Office. "Let them watch," he grumbled; they were about to stand witness to history yet again. Only two of the watchers had ever done what Tinsley had planned to do on this day. Even then, those two had not gone to the lengths in their actions that he had in mind for America at this moment. He wondered who would paint him and what his vision would mean for the future of this office and the country.

Bold actions, he realized, might be among the bullet points future historians would associate with his Presidency. No President, not one, had had the spine to take on the gun lobby with the ferocity and resolve that he did. An action justified, he felt due to the mandate he claimed following the landslide election and overhaul of executive and congressional branches. Tinsley had political capital and he dared not waste it. Pushing for the Amendment to repeal American's rights to bear arms was bold. No person could doubt that. He reflected, given the chance for a do-over, he would fight this fight again. *How many people needed to die for America to see he was right? What was that guy's name up in Minnesota?* Tinsley didn't even remember, it seemed so long ago. Deciding that the man was simply a pawn for his agenda, he wasted no further effort to recall it.

The President imagined his push for the gun legislation would trigger some push back from his opponents, even scattered protests. What had happened on the National Mall however was an eventuality that he never considered. Failure to imagine the possibility was not just his shortcoming, not a single advisor had foreseen the extent Americans would go to in actual action to stand up against his administration. Declaring martial law following the calamity had been a bold move of necessity. He couldn't lose control of the country now, not this early in his term. There was much to accomplish before his legacy would be set in the annals of American history.

Had I just done then what I'm going to do today, I could have avoided the issues plaguing me now! Voices of restraint that held me back then will not be heard today.

Awaiting President Tinsley in the Oval Office were the handful of advisors and political appointees he felt had earned the privilege to be here now when he announced the next bold landmark decision of his Presidency. The actual announcement to the American people would happen soon after he briefed those who advised him. As has been the case for past seminal moments in American history, the public would hear of it from this office. A few of his advisors were seated on the matching furniture while others stood nearby in quiet conversation. Of them, only his Chief of Staff Marvin Miller was privy to the details the President was about to share.

Tinsley cleared his throat from the Resolute Desk, "Thanks for coming, you will all no doubt want to hear what I am about to tell the American people." The President opened a folio with the seal of his office stamped into the cover. "I've spoken with the Attorney General to ensure I am within the purview of my duties. Today, I will invoke the Insurrection Act to restore control of the country."

Vice President Whitmore spoke first following a short silence. "Excellent choice, Mr. President. Might I ask how exactly you plan to implement the order?"

Marvin Miller offered on behalf of the boss. "Mr. Vice President, this will allow the White House and Department of Defense to coordinate and plan operations within our borders freely to shorten the unrest. Our military will be able to restore order to communities and put an end to the outbreak of violence being perpetrated by misguided antagonists throughout the nation."

"We would all like to curb suffering across the country and restore normal life to Americans, Mr. Miller. I am not intending to come off as the voice of dissent. What I am asking, perhaps poorly, is *how* we envision this actually working. Are the men and women in uniform going forth into the communities under the banner of peacekeepers or are we going to ask them to conduct raids and offensive operations? Are they mediators or combatants?" Adam Whitmore's demeanor was one of calm strength.

Tinsley answered, "I suppose that question is one of perspective, Adam." A short silence followed the President's statement. While simplistic and straightforward, nobody missed the implied threat. At least a portion of the population would see the President's plan and purpose as a threat and Tinsley had no apparent desire to hide that fact. The President was not ruling out openly waging conflict on his constituents in the name of restoring his vision of order.

Secretary of Defense Smithson next ended the silence with a question of his own, "Mr. President, there is past precedent for invocation of the Insurrection Act. Without digging into reference material, I seem to recall this type of action being taken for civil unrest in smaller localized events such as race riots and desegregation initiatives. Even the Lincoln County War incident was not so vast an undertaking as what you suggest here. You want to deploy our military forces nationwide? The sheer logistics..."

Once more Marvin Miller interjected. "Mr. Secretary, obviously blanket coverage of the entire nation is not realistic, even for our military. Simply put, utilizing the Insurrection Act gives the White House flexibility to move around forces as needed to the most crucial areas. A rebellion cannot be allowed to take root; it must be stopped."

NSA Director Flynn added his voice to Miller's. "What reduced intelligence we are still able to glean electronically after the people have had their cell phones crashed and internet restricted is not encouraging. Rather than breaking the defiant spirit we had hoped to curb, the opposite effect seems to be the case. People are mad, mad enough to take action. Most people are guilty of no more than nuisance talk of sedition. The others, while in the minority, have far more harmful intentions. Worse yet, they are on the move. Mr. President, perhaps you remember when we discussed Houston? What I warned about is, in fact, coming to pass. We're not talking local law enforcement issues, they're sweeping across state lines and growing."

General Adams quietly listened until he'd taken in the information and had time to process a spectrum of ideas.

"Mr. President, if I may, might we consider a posture of simply showing force to maintain peace instead, with an emphasis on humanitarian missions? We can put ROEs in place to protect our men and women in uniform. You can direct them to only fire weapons to protect themselves or others in imminent peril. I fear asking them to carry out offensive operations will fail to have the effect you seek."

The President fixed his Commanding General with an imposing stare. "Explain that last part, general."

"Mr. President, our military service members are among the best in the world." Adams stood his ground tactfully. "They are loyal and fearless, truly an imposing force. What makes them the envy of other nations is how savagely they fight for America and our values. They are however flesh and blood, with strong moral codes and values. They are loyal first and foremost to our *nation*. Some will undoubtedly follow commanders and their President in whatever is asked of them, but it will not be because they are mindless robots. Rather, they will do so because they share your values. Others will see prosecuting an offensive against the nation they took an oath to defend as an unlawful order. Some will turn on you as their ancestors did leading up to and throughout the Civil War. I fear that asking them to attack people they swore to defend will lead to an exodus among their ranks, and they will run to the other side growing the ranks of those you hope to suppress."

President Tinsley quietly considered the general's assessment, while everyone else in the room remained deathly silent. "General, can I count on you to take my directive forward and issue the orders?" asked Tinsley.

Adams answered frankly, "Yes, Mr. President, you can count on me to distribute your orders. I do however fear that

294 · MATTHEW H. WHITTINGTON

not all commanders will be so diligent. Some may have already taken initiatives of their own, such as what appears to be happening out west. It is my opinion that this action is very likely to weaken our position on a national level, sir."

Tinsley signaled that he had endured enough. "Understood, general; prepare the orders. Through your channels, I suggest you make it clear that those who *'take their own initiative'* will suffer the fate of traitors. I will not tolerate sedition." The President closed the folio on his desk and adjourned the meeting. Soon the media would be in the Oval Office. Cameramen would fuss over positioning and networks would bring word forth from the President of the United States.

CHAPTER 69

Davis-Monthan Air Force Base
Just outside Tucson, AZ

Davis-Monthan Air Force Base just southeast of Tucson, Arizona, is perhaps known best by Americans as the Boneyard. Before the United States military assumed ownership of the property, the small airstrip had been a popular re-fuel stop for the likes of Earhart, Lindbergh, and Doolittle. Among the first airframes to be retired at the Boneyard were B-29 Super Fortresses and Douglas C-47s following World War II. At first, the airfield served the Army Air Corps then Air Force exclusively. That changed in 1965 when aircraft storage across the branches consolidated. In the 1990s, hundreds of B-52s were destroyed at the Boneyard by an enormous guillotine under the START treaty. The savage destruction of the bomber fleet was conducted in the open so that Russian satellites could fly over the site to document America's compliance.

The Boneyard was far more than an airplane graveyard. A handful of military aircraft ended up being restored to full mission capable status while others find forever homes in museums after visiting the base. Airframes that wind up in purgatory though are destined to endure heavy cannibalization in the name of mission readiness for their counterparts still active around the world.

Henry found himself seated aboard Captain Michaels' Osprey adjacent to one of the few portals with a view to the world below. Wrapped neatly at his feet were the three bodies of his dead comrades while below a sea of dead and forgotten aircraft opened to his view. The Marine pilot expertly transitioned the rotors from forward flight to an approach hover orientation. Henry barely noticed the change. Within just a few minutes Captain Michaels had eased her Osprey onto the deck and smoothly taxied to a stop.

Hot arid air and Arizona sun filled the cargo compartment as the Osprey's ramp lowered. A desert gust blew in as if the ramp had been holding it back, the breath of wind felt like a hairdryer on O'Brien's face. More jarring than the sudden southwest weather however was the spectacle awaiting their arrival. Lined up in parallel rows in ramrod straight attention were airmen who called the Boneyard home.

The Marine had not expected a formal welcome, let alone one free of tension or even possibly passive hostility. Henry had worried that their movements would be at best, tacitly allowed. At worst, violently opposed. Logically he knew that what Graham had started would be viewed by those in power as illegal, some would even view their actions as traitorous. Every story had two sides. Nobody set out to be the villain or to occupy the shaky ground of immorality. Even as the men of Patriots USA had set out to right perceived wrongs, there would be those on the other side who would fail to see their actions as just.

In the middle stood the United States Military. An all-vol-
unteer force drawn from the melting pot of Hometown, USA.
Brave men and women raised on sets of values as different as
black and white. Yin and yang. Those who shared Graham's
views and those who did not. All sworn to the same oath. One
mission, to defend the United States of America. Against all
enemies, foreign and *domestic*. The problem that troubled him
was a matter of definitions. Who decided which Americans
were enemies?

The government or the people? Was it even that simple?

Clearly, matters were more complicated than lines in the
sand. Spurgeon Gorlick's canvass of the checkpoint turned ambush site had revealed they were jumped by their own fellow
Americans. Non-military to be more specific. What weapons
and belongings that escaped incineration and destruction indicated they had been a hastily assembled militia force. Not
dissimilar from their own. Had Patriots USA approached the
ambush without the force multipliers hovering above, the outcome may have been starkly different. There were newer small
arms strewn about with enough ammunition to match that of
Graham's mobile force. Strangely, there was cash on hand as
well. Lots of it. A logical inference was made that these people
were paid to be there. The amount of cash meant that whoever
employed them didn't want that fact traced backward. Henry
suspected that if he survived long enough the enigma would
solve itself in time.

Whatever sentiments the command here at the Boneyard
held about the political climate gripping the country, it was impossible to gauge them based on those solemnly assembled on
the tarmac now. Obviously, someone had notified the men and
women stationed here about what cargo the Osprey carried, and

the emotions in seeing their response washed over Henry. The dead were not active duty, but they were veterans. The fact that these airmen ignored the distinction made Henry swell with pride.

Remaining aboard the Osprey, Henry watched as each body was carefully and respectfully raised in the arms of their service brothers and sisters who then in turn slowly walked them down the ramp to the base coroner's vehicle. Reference to time seemed to fade even as Henry watched Graham's body make its journey from his custody to that of those who would prepare it for final rights. As each body passed by the rows of airmen, they offered a somber salute. Only when the dead had all been moved away did the gathered in uniform disperse.

Henry descended the ramp where an Air Force Major greeted him. "Come with me please, sir."

***

By Air Force standards the operations center at Davis-Monthan lacked in style and amenities compared to others around the country and world. While a visitor may have found that fact odd at a glance, it made perfect sense upon reflection. In the way that people commonly observe how dogs resemble their owners, the Boneyard operations center assumed the personality of its inhabitants.

Two active squadrons operate from the base, each flew the venerable A-10 Thunderbolt, or as the soldiers who count on the plane's presence overhead prefer to call it, the Warthog. What the old bird lacks in technology, looks, comfort, and several other features it more than compensates for with grit, toughness, and firepower. A lot of firepower. In many ways, the Warthog is a throwback to generations past in aviation. Plainly said, it is an aviator's plane and a grunt's best friend.

There is nothing clean about how the Warthog and its drivers do business. With the Warthog prowling the battlefield one simple fact comes into razor-sharp clarity, the fight is on and the enemy's teeth are going to get kicked in by the Red, White & Blue.

Henry O'Brien took in his surroundings as the major led him into the room. To his relief, he saw a few familiar faces. Most notably two of the Cobra pilots, Major Harrison *Sugarbush* Holder and Captain Brent *Merle* Avery, were in conversation with their Air Force counterparts. Their hair was heavy with sweat and they sported a hairstyle Henry thought would best be described as 'helmet head'. The room itself smelled of worn flight suits, coffee, and sweat. Conversation among the aviators was at a low murmur, nobody carried on in the animated fashion commonly depicted in movies. Henry had only been there for a few minutes when a colonel walked in and assumed a commanding stance at the lectern.

Both Air Force and Marine officers found seats and Henry followed their lead. The chair he settled on was cushioned though beyond worn. Lumbar support was not to be had and Henry wondered if he wouldn't be better served to sit on a simple wooden chair. Aside from the lumpy discomfort provided by the seat, it was also heavily stained with sweat and possibly coffee. Henry had always heard that Air Force amenities were plush. Apparently, Warthog drivers preferred to live with amenities on the modest side. He wondered if it was a psychological tool the aviators employed to condition their minds to connect with those they flew combat missions for.

Henry's reflection on the subtleties of squadron briefing rooms was curbed when the colonel cleared his throat. No screens were turned on; nothing was written out for visual display. Whatever the man had to say was off the cuff and most definitely off the record.

"Word from the Pentagon isn't good, folks. The President has invoked the Insurrection Act. Early indications point toward a broad application of the emergency power. Rather than using the armed forces to control a specific localized event or maintain order, our commanders warn that the Commander in Chief intends to utilize us offensively. As yet it is unclear what that would entail for this command specifically, but the possibilities are chilling. I for one do not relish the thought of strafing our local communities."

A long silence fell on the room as each person let the colonel's words soak in.

Troubled, the colonel continued, "I've put too much time in to adopt an openly defiant stance. We will need to be calculated in our actions. Numbers and records can be fixed to tell any story we desire. Airplanes may develop mechanical issues. In this volatile environment, it isn't a stretch to believe that logistical channels will be strained and unreliable." Just then Henry caught a side glimpse of Patriots USA's new boss, Spurgeon Gorlick, sitting a few chairs away. Somehow, he hadn't seen him until this moment. The former Ranger looked worn. He looked like a person whose whole world was falling apart around them yet still stood, like a lone stubborn tent pole in a windstorm. Whipped. Beaten. Resilient.

The colonel's eyes must have fallen on Gorlick as well. His tone softened as he addressed the beleaguered veteran.

"Your people have done this community a great service today. Those thugs you encountered at the checkpoint were creating a lot of problems for the locals. Nobody seems to know where they came from; I don't think they were from the area. Those bastards just showed up a few days ago and started causing problems. Barricading pharmacies. Blocking off hospitals and as you know they took it upon themselves to chokepoint arterials. Why they were doing what they were doing was unclear. What is clear, somebody had to stand up to them. On behalf of my command and the greater Tucson area, thank you. We stand beside you in mourning for your losses." Spurgeon nodded graciously.

As if adding an afterthought, the colonel said, "We're expecting a flight from Miramar, you'll want to be there to greet it, Mr. Gorlick." No further guidance was offered; no questions were taken. He simply concluded, "Dismissed," and walked out.

Henry sat for a minute and puzzled over the officer's message. Was the colonel sympathetic to their mission or simply empathetic over their losses? Had he and the men come to a place of shelter and support or would their mission fail? Would the men even be willing to fight on or had their resolve died with Graham? Anxiety threatened to bubble up and tear down the warrior façade he had erected for those who followed his example. Henry knew he couldn't allow that to happen, if the men smelled fear on him or any of the leaders, all future operations could be clouded by doubts. His introspection was curbed when Spurgeon stood up and motioned for the men to move out.

CHAPTER 70

Davis-Monthan Air Force Base
Just outside Tucson, AZ

Henry stood next to Gorlick on the tarmac where they watched a C-130 slowly navigate the taxiways to their position. Temperatures were becoming insufferably uncomfortable as the two men stood waiting for the bird's arrival. A modest breeze out of the north offered slight respite in the unforgiving desert. Four idling turboprops filled the air with the only noise the men could hear. Henry found the noise comforting, it was like white noise from a house fan one might use to sleep to, only on a much larger scale. Deafening yet smooth.

As the venerable aircraft rolled to a graceful stop, Henry admired the pilot's precision. He put the front tires directly on top of a small yellow 'T' painted on the deck. One by one each engine was powered down and finally, the ramp lowered. Single file, men in desert fatigues disembarked, encumbered with gear. At a glance, there was vague recognition. They were warriors, Henry had no doubt, he could see it in their bearing. Yet, they were not his fellow Marines.

One by one the men staged their gear neatly on the flight deck. Most of them walked back up the ramp, Henry surmised there must be more equipment they needed to offload. A lone figure walked toward him and Gorlick. As the man drew nearer, Henry noticed bronze maple leaves on his lapels and U.S. Navy embroidered above his breast pocket. The stranger stopped just in front of him and Gorlick and offered a handshake.

"I'm Lieutenant Commander Bobby Simmons; I command SEAL team 2. Your medical officer reached out to us through Jim Creek. Apparently, one of ours was killed in a gunfight. We're here to pay respects to our fallen brother. Can you tell me what happened?"

Henry listened respectfully as Spurgo debriefed the commander. As his boss laid out all of the known specifics, Henry felt a great force pulling on his guts from the inside. He'd known loss before, it was awful and devastating. Before, he felt guilty for being the one who came home. He was swept in sadness when a friend's loved one would ask *how it happened* as if they could understand the horror of war. He even felt anger for having been powerless to change the outcome. Yet each time a brother or sister had been lost, it had been in war. In war, people die. Death in wartime was terrible, but to be expected. What he felt now was different, far more powerful and devastating. The mechanics of Graham's death were the same as the other losses Henry had known over time. What made this different was the trigger puller on the other end. An American. A faceless person they hadn't known, yet had sworn an oath to defend. Henry realized what he felt now as Spurgo recounted the checkpoint battle was a betrayal.

The entire debrief between the two commanders could have only lasted minutes. Lieutenant Commander Simmons asked a few follow-up questions where Spurgo left gaps such as; *where is his body* and *have you established a perimeter?* Henry thought, *we're on a military base, isn't the perimeter established?* Yet, even as he puzzled it over Henry realized that all security assumptions ought to be recalculated. Assuming to be safe anywhere could get him and the men killed.

"I'll get a fire watch set up," Henry offered. They nodded as Henry turned on a heel to track down the men.

***

When a person, man or woman, considers committing a portion or whole of their life to the United States Military they might consider any number of benefits that are worth risking one's life for. Despite what one might say, it is almost certainly not the college money that truly pulls on a soul. Life experiences? Perhaps. The privilege of wearing the uniform of a given branch? Sure, to some extent. Some might say taking the oath was their only escape while others simply wish to write their own chapter in family heritage. Those who hit closer to the mark could talk about long and rich traditions. Most of all, on the most basic and truest level, it's all about camaraderie. What is a person willing to do for their fellow brothers and sisters in arms? One might get in for any or all of the previous motivations, those who find joy in service do so because of the company they keep. *That's* what it's all about. It is the bonds of relationships forged through shared adversity that stand the test of time.

Skeletal remains of aircraft from eras past lined the funeral procession path. Stripped from their exposed remains were all that once made them rulers of the sky. Hydraulic pumps, jet engine parts, and life support systems alike, yanked from their innards like some old Chevys at a countryside junkyard. What had once been the backbone of America's projected power now stooped sorrowfully over the scene unfolding under their plastic-covered nose cones.

Gathered among the assorted old sentries, were the men who had followed Graham Pinchot across the Mojave. Beyond them, the warriors of SEAL Team 2 stood at attention opposite each other, forming a corridor. The Arizona heat had reached its apex hours ago. While the aircraft graveyard was still stifling hot with the sun falling in the west, nobody seemed to be overly mindful of the fact.

Murmurs among the men could not penetrate and carry through the assembly for any great distance thanks to lines of aircraft carcasses. Henry found the scene to be devoid of life; the observation saddened him. What sparse whispers had been present faded to silence as a hearse backed into the column of men.

The black Cadillac was driven by an older man. He slowly lumbered from behind the steering wheel. Henry thought the man looked as though he were trying to wait for his joints to warm up. The driver's stroll to the Cadillac's rear went painfully slow. Finally, he managed to open the door to reveal a simple cedar casket. SEAL veterans working for Patriots USA led by Parker Jefferson, who worked logistics, and Dakota Grant, the medic, assembled to remove Graham's remains from the car.

No verbal communication was necessary. They simply and deliberately pulled him from the vehicle. With each man assuming a position around the casket's perimeter they carried their boss through the corridor of men. As their walk began, only men who hardly knew the man bowed their heads in respect. Airmen from Davis-Monthan and Marines from Camp

Pendleton, Yuma, Twenty-Nine Palms, and Miramar each, in turn, stood by in their uniforms and offered a salute. Next to witness his passage, were the men he employed and led. Tommy Sullivan, Spurgeon Gorlick, Henry, and the rest of the men hung their heads in reverence for the leader they chose. If any man dared look to either side and could see through a sea of reflective Oakley sunglasses, they would have seen hardened warriors heavy with tears.

Finally, the procession came upon the lined-up men of SEAL Team 2. Inch by inch Graham's pallbearers made their way to the head of the column of mourners. As they drew even with each sailor, a slow sharp salute was rendered. Rendered out of tradition. Rendered for the shared respect of donning the uniform. The salutes were given for honor. Honor for a fallen warrior who shared the brotherhood of their exclusive community. Few of them had known Graham Pinchot when he still wore the uniform, it didn't matter. Graham wore the same Trident they had each earned. They didn't need to know Graham on a personal level; he was their brother nonetheless.

After passing by the last salutes, Graham's casket was respectfully set on a pedestal. Lieutenant Commander Simmons stepped forward with three of his men. Two of them smartly unfolded a banner. A star-filled blue field was flanked by thirteen red and white stripes. Each of the four SEALs assumed control of a corner and snapped the flag taut. They then draped it over Graham's remains.

Aside from those who had gathered there was no fanfare. No photographers. No emotionally ravaged next of kin, Graham had none left. What ceremonial steps happened next were for the traditions, not a crowd of mourners and onlookers. What could have been said for the assembled warriors?

At first, the sound was faint, as if whispered into the wind. With each passing note, it became more apparent what was happening. Bagpipes wept the notes of Amazing Grace.

When the final notes inevitably fell silent, there was a brief pause before a detail of airmen offered their salute. Twenty-one sharp reports later their ceremonial rifles fell silent as well. What few grisled warriors managed to conceal their manful tears up to that point were soon put to the ultimate test as a Navy bugler piped the world's 24 most sorrowful notes. Taps rang across the Boneyard with powerful finality.

Two of Commander Simmon's men then removed the American Flag draped over Graham and neatly folded it for presentation. There was, however, nobody to present it to. No family to receive a nation's gratitude. No family left to hear words of condolence. Instead, the standard was simply placed into the casket with him.

With all military funeral traditions met, there was one final tradition specific to the SEALs left. Airmen, Marines, and veterans of Patriots USA were left on the periphery to watch as one of the most exclusive displays in all of United States Military history transpired. One by one, each man approached the casket, where he then removed the Trident from his uniform and pounded it into the coffin. Offering proffered, the SEAL would then render a salute before turning on a heel and making way for the next man. When they were done, Graham's casket shimmered gold in the setting Arizona sun.

CHAPTER 71

Davis-Monthan Air Force Base
Just outside Tucson, AZ

Sneaking onto the base undetected had been easier than Carlos Gutierrez expected. Avoiding the gates was obvious.
Military police had established a series of barricades to slow
down incoming traffic, just as military bases had following the
September 11th attacks. Breaching the perimeter was simply
about finding a weak point and patience.

An opportunity to infiltrate the Boneyard presented itself
when Gutierrez circled to the east side of the installation. The
security weakness he discovered was not brilliantly obvious, a
casual passerby may not have even noticed what he had detected. At the base of the fence near one of the poles, an animal
had burrowed underneath, perhaps feral cats or a coyote attempting to pursue a desperate meal. Whatever had created the
shallow depression beneath the wire had provided the agent
with an opportunity.

At first, Gutierrez concealed himself amongst the desert
fauna to observe his entry point. How often would the MPs pass

by? Did aircraft on approach fly over this spot? Could he be deliberate during infiltration or would he need to move fast?

Hours of watching the spot revealed an ideal scenario. No patrols rolled by and save a lone C-130 arrival, the skies were eerily quiet. Gutierrez was mentally rehearsing how he intended to slide himself and gear under the wire when he heard gunshots. Crisp reports, not those firecracker-like pops of handguns. He thought they must have been rifles. The incongruous discharges left him perplexed. Alert. No incoming shots snapped over his head and oddly it seemed one-sided. There was no answering volley.

Gutierrez laid in wait once more in hopes of observing where the shots had come from. He thought they must have come from the base itself, though the landscape in front of him only revealed hundreds of defunct aircraft.

Clarity didn't come; he just needed to move.

Wide-eyed, Gutierrez moved smoothly to his planned entry point. First, he slid his gear into the breach. His backpack was compact, yet it was still caught on the loosened fence. Gutierrez pulled it back out and dug sand from the hole with his hands until it seemed deep enough. On the second try, his backpack went through without incident. Next, Gutierrez laid down with his head pointed toward the opening. Using his shoulders, he began to shimmy through. The fence seemingly worked to forbid entry. Each inch gained was challenged. Fabric from his shirt kept catching on protruding wire edges and tearing as he tugged. Upon finally gaining passage, Gutierrez looked down to see scratches and scrapes on his arms and torso. His clothing looked as though it may have been cleaved by an angry, feral animal.

Considering his alternatives, the agent considered himself fortunate. Gutierrez felt confident that while his clothing may have been torn, his cover remained intact. His next objective was simple in principle while possibly dangerous in execution. *I need to establish an observation post to find out what's going on here.* That required movement across a large area before cover was available. Runways. Taxiways. Flat ground with great visibility all had to be crossed undetected until concealment opportunities became abundant.

While at first the task seemed daunting, an encouraging realization surfaced in his mind. *Only one aircraft in hours has flown into this airfield. People up in that tower with the best view of my movements will be less vigilant considering their lack of work. This Boneyard is a ghost town today, something is going on. I'll just need to avoid flashy movement.*

Carlos set out across the airfield to where he thought bountiful opportunities for concealment would be, the vast airplane graveyard.

***

The movement to his hiding spot went painfully slow. Hypervigilance mixed with the afternoon heat worked in concert wearing Gutierrez down both physically and mentally. His walk seemed to last all afternoon over a relatively short distance. For the entirety of his movements, Gutierrez could see his end goal shimmering ahead. At times he wondered if his destination was a mirage. While he had heard tales of men seeing lush oases on sandy horizons, Gutierrez observed nothing to that effect. Rather, he worked to focus on shifting hulks through the distorted air.

When he finally arrived among the resting metal giants, Gutierrez looked up and down their ranks to scan for appropriate observation posts. The coming darkness would be his friend. Not only would detecting his movements be made more difficult for his quarry, using the abundance of natural cover would be far more bearable at night.

All this metal has to be murderously hot to the touch.

Gutierrez methodically worked over his options when his eye caught an incongruous feature. *A mirage?* Where the countless aircraft each had a certain aerodynamic flow, even to the eye while parked on the ground, these objects were block-like. *Not aircraft. Conex boxes, dozens of them.* Gutierrez wondered what he would find inside the huge storage containers.

Using the approaching twilight to his advantage, Gutierrez moved among the shadows toward the containers. Fuselages and wings provided all the shade and concealment he would need. Even still he moved with deliberate caution to avoid careless mistakes.

Reaching out with a gloved hand he touched the nearest Conex box. *Still pretty hot.* Gutierrez looked up and around to ascertain what the view might offer should he clamber up for a look around. With the whereabouts of base personnel uncertain, Gutierrez had to get his situational awareness right. That would mean getting himself higher to see over the rows of aircraft. *The sun is going down, the metal is as hot as it's going to get.*

Gutierrez circled the boxes at ground level to see if any had been left unsecured. To his disappointment, each was latched and secured with padlocks. A good bolt cutter would easily gain him entry, but he had no such tool. *What's in here? Parts? Weapons?*

For now, the answer to his question would have to stay a mystery. Gutierrez looked up at the stacked containers. They were double stacked and five wide with a lone container starting the third row in the middle. *If I can climb on top, this might be the vantage point I need.*

Cautiously, Gutierrez searched for a spot where his feet could find purchase to clamber up the side. The sides were corrugated and looked slick. He didn't want to stack objects to boost him up. Any person walking by could notice the stacked objects as suspicious and deduce their purpose. It appeared his only realistic option was to use the latches for footing and pull himself up. Gutierrez would have preferred if his chosen ascent path were more discreet, obscured by other features. Unfortunately, it wasn't; he would have to climb where detection would be easy if anyone was about. Ultimately, he knew the elevated ground was worth the risk.

Double-checking to make sure his pack was fully zipped and cinched to him; Gutierrez backed up a few steps. A glance in each direction to see if he was being watched. No one. He exploded for his target. One stride before reaching the container Gutierrez leaped, deftly landing the ball of his right foot on a hinge before exploding upward to reach for a handhold. Finding his grip, Gutierrez pulled up. Thankfully the containers were not stacked perfectly flush to the edge he had scaled. A small lip formed where the second container rested just about eight inches back. With the first stage of his climb complete, Gutierrez realized summiting the second wouldn't begin with the benefit of a running start. Still, he had to move. Gutierrez felt naked perched in this spot, out in the open for the whole world to see.

Pushing exhaustion down and gathering his breath, Gutierrez climbed the second container. The metal was scorching and traction was poor. It didn't matter, he had to succeed. Agent Gutierrez gained the top. Crouching to reduce his profile he was finally able to look around a bit over the acres of aircraft.

Something *was* going on! Even from hundreds of yards away, the C-130 which had flown over just a while ago was easily visible. Gutierrez could make out personnel movement, maybe a dozen or so stood around its ramp. Beyond the cargo plane, a Marine Corps OV-22 Osprey sat idle, only one or two figures milled about it. *Plane captains or maintenance crew maybe?* Still further on, a division of slender helicopters settled on their skids, tie-down straps keeping the rotor blades in place.

Far more interesting than the non-Air Force aircraft though were large groupings of personnel. Some were clearly in military uniforms while others wore tan BDUs, non-descript tops under gear harnesses, and ball caps. Slung over many of their shoulders were weapons. *Contractors! Militia!* Ignoring the discomfort from lying prone on the hot metal, Gutierrez unslung his gear bag and opened it. From inside he retrieved high-power binoculars and his briefing. *I may have just found that Pinchot bastard!*

Gutierrez pulled out his cellphone and made a call. "How soon can you get a Predator over the Boneyard?" he growled.

CHAPTER 72

Davis-Monthan Air Force Base
Just outside Tucson, AZ

Spurgeon and Tommy were in deep conversation when
Henry walked up to them after Graham's ceremony. From what
he could tell, their debate was more pointed and measured than
it was confrontational. Henry's two senior officers were all that
remained of company leadership, officially. He often described
his position to anyone who would ask as, "middle management
mixed with mentorship." In truth, Henry assumed ownership
over many of the training evolutions and Graham had often
confided in him. Besides that, Henry was well connected in
Marine Corps circles, a nice benefit that likely saved many lives
over the past few days. What the two men were discussing now
centered around the future. Would the company follow through
on what Graham had started or would they dissolve and disap-
pear, cutting their losses in the name of survival?

"I'm just saying, we have a long way to go," Tommy said.
He nodded at Henry's approach. "Those assholes that jumped

us on the highway the other day; I think that's just the beginning. Coast to coast is no cakewalk. We're in for a lot of
dogfights, Spurgo. We're not all going to walk away."

Spurgeon's counterpoint seemed equally valid. "There's no
going back, Tommy. The minute we pulled off the lot back in
San Diego the die was cast. We're committed. You think we
can turn around, go back, and get future contracts from the government? No, we're wanted. We either fight, go to prison, or
die. We can't run from this; the only choice is to see this
through."

Tommy pressed the uncertain support angle. "What did that
colonel say in the briefing? Something to the effect of not
openly committing his forces to our side or at least not taking
our asses when we pull out of town? Didn't he say he wouldn't
be openly defiant with the Insurrection Act invoked? Don't you
get it? *Our side* is the one of defiance! He's not backing us.
Without air support, we're lost."

"The choppers," Spurgo protested.

"Limited range, logistical considerations across the country.
We'd have to establish a massive network of FARPs," Tommy
shot back. "Not to mention there are only FOUR! What happens when sand gums up the cannons and they start having
major mechanical issues? Or get shot down?! What happens
when this colonel gets convinced that we are his enemies and
these A-10s take us from behind?!"

"We can't give up, Tommy." Spurgeon shook his head res-
olutely. "We'll just have to find a way. We'll just have to
convince the colonel to look the other way. I think he sees the
tyranny. He doesn't want to fuck us; I think he's looking for a
reason to fight. I think he *might* back us."

O'Brien seized on a pause in the debate.

"I told the guys to make sure that any vehicles not parked undercover get some of that China Lake netting thrown over them. Also, I spoke to Charlotte; she's had her drone up there almost all day looking for other militia checkpoints and threats. She's spotted a few troublesome groupings back toward Phoenix, but nothing in our way should we continue east. Should have the drone back soon."

Spurgeon and Tommy nodded their approval. They were about to continue their discussion when they spotted one of the team leaders jogging toward them. Frank 'Franko' Wilson stopped a few feet away.

"Drone spotted something close! *REAL* close!" he announced.

"What is it, Franko?" Spurgeon's demeanor flipped from diplomat to commander in front of their very eyes.

"She was orbiting overhead and just happened to pan the camera down, the sensors picked something up out in the graveyard. Not base personnel or one of ours. She said the subject appears to have set up a surveillance post. We're being watched!"

Spurgeon turned to Henry. "Get a team out there to check it out!"

CHAPTER 73

Davis-Monthan Air Force Base
Just outside Tucson, AZ

From atop his observation post, Gutierrez searched for his contract. The call had just come, a message relayed from the drone control team, he found the Patriots USA militia. Several thousand feet overhead a drone armed with a pair of Hellfire missiles had positively identified a handful of the men known to lead the outfit. They had not however managed to positively ID the man he wanted. He had only two shots from above, one of them needed to land on Pinchot.

Gutierrez restarted his canvas of the civilian militia; he must have missed Pinchot somewhere. Minutes ago, they were all walking around casually, almost slowly. Now as he scanned their faces the challenge became more daunting. They were moving more quickly, some had unslung their weapons and huddled up like they were about to run a football play. *Something was happening.* Gutierrez relayed his observations back to the drone controllers. An alarm had been raised. *Did they know the drone was overhead?*

He was still working the binoculars looking for Pinchot when the call came through.

"Standby for a strike, verifying identities."

There was nothing Gutierrez could do to stop the attack; it was out of his hands. Even still he felt anxiety. *No; it's too soon! Give me time to find the guy I came for. He might escape!*

CHAPTER 74

Davis-Monthan Air Force Base
Just outside Tucson, AZ

Lieutenant Commander Bobby Simmons picked up on the word of a possible unknown spotter surveilling the field and insisted some of his men get in on the patrol to ascertain the person's identity and purpose. Also, in on the situation was the Air Force colonel who greeted the Patriots in the briefing room just hours before. Upon learning of the intruder, the colonel quickly made his way to meet with Patriots leadership escorted by his security team.

With the help of base military police, Henry and Commander Simmons were able to orient themselves with where the mystery observer was spotted and what terrain features the men could use as they approached. The target's apparent position on top of stacked shipping containers offered a defensive advantage the patrol would have to overcome, especially if he was armed well enough to fend off an assault. All indications however pointed to a single person. Even a single well-armed expert rifleman would be strained to defend against a well-planned flanking approach.

320 · MATTHEW H. WHITTINGTON

Unfortunately, Henry pointed out, the spotter would have one other distinct advantage. "This guy will see us coming from a mile away. Even if we wait for dark, I'm assuming he'll have night vision goggles."

Commander Simmons considered the point a moment. "How about we make it look like wire checks, night patrols? As we set out, make sure nobody looks panicked. Send some of your guys out in different directions like we're canvassing the area in 360 degrees. I'll lead a detail to go flush this guy out. Even if he picks up and moves, we'll track him down."

Henry thought the commander's plan was as good as any he'd come up with. A moment of consideration passed and then he acquiesced. "Good plan, we're in under one condition. Four of our guys embed with you, I'll lead them. We'll get a radio to our drone operator and I'll hold the other. If he moves, the eye in the sky will see where. Also, if you don't mind, I want to be on the front assault. Whoever this is, they came for us"

Knowing that Pinchot had trusted Henry was enough for the SEAL. He agreed to Henry's suggestions and the plan was set in motion. Henry realized Simmons's tactical genius when the commander considered even the most subtle details in executing the plan. The SEAL commander had his men change into clothing that matched the other patrols, so his team wouldn't stick out. Satisfied that all were ready, Henry dispatched 3 patrols in opposite directions away from where he and the SEAL strike team were heading. Then he and Commander Simmons stepped off with their men for the mystery watcher.

CHAPTER 75

Davis-Monthan Air Force Base
Just outside Tucson, AZ

Anxiety built and his heart raced. Gutierrez hoped the missile would have struck by now. The men were all relatively closely grouped just a moment ago. The strike may not have wiped them all out, but how many would have walked away cleanly with no debilitating injuries? That was then. Now with each passing minute, the militia was spreading further apart. Left at the origin point were just a small handful of people, maybe a dozen or so. None of which were Graham freaking Pinchot. *Where is he?!*

Anger and anxiety ebbed, replaced by excitement when Gutierrez got the call. "Missile launched."

"Is target the primary objective?" he asked.

In a clipped response his contact's answer was simple and disappointing, "No, other senior leadership."

Gutierrez curtly replied, "Copy" then ended the call.

To his horror, Gutierrez then realized he had lost track of the patrol nearest him. *Where the hell are they?!*

CHAPTER 76

Davis-Monthan Air Force Base
Just outside Tucson, AZ

Commander Simmons gave his directions in hushed tones. "Mike, Craig, and Deshaun I need the three of you to circle behind the containers. If this guy flees away from the pressure you guys will be the grab team. O'Brien your guys will stay on this end with a few of mine, the idea is to make him move away from you. If he so much as wrinkles his nose in a threatening fashion, cut him down. I'll lead a detail to the long side on his flank and initiate contact. Hopefully, he'll just surrender, if not we'll push him back to the grab team. Any quest...."

A sudden whoosh preceded a violent explosion behind them. The initial shock had each man ducking down before reflexively turning to face the unknown threat. Weapons raised, they could only see a pillar of smoke reaching for the sky against the Arizona sunset. With confusion settling on them like a layer of fog, it was Simmons who brought the men back into focus with purposeful direction.

"O'Brien, get on that radio and get a handle on just what the fuck is going on! The rest of you move into position NOW!

Whatever is happening I'm sure this bastard up here has something to do with it!"

With that, the men sprang into action. The frontal assault team raised their weapons in the direction of the container and popped suppressive shots over his head. Commander Simmons sprinted with his flankers to the left side as planned while the grab team sprinted around the right side. Seconds later, flank established, Commander Simmons and the men with him popped shots over the containers as well. Boxed in on three sides, one of which being the lone container starting a third row, the unknown spotter had only two choices; fight or run.

Meanwhile, Henry crouched behind the landing gear of an old B-52 and keyed his radio, hopeful that the explosion had not enveloped his drone pilot Charlotte as well. "O'Brien to Washington, do you copy?!"

A long moment passed with anxiety and uncertainty building within Henry. *What happened? Are we under attack? Am I all alone now?* Henry felt desperately powerless. All he could control at this moment was the radio, and even that only worked if there was someone to answer him. Agonized, he keyed it once more. "O'Brien to Washington!"

Finally, after a few painful seconds that seemed to linger in purgatory, a voice did come back. "This is Franko. I'm with Charlotte in her vehicle."

Henry felt the weight of the world lift off of him. Gunshots rang out nearby; he barely registered their reports. *I'm not alone.* Composing himself Henry keyed up once again. "Copy, what's going on? Was that an airstrike?" Henry felt bad the minute he asked the question. *Like Franko has any more idea than I do.*

Franko came back over the radio, clearly trying to sound as in control as he could manage, "Franko to O'Brien, unclear about what happened. That spot where everyone was gathered seems to be where the explosion took place, I didn't hear any jets or helicopters."

Henry knew he had narrowly escaped death; he been standing in that location just minutes ago. *Who was still there? Anyone? What combustibles were laying around? None. This has to be an attack.* Clarity struck him like a thunderclap. Henry keyed the mike.

"Have Charlotte scan for other drones, if any are present eliminate the damn thing before anything else gets dropped on our heads!"

"...Copy...how exactly?"

Henry fired back. "She knows what to do."

CHAPTER 77

Davis-Monthan Air Force Base
Just outside Tucson, AZ

Damn, how did they find me so fast?! Gutierrez cursed as lead zipped over his head. *SNAP.* In training, the sensation of rounds flying over him had been a little thrilling. This wasn't the same thrill; this was unsettling and desperate. He was trapped. Attempting to problem solve while under fire was not a skill he had been forced to develop. Some men run to the sound of gunfire while others run away. Gutierrez could do neither. Rather, he simply felt paralyzed. Pinned down. *SNAP. Was that the point? From their angle, they can't hit me.*

They can't hit me! If I move slowly away from them, maybe I can slip down the back end of this container and sneak away! SNAP. Remaining in the prone position, Gutierrez hurriedly shoved gear into his bag. *Hurry before one of them climbs up here!* SNAP. Sliding his arms through the straps, Gutierrez cinched them down tight and began low crawling away from the gunfire.

Gutierrez hoped they couldn't hear him moving, he thought they probably wouldn't over the gunfire. SNAP. Still, in his brain the risk of being heard was real. So, he methodically dragged himself and gear one elbow at a time until the back edge was only feet away. SNAP. *How far is the drop?* He remembered from the climb up that the second container was slightly offset toward the back, which at the time had worked out nicely. It had meant a ledge to work with. SNAP. What that meant now, however, was that his container overhung the bottom one slightly. No ledge to work with on his way down. *Damn!* SNAP.

Inch by agonizing inch Gutierrez snuck the last few feet until his head was nearly able to poke out and have a look below. SNAP. He felt he couldn't possibly get any closer to the container beneath him without becoming one with the metal. Gutierrez feared a round slamming into his head the minute he stuck it out over the edge to have a look around. Yet, he couldn't stay here. Eventually, they would run out of ammunition and come up to physically remove him. SNAP. Squinting his eyes as if to anticipate the impact he gradually moved far enough out to look around.

Nobody down here! Just an old hunk of airplane! Now I just need to find a way down! Spirits buoyed, he slid toward the next container over to see if it had been set in place offset in the other direction. SNAP. To his disappointment the container had been placed differently than the first, only this one was set down exactly right, flush. SNAP. He moved for the next container; this one too was flush. Running out of options he arrived at the final container, also flush. *FUCK!* SNAP.

All that was left for Gutierrez were a handful of bad options. Sit them out or drop down. SNAP. Sit them out and they'll come up; I'll be captured or killed. Drop down, I may get hurt.

But…I may escape. SNAP. He looked out again, *that's easily a fifteen, twenty-foot drop.* SNAP.

If I can get to the ground and get far enough away, I'm going to get that other missile dropped on these bastards. The thought of dropping a Hellfire on the heads of his tormentors was enough to compel his decision. Injuries be damned, he was getting off these containers. SNAP. SNAP. I'll hang off the edge, that will cut the distance by six feet, then I'll drop and roll. I may sprain an ankle and jack up my back, but I'm getting out of here.

Gutierrez pulled his gloves off and shoved them into his pockets. He wanted to feel the metal on his skin, he wanted no false sense of grip. Assured of his hold, Gutierrez slowly edged his legs over the side, pushing into the metal trying to gain whatever traction was there to be had. There wasn't any. Still, the rubber in the soles of his boots had been warmed by a combination of ambient heat and friction from crawling, thus softened. His feet did not just slide as if there were no drag. Rather he thought the sensation akin to going down a hot metal slide in the summer in shorts. Like when the skin met the metal going down; you still slid, but much slower.

Arms fully extended, he realized a lull had come in the persistent potshots over his head. *Odd.* This was no time to dwell on it, he took a breath in and released his grip. At the first indication of feet touching the ground, he expelled his breath and allowed his body to collapse into a roll. Gutierrez rolled a few feet from his landing spot before coming to a stop.

I can't stay here; got to move! He rolled to one side and then up on an elbow. *Achy, battered, not broken.* Gutierrez then got onto one knee when he felt the pain shooting up from his feet and ankles. More concerning than the pain though was the sound rushing up from behind him.

Gutierrez turned his head in time to glimpse a blur before it hit him in the back, driving him face-first into the ground. On each side, his attackers held him in place with weapons and terrifyingly null stares. One of them spoke so matter-of-factly into his helmet-mounted headset, "Subject captured."

CHAPTER 78

Davis-Monthan Air Force Base
Just outside Tucson, AZ

Franko's voice cut the air so abruptly Henry thought it sounded as if the man were shouting directly into his ear. Of course, he wasn't, it was a radio hail. With the cacophony of gunfire at an end though, the voice just *seemed* insanely loud.

"Franko to O'Brien; she found the other drone and smoked it!"

Relieved that the dagger at their throats from above was removed, Henry sighed deeply. Already slightly more relaxed he answered, "That's great news, Franko. We're wrapping things up out here. Any idea yet about damage from that strike?"

Henry could practically hear Franko shrugging his shoulders through the radio. "Not yet. Base fire crews are over there working to contain the blaze."

O'Brien cursed under his breath, someone had died, he just didn't know who. What Henry did know, everyone else who went out on patrol must have seen the blast. They will all be headed back soon to muster up. Only then would Henry have a true sense of what had been lost.

***

The accountability muster had revealed a terrible human cost, far higher than Henry was emotionally prepared to pay. Killed in the drone strike were Spurgeon Gorlick and Thomas Sullivan, thus decapitating the Patriots' official leadership and the colonel in charge of Davis-Monthan Air Force Base along with his entire security detail. In an odd paradox, discovering the man atop the containers had actually saved countless lives. Had he gone undiscovered, there would not have been patrols or a hunt. Rather, Spurgo and Tommy would have had a much larger cadre of their men about them. The death toll would have been staggering, even paralyzing.

Thankfully that terrible scenario was not reality. Nearly all the men had survived the attack physically unscathed. Angry and vengeful beyond words, emotionally distraught, yet physically sound. For that much, Henry was thankful. His gratitude was tempered however by a pair of new problems. The men were mad; mad enough to act. At this point, the prospect of disbanding and fading away from the fight retreated away like the horizon in a rearview mirror. Even if Henry wanted to go home and lick his wounds, the men would hear nothing of it. Second, and perhaps more pressing in urgency was the vacuum of leadership. Who would lead them?

Whether it was Graham's influence from beyond the grave or simply his amicable approachable nature as an instructor, the men seemed to solve this problem for Henry.

Franko approached the shell-shocked Marine and asked, "What now, boss?"

What now? I have no idea. His first instinct was to ensure no more of his men died today. "Get everybody out of the open." He paused a moment to clear the cobwebs and channel what he thought Graham might do. Graham would surround himself with smart counselors and act decisively. "Track down every officer you can find. We need to re-group; fast. Whoever pulled that trigger will not be happy about the lost drone, they'll be back and with greater ferocity. I think it's time we play offense."

Franko's shoulders noticeably raised from defeat to hope. "Where do you want everyone? What will you do?"

Henry already knew his next step. "Get everybody over to that hangar." He pointed in the direction of the one nearest their position. "I'm going to check in with Commander Simmons to see what he's managed to learn from our guest."

CHAPTER 79

The White House
Washington, D.C.

Security threat assessments, briefs, and memorandums piled up on the desk in front of the President. They seemingly multiplied by the hour, faster than he could absorb them. Unrest, rioting, and in the best-case scenarios, peaceful protests all spread throughout cities and smaller towns across America. Even in communities where he had great support, massive disturbances were becoming the norm. Federal, state, and local law enforcement agencies were in crisis as they stretched their resources and manpower to the brink in the name of maintaining peace.

Tinsley had been sitting at this desk for hours. A half-empty plate from dinner still sat to one corner of his desk while a carafe of coffee rested just beyond arm's reach. A large flat screen was on though he had muted it hours ago. Disturbing images colored the screen like a silent movie, giving life to the reports at his fingertips.

Meanwhile, beyond the White House lawn, he could see the massive fence which had been erected around the grounds, highlighted by watchtowers and firing positions. No doubt the Secret Service had played a role in bolstering defenses as if preparing for a siege, but they weren't the ones standing sentry at this late hour. At least not where they could be seen. From his reports, Tinsley knew his perimeter had been bolstered by Maryland and Virginia National Guard units.

Tinsley considered, *What would it take to overrun that perimeter?* Entertaining the possibility triggered an involuntary shudder. The thought of a war zone in his yard was terrifying. *I cannot allow that to happen.*

Even as the President retreated into his mind to ponder his options, the phone rang. It was Anthony Flynn.

"Yes, Anthony."

"Apologies for the late hour call, Mr. President. I have something to report that I thought may please you." The Director's words sounded like good news. There was, however, something about his tone that betrayed an underlying issue.

"What is it?"

"Mr. President, do you recall the San Diego terrorist cell?"

"Of course, Anthony, what about them?"

"One of my operatives tracked them to Davis-Monthan Air Force Base in Arizona. Upon discovering their position, the agent made contact and requested a drone strike. The drone team successfully made a positive identification on a pair of senior leaders inside their organization. A strike was executed and the men were eliminated."

Director Flynn's news was good, Tinsley puzzled over the underwhelming delivery which carried all the exuberance of a doctor delivering bad news to a patient. "That's great news, Anthony. What about Pinchot? Was he among the party?" A long pause revealed the answer without Flynn having to say a word.

"We're still working on locating Pinchot, Mr. President."

There it is; this call was over the elimination of middle management. A partial victory. The snake's head is still firmly attached. Still, I don't want to discourage the efforts. We seem to be shrinking the dragnet. "I see. You say this was a drone strike? What else has been observed? Have they dispersed? Which direction did they go? Any clues at all about Pinchot's whereabouts?"

"We're still analyzing imaging, Mr. President."

Analyzing imaging? That's a non-answer, a dodge. Annoyed, Tinsley leaned back in his chair and looked out the window. Across the White House lawn, Tinsley thought he caught movement. *Has security been breached?! Are they coming for me? Secret Service should have come for me by now. Maybe I'm just seeing things.* Tinsley shook his head as if to rid himself of fear and paranoia. He closed his eyes and reopened them trying to reset the images in his mind. "Still analyzing? Do you not have footage from the strike and aftermath?"

"There seems to be a technical glitch we are working to patch regarding the footage, Mr. President. As soon as the issue is resolved I will follow up with answers to your questions," Flynn said carefully.

Stymied, Tinsley ended the call. At this late hour, only essential staff occupied the West Wing. The President knew that only his secretary and Secret Service were around him. Or did he? The halls were quiet. *Were those footsteps?* Tinsley stilled himself to the point that his heartbeat sounded as if it might be plugged into an amplifier. He once again closed his eyes, trying to quiet the noise. Focusing on his breathing, the heart seemed to calm, though when he re-opened them once more Tinsley thought he heard whispering outside his door.

Jumping up he quickly jerked open the door to spy who might be fomenting sedition in his midst. Only, there was nobody there. He looked in each direction within the halls, they were empty. The President of the United States was alone with his thoughts.

Returning to his office Tinsley unlocked his phone and dialed his Chief of Staff.

"Marvin, I need you in my office, right now!"

CHAPTER 80

NSA Headquarters
Fort Mead, MD

Director Flynn fumed as he listened. Even on a night when he should be basking in success, only bad news and excuses seemed to be what his contact had to offer. Cutting the caller off Flynn fired his first shot in a salvo of frustrations.

"What do you mean your men are gone?" He paused as the contact explained the carnage. "So, they're all dead," he restated.

Anthony rapped his pen nervously on the desk while the caller outlined his next talking point. Disgusted, he cut the man off. "So, no sign of Guttierez? Any chance he's simply moved to avoid … wait what was that about a crash?! You saw it fall from the sky?" Flynn set his pen down to focus on the report with renewed interest. Calming himself, he asked, "Do you think you could find the wreckage?"

***

Hope renewed that he had some fresh information to work off of, disturbing as it was, Flynn's next call was to Annie Nguyen. After a pair of unsuccessful calls, she answered sleepily. "Director; everything ok?"

"Yes, yes, Annie. Listen, I think we may have an angle to work on these nuisance drone malfunctions. I don't think they are malfunctions at all. It may be possible the terrorists have come up with a method to shoot them down. The second drone crashed near the strike site. This can't be a coincidence."

Annie's reply was slow as her mind turned to work what her boss was saying, "I see sir. What is it you want me to do?"

"I need you to get to the office and start working on the problem. I need to know how they're being destroyed. I have on-scene assets searching for the wreckage, maybe their search will turn up some evidence we can work with."

CHAPTER 81

The White House
Washington, D.C.

Marvin Miller appeared in the West Wing within an hour of Tinsley's summons. Despite the advanced hour, Marvin had at least taken the time to don a suit. He knew immediately upon entering the President's office that the Commander in Chief had not slept. The President's appearance was disheveled. Tinsley had obviously been running his fingers through his hair, the tie he had worn the previous day was on the floor, and he had not shaven. Frankly had the Secret Service told Marvin that the President had just dragged himself in from a night in Las Vegas, the claim would have been convincing.

Spotting the carafe of coffee, Marvin poured cups for the President and himself. Handing the lukewarm beverage to his boss, Marvin settled into a chair opposite Tinsley and took a drink. Finally settled Marvin asked his boss.

"What's going on, Mr. President?"

Tinsley's eyes were heavily bagged, a detail Marvin had not glimpsed in the dimmed lighting when he initially entered the office. On the desk between them, reports seemed to spill together. Briefing papers co-mingled with internal memos which in turn mixed with intelligence briefs. Marvin thought the desk looked like a feral ven diagram. No, not a ven diagram. A ven diagram had organization, and where the confluence of information merged one might then uncover a central truth. This chaotic mess looked more akin to a kaleidoscopic mural of tidbits and factoids without context. Frankly, the scene before Marvin reminded him more of a link diagram, only it lacked the actual strings connecting the dots from one page to the next.

The President shuffled some papers around as if noticing his mess for the first time and feeling compelled to tidy up. After a moment he finally revealed his reason for the midnight summons. "Marvin, I'm concerned our situation may be slipping out of control."

Inclining his head slightly Miller answered, "How do you mean, Mr. President?"

"Just look at this desk, Marvin! You would think with the margin of victory we enjoyed last year, the American people would give my administration more grace! Yet, it seems each time we address an issue, new threats spring up like weeds! I have the world's greatest military and all the resources of our massive intelligence network at my fingertips, yet we can't find those who want to undo our work within our borders! We've practically lost the state of Texas, even the cities! One of these reports talks about Houston. Did you know that Houston has been completely cut off and barricaded by anti-administration forces? What more can be done to curb these out-of-control insurrections all over the country?" Tinsley turned to look out his window, seemingly straining to look across his embattled nation.

Marvin quickly unlocked his cell phone and fired off a text message; *He's in crisis, hasn't been sleeping. Intelligence has him unnerved.*

A response came quickly; *Nudge him where he wants to go.*

Marvin stood up and circled the desk. "There is an outside the box solution we might consider, Mr. President."

"What is it, Marvin?" Marvin Miller thought the emotions painted upon the face of the President of the United States were a mix of relief and anxiety. Almost as if the man was thankful he wouldn't need to conjure up solutions on his own, yet reticent to relinquish control.

"You say we've lost control of Houston? I say the fastest way to regain control of that city is to undermine the political power of the opposition on a local level so that it doesn't look like the work of the federal government. Let the local populace fight that battle for you while keeping your hands clean in the process." Miller drank deep from his coffee.

"How do you propose we do that, Marvin?" Interest piqued, Tinsley's bearing seemingly gained steam as he retreated from the precipice of a breakdown.

"Do you recall being briefed on EMPs, sir?

"Yes, of course, Marvin. A bit heavy-handed don't you think?"

Marvin countered, "Not necessarily sir. Many factors must be considered when deploying an asset such as this. For example, setting off an EMP in the upper atmosphere greatly increases the coverage area of a prospective blast. Conversely, a device used at sea level, while devastating within a certain radius is limited in reach. Of course, the power of the device itself must be considered, which brings me to what I propose."

If the President were seated, he would have been on the edge of it. "Get to it already!"

"Yes, of course, sir." Miller knew in Tinsley's exhausted state he was practically begging to be spoon-fed an out, a solution regardless of damages to those who opposed him that would ensure the survival of his administration and legacy. "Out in New Mexico, the White Sands Test Range, we've had a team working on honing, perfecting the weapon known as EMP. No longer is it a blunt force device that affects large swaths of land. For lack of a better term, think of them as strategic tactical devices. We have finally developed this technology to the point where we can use them to cripple a grid, a few blocks, or even a city. It all depends on how and where we choose to deploy the device."

Tinsley's mouth opened without a word, an apparent temporary indication of shock before he gathered, "So, are you telling me you want to deploy this weapon to cripple the city of Houston?"

Marvin shook his head. "No, Mr. President. We will make sure the people of Houston know it was those who have engineered this insurrection that crippled their city. You will then provide leadership and salvation in the aftermath. That will be the end of this terrorist movement."

The President of the United States smiled widely and nodded his head.

342 · MATTHEW H. WHITTINGTON

CHAPTER 82

Davis-Monthan Air Force Base
Just outside Tucson, AZ

Resting on a desk among the men was the cell phone of their captive. Despite an intense session that played hopscotch with the gray line between torture and harsh questioning, the captured man would not break. In fact, only two details had been gleaned since he had been captured. His name was Carlos Gutierrez, and he was an American.

One of the men present for this meeting, a scout named Brian, who had been recruited to the company by Tommy was the first to speak up.

"So what do we do about this guy? Can't we just kill him?"

Around the grouping, everyone seemed to shift uncomfortably in their stances. The primal thought had also been on their minds. Henry's voice was the first to offer definitive guidance.

"No, we can't kill him."

"Why not?" Brian practically fired the words.

"We can't kill him because it's wrong. He's a captive, an unarmed one. At this moment he is not attempting escape or conducting himself in a violent way toward us. He has rights,

Brian, have you forgotten?" Henry's words came without the edge of condescension, rather they sounded more like a hopeful query into the man's moral compass from their past lives. Before their own government's efforts to hunt them. Before America lost its way along the road of decency and tolerance.

Only slightly shamed while still heated Brian persisted, "The President of the United States declared martial law. *He* suspended those rights. *This* man isn't some common criminal. He's made the decision to openly wage war on American citizens. *He's* committed *treason*."

Lieutenant Commander Simmons picked this moment to interject.

"Be careful with that 'T' word, brother. Seems to me there are some folks in high places who have hung that mantle on this group. We may not understand his reasons, yet I can assure you he feels as though his decisions and values have him believing he's on the side of righteousness."

"So that's it? We just give up and let him go?" Stymied by the flanking maneuver the scout threw his hands in the air.

Commander Simmons smiled wryly, "Now, nobody said that. We haven't played all our cards just yet." The commander then looked down at the cell phone.

"I thought the cell phone was a dead end? When you finally broke into it, weren't all the numbers unknown callers?" Henry asked the SEAL officer.

"Yes, that is the case. It would seem our friend has taken great efforts to make sure his puppeteers remain in the shadows, hands unsullied by the blood of the murdered. Plausible deniability is what his handler had hoped for. Frankly, in just about any circumstance their efforts would accomplish just that. Typically, an investigator would need a warrant and cooperation from the cell phone company to uncover who Carlos was talking to. Unfortunately for our friend, his circumstances aren't typical. Those of us in the Special Forces community have ways of using devices like cell phones to follow bread crumb trails."

One of the pilots who had walked in and stayed to observe the meeting quipped, "I knew it! No wonder you guys seemed to be on the heels of all those HVTs in Afghanistan and Iraq."

"You see, every electronic device has a unique signature, Simmons continued. "Think of it as a tech fingerprint. When they connect to your Wi-Fi, cell phone towers, and satellites their locations are logged and tracked. In most cases, a normal person with nothing to hide finds this useful. Updating social media, searching for your nearest hardware store or updating directions on your navigation in real-time are all possible because of this. Your life is made easier by convenience. If, however, you don't wish to be tracked and found, then connecting your device to any network is the last thing one should do. Just ask the countless HVTs in the Mideast. Learning that lesson took some time for them. Most people have heard of this technology by now thanks to congressional transparency. Thankfully what hasn't been made widely known just yet has been the capabilities the Special Forces community has developed to track other people through a device they've never possessed. We can now go through one device and locate with varying levels of precision all the devices it has ever communicated with. Our friend Carlos either isn't aware of this capability or he figured his tracks were sufficiently covered. We can backtrack his communiques all the way to their origin. It will just take a little time."

"That's amazing!" Even with numerous deployments and involvement in tracking the enemies of America, Henry had never even heard whispers of what the commander claimed could be done. "What variables factor into your ability to pinpoint who and where this guy's handler might be?"

Pressing his lips into a thin line Commander Simmons answered as best he could. "We can get an idea about the person's general area from more than 500 miles away. As we get closer to the source, precision improves. I am not willing to discuss our tactics in detail, Mr. O'Brien. I will say, given time, there is no place on Earth the handler can hide if they stay plugged in."

Satisfied Henry asked, "How long will it take?"

"I cannot give an estimate until my tech guy has the device." Simmons motioned toward the idle phone.

"It's yours, let me know what you find." Henry then turned to his Air Force liaison. "How many aircraft can be restored to mission readiness from the Boneyard?"

Major Cassie Morgan had served with the murdered colonel since her transfer from airlift command, "The question, Mr. O' Brien, lacks a simple answer. Ultimately dozens could be made airworthy in short order. That is, provided access to replacement parts that have been pulled for cannibalization to maintain other aircraft. The turnaround time would depend on how fast logistical channels could be opened and streamlined in this current social-political climate."

"I see, where do we need to go to acquire the parts and equipment?" Henry asked.

"Apologies, Mr. O'Brien" Cassie met his hopeful gaze. "Exactly which aircraft are you hoping to make whole again? I ask because the answer depends on what you need. Air Force

346 · MATTHEW H. WHITTINGTON

logistical squadrons stage parts regionally in support of our on-going missions around the world with consideration given for which airframes they are tasked with supporting. For example, you would not expect to find an abundance of parts for A-10s at March Air Force Base. That said, there are a handful of hubs centrally located with means to move logistics around the world quickly that will have a surplus. Tinker for example."

Henry wore his disappointment like one might wear a scarf. It seemed to choke back his enthusiasm and that fact was not subtle. He sighed, "Alright, what kind of support can you provide?"

"That would depend, sir."

"On what?"

"Simply put, your objectives, sir." Cassie betrayed no emotions, her answer was matter-of-fact. "If you would ask for our help to carry out strikes on the American people or the government, then the answer would be no. If however, your purpose embraces the preservation of American lives and our Constitution I would think we could find common ground."

"What happens when one threatens the other, Major?" Brian interjected. "What happens when the government murders those you've sworn to defend and throws the Constitution to the wind?!"

Major Morgan met Brian's fire with icy resolve. "If that can be proven, then I believe the oath speaks for itself."

Just as it looked as though Brian might rupture veins in his head, one of Commander Simmons' communication SEALs briskly walked through the door and approached his boss. The SEAL commander leaned his ear closer to the intruder while the man delivered a silent and succinct message. When he heard

everything, Simmons looked at him as if to affirm his serious-
ness. Henry thought the whole room might have stopped
breathing; as if their whole lives hinged on the news of this unexpected messenger.

When the SEAL commander finally shared, petty squabbles
over conditional rules of engagement and logistical puzzles fell
away into the realm of unnecessary minutiae. The experimental
weapons division at White Sands Test Range in New Mexico
was under attack.

Lieutenant Commander Simmons asserted control of the
meeting with a chilling command. "This is a crisis that threatens the lives of *every* American. We need to mobilize *now!*"

CHAPTER 83

Davis-Monthan Air Force Base
Just outside Tucson, AZ

"One more time, the abridged version for Marines!" Henry shouted at his Navy counterpart over the gathering storm of turning engines all around him.

Lieutenant Commander Simmons' movements were controlled yet urgent as he directed his men around the tarmac. Some were riding with him in the Osprey while others were hastily donning jump gear and loading onto the C-130 they flew in on. Simmons didn't care to drop what he was doing to draw Henry a diagram, yet he was attempting to relieve Henry of the Osprey a general had attached to the Marine's cause so some explanation was warranted.

"White Sands Test Range is a NASA facility! It's where they develop and test volatile fuels and other hazardous materials. Due to the remoteness of the facility, the military will often hide secret projects that are unconventional there under the guise of 'scientific testing'. Should they be disclosed by loose-lipped politicians or lobbyists, the military will just double down on the scientific advances rhetoric. We both know though, that if DOD is dumping money into anything, it's not philanthropic."

Somebody was trying to steal weapons, ok. Deducing the military had married warheads to space rockets he shouted back in the SEALs ear, "Must be one hell of a rocket they develop there. Bet D.C. is scared shitless somebody will launch their own creation at them!"

Simmons scrunched his face and laid it out. "I don't give a fuck about some piddly ass rocket! What do you know about electromagnetic pulses?!"

Electromagnetic pulses? "Isn't that when the Sun throws off huge solar flares?! I've read that preppers believe large solar flares will one day crash the grid! A weapon though?! Sounds like science fiction!" Henry responded.

"Not science fiction, science fact," Commander Simmons shook his head. "I read a brief on it last year. An EMP detonation over America would not only crash the grid, but it would also alter life as you know it! Our society would be set back centuries! MILLIONS will die!"

Henry felt his skin turn cold while every hair on his body went erect with electricity at the statement. He moved to action. Henry grabbed the first man from his company he saw and shouted, "Get my best assault team on that Osprey right now! No time to explain, just do it! Get the word to everybody else to follow by land to Las Cruces, New Mexico!"

"When should they leave?" he asked as Henry turned to board the idling aircraft.

"Right now!" Henry shouted over his shoulder.

CHAPTER 84

Skies over Easter New Mexico
Approaching White Sands Test Range

Henry reflected that having inserted himself and the men into this evolving sortie might end up being a seminal moment in his journey as a leader. Before the mission, while certainly not ignorant enough to believe he set the gold standard in leadership, Henry felt his background as a Marine and training instructor at a private military company made him a capable decision-maker and tactician. The hasty tarmac mobilization at Davis-Monthan under the circumstances had been a true learning moment, Henry only hoped they had moved fast enough.

In itself, simply getting the entire SEAL team and Henry's detachment loaded with gear and weapons as fast as they had was no small feat. Those aboard the C-130 had to don their parachute gear for a static line jump on top of readying their weapons. Their mission would be one of heading off a retreat from the unknown hostile force they were flying to confront. Allowing White Sands' intruders to abscond with the technology Commander Simmons feared they were pursuing was not negotiable. Aboard the Osprey with Henry and Simmons was a smaller strike team, yet no less lethal. Each leader had hand-picked their most capable warriors for the infiltration and assault. Should they meet a force short of other operators in expertise, the scales were greatly tilted.

Observing merely the speed and composure would have been instruction enough. The lessons Henry took from the man he sat across from now did not stop there though. On the fly, even as the aircraft taxied away from their chocked positions, Lieutenant Commander Simmons had the foresight to request their Osprey pilots coordinate a follow-up wave from the division of Vipers left behind. Henry heard him casually reason to Osprey pilot Captain Michaels, "The snakes can't keep up with us in transit at top speed, but that doesn't mean they need to be out of the fight. We may end up needing them if we get pinned down."

Henry thought the coordinated assault plan was already coalescing beautifully when the call came in from Davis-Monthan. The Air Force officers and pilots of the storied A-10 squadrons stationed there were still licking their wounds from the base being hit and their commanding officer being lost. Even as the Osprey and Hercules made for the eastern sky they had held a briefing. Major Cassie Morgan filled them in on the situation. A quick straw poll ended with a near-unanimous decision to send a section of Warthogs to support the interdiction. They all agreed that launching a sortie with hot weapons amongst Americans was a moral gray area, but tacitly allowing a potential EMP event to happen by standing on the sidelines was inarguably wrong. It had been Captain Michaels who relayed the good news, "Looks like you guys will have Warthogs flying air cover. Call signs will be Dragons 11 and 12."

Lieutenant Commander Simmons didn't clap or smile. He simply nodded acknowledgment. Henry marveled at his professionalism and ability to so quickly assemble a legitimate QRF in so short a time. Henry met his focused gaze and asked, "Want to review the plan one more time?"

The SEAL nodded.

"We're going to set down just west of the weapons facility and push our way in. If after making contact they flee, we will make contact with the C-130 orbiting above. The remainder of my team will static line jump in ahead of their retreat and cut them off. At that point, we will have them trapped. The A-10s can strafe in parallel to our lines. Should the snakes show up and we are still in contact, they will racetrack around the perimeter to track down any squirters. It is *absolutely imperative* that these weapons not make it out."

A call came back from the cockpit. "Five minutes out."

Just outside, the Osprey's enormous propellers gradually made the transition from high-speed forward flight to a low-speed hover. Captain Michaels seamlessly set the aircraft down and lowered the ramp. Simmons and Henry's men charged out to set up a perimeter while the Osprey lifted off.

Behind them, the sun was falling into the west. O'Brien could hear the drone of four turboprop engines circling somewhere overhead, *that would be the others*, he thought. No other sounds cut the arid New Mexico evening. No gunshots. No equipment. Nothing.

Just ahead a lone building serenely rested. It seemed that nobody occupied it. If anyone was here, they were laying low. Henry whispered to Simmons, "Is this the place?"

The SEAL just nodded. It appeared something about the environment had him unsettled. Something was wrong, out of place. Led by Simmons, the men advanced on the building to evaluate what had transpired. Only the sounds of boots crunching sand could be heard. Their objective had the feel of a ghost town, the silence was deafening.

Drawing closer, the first thing Henry noticed was the smells. Barely noticeable at first was the unmistakable odor of feces. It smelled like someone had lost control of their bowels in their pants. Time seemed to slow as the men closed on the building, had seconds passed or minutes? Just feet from the building Henry caught sight of a crumpled mass just outside a door. It was a corpse. Blood pooled around the dead man. The sentry's death was fairly recent as the pavement and sand had yet to fully absorb the puddle. It had not yet turned black and Henry caught the tang of iron in the air as he drew closer.

Commander Simmons' SEALs were lining up to breach and clear the structure, while Henry already suspected he knew what they would discover. The heist they came to prevent had been a fast one, the intruders were long gone. *We're too late! All we'll find here are the slaughtered, poor bastards who were overmatched.*

All the same Henry and his men loaned their assistance with the sweep and search. Whoever came here to make off with the experimental weapons overwhelmed meager defenses and a skeleton crew. They counted just over a dozen murdered men and women before coming upon a lone man who had run into a mop closet where he had jammed the door shut with brooms and mops. A gunman had known he was in there apparently, or at least so the half dozen bullet holes in the door would suggest. Faint sobbing had given away his position to the SEALs, it seemed the barricaded man thought those who had shot up the place had come back to finish him off.

A pair of SEALs were discussing breaking the door down to get him, just in case the man was feigning victimhood only to pop out and ambush them. Thankfully calmer heads prevailed, Simmons didn't want the man harmed. He hoped the man would have some nugget of helpful information to offer.

"Sir, my name is Lieutenant Commander Simmons, United States Navy SEAL team leader. My men have not come to hurt you, we came to help. Come on out, I personally guarantee your safety."

At first, Henry wasn't sure if the calm plea had softened the frightened man's resolve. He could hear the man shuffling beyond the door as if he were dragging a foot. Then slowly one by one he heard the man moving items away from the door. Each step he took within sounded painful and slow. Finally, the man cracked the door open. The eyes that peeked out appeared sallow and drained. A strong odor of urine cut the air as the door opened wider.

Slowly the barricaded man pushed the door fully open to reveal a nightmarish scene. Bullets fired through the door to silence him had missed their mark on the original trajectory. Unfortunately, they had ricocheted about the tiny space and struck glancing blows. No major organs had been hit, thankfully, but he lost blood via the flesh wounds. He had done his best to compress the pair of wounds and stop the bleeding which now begun anew. It appeared when they had initially approached the door, he had sought cover behind a mop bucket. The bright yellow bucket was awash in red, as were his torn pant legs and mangled foot.

Collectively all of the men lowered their weapons while a corpsman sprang into action. The medic worked to stabilize and treat the man's wounds. Even while his injuries were being attended, Lieutenant Commander Simmons worked to learn what he could. Relieved to be out of hiding and in safer hands, the stranger was quick to offer his name, Todd. As it turned out, Todd was one of the engineers working on the EMP team. He had been outside smoking a cigarette when the attack began. A pair of UH-60 Blackhawks painted all black set down just outside, and each unloaded a team of armed men dressed in street clothes.

Commander Simmons held up a hand. "Hold up; you're sure they were Blackhawks and you're certain they were not in uniform?"

Todd shook his head. "I've seen plenty of movies, Commander. They were definitely Blackhawks; two of them."

"What kind of weapons did they carry? Were they military-style or did they seem civilian?"

Todd winced as the corpsman flushed his foot in disinfectant. "I'm not sure what you mean."

Did they all have assault rifles or was it a hodgepodge of firearms like handguns and shotguns?"

Todd jerked as the corpsman worked on his foot. "Damn, that hurts; can't you do anything to dull the pain?" The corpsman pumped what lidocaine he had around the wound. Todd answered the commander, "I'm sorry, guess I didn't get a good look. I was scared. They just jumped off. One raised his weapon and fired. The guy I was smoking with, Kyle, fell into a heap next to me. I ran inside to look for a place to hide. Only thing I could think of was that damn mop closet. I must have just shut the door when those bastards came charging in. Sounded like each person they came across got shot. They didn't bother asking any questions or demanding anything. It's like they simply came here to shoot up the place. They tried to open the closet; thankfully I had it blocked pretty good. Seemed they were in a hurry, rather than trying to force in to kill me, somebody just shot up the door. I guess they killed whoever they came for; as fast as they came, they left."

Commander Simmons looked slightly confused. "You say two Blackhawks, each full of men? There wasn't a third aircraft?"

The corpsman bandaged up the damaged foot well enough for transport to a hospital and moved on to treat cuts on Todd's arms. Todd looked as confused as Henry felt.

"Third aircraft? What the hell are you talking about? Why would they need another team?"

Simmons shook his head. "No, not another team. They would have needed the added floor space to load up the EMP weapon and haul it out of here."

The shock from his injuries transformed compounded with shock over what the SEAL was asking about. "The EMP, they came to take it? But...why?" Todd whispered.

Running low on patience and frustrated over having been too late, urgency crept into the SEALs' voice. "Look Todd, I don't *know why*. I *need* to know *how* they got it out of here so I can chase them down before something terrible happens! Now think! Did you hear a truck pull up? Are you certain there were only two choppers? Maybe they said something? Did you hear any talk about who would ride in each aircraft to make room for the device? Anything?!"

Reality finally seemed to crystalize within Todd. He practically choked on his words. "We've made significant advances in scaling EMP technology in the past months. Our team made the device small enough to carry in your laptop bag. You could carry an EMP weapon out of here like a textbook."

Todd's words hit like an uppercut from a heavyweight boxer; the air left the room along with their collective hope. The weapon was long gone, highly mobile. Henry knew the weapon's location would inevitably be discovered. However, the knot in his stomach told him it wouldn't be until after it had been used.

CHAPTER 85

Houston, TX

Twilight stretched across the wide Texas horizon. Where its fingers had not yet reached, the sun's receding orange glow provided a beautiful water-colored midwest sunset. Blue skies burned in shades of amber, orange, and champagne before yielding into hues of violet and finally black. In turn, the stars and visible planets above popped into sparkling view; first Libra and then Ursa Minor while Earth's celestial sisters danced around the solar system.

Streetlights around River Oaks in Houston, Texas cut the darkness. Sleepy streets ordinarily occupied by early evening bike rides and dog walkers now stood starkly lit in an eerie void of inactivity. Only the occasional rumble of neighborhood patrol vehicles threatened to disturb the still evening air while scores of custom-built homes flanked to either side in solemn repose.

Nestled in a quiet cul de sac between two beautiful colonials stood the home of systems integration specialist, La'Ron Buckner. La'Ron had jumped at the opportunity to relocate for his dream job at the Johnson Space Center in Houston. Transplanting from San Diego to the Lonestar state had been a significant cultural adjustment at first. Over time though, he had come to love his second home. What had truly accelerated La'Ron's assimilation had been the purchase of his first home, a contemporary masterpiece of architecture. Massive windows flanked his front door looking west, a feature particularly appealing to him after the move for two reasons. First, his heart still loved and yearned for lazy southern California days. Gazing west from his new home kept La'Ron grounded in his roots. His second reason for desiring a west-facing facade was grounded more in practicality and preservation. Friends he had met from Texas had mentioned that most thunderstorms moved from west to east, therefore having a superb west-facing view would allow him to see what was coming.

Truthfully, most of the troublesome weather since his move had not come from the west at all, hurricanes threatened from the southeast. La'Ron had been through exactly two of nature's monsters since taking the job in Houston, each of which had taught him sufficient lessons about survival along the Gulf Coast. Two of the storm preparedness steps he'd learned seemed to be applicable now in America's current state of duress; power up anything run by fuel or batteries and assemble an emergency kit.

Maintaining full gasoline in his generator and Audi had been crucial. La'Ron had not expected the city of Houston to roll blackouts. As yet he did not understand why blackouts were happening, though he suspected that many who worked for the local energy company were in a situation similar to his own. NASA had dictated weeks prior that La'Ron telecommute. Their reasons for keeping him home had been for public safety.

As one of the city's largest employers, NASA did not care to add their people to the surface streets where violent carjackings, gunfights, and mobs had become commonplace. Rather, it had been hoped that the unprecedented civil unrest would run its course and mellow out. As proficient as NASA had become at examining the solar system and beyond, they had failed to foresee the cataclysm back on Earth. Even during daylight hours, driving to the local grocery store for essentials and gas stations for generator fuel was risky. Texans with far fewer resources than La'Ron staked out public gathering places to handpick who they could victimize for their own survival. Local law enforcement was far too overwhelmed to intercede, their apparent inaction only served to embolden the desperate. Where the local law failed, Texans stepped forward. Gunfights were now the norm.

When the sun went down what had been risky turned into an outright nightmare. Rather than mortal struggles over food and medication the downtrodden predators escalated their tactics toward far worse atrocities. Abductions, rape, and human trafficking cases didn't merely multiply, they expanded exponentially. Even the media declared that leaving your home without a firearm almost certainly guaranteed victimhood.

Venturing out for survival being so risky made La'Ron's emergency preparedness stash all the more vital. He carefully rationed non-perishables and only risked trips outside of his home for essentials every tenth day. Even then he was careful to take every precaution.

Then, the real problems started. Large swaths of the city came under siege from organized groups from out of town. Nobody seemed to know where they came from, but it was quickly evident what their purpose was. Someone sent them to seize control of the city. Among Houstonites the invaders came to be known as the "Out-of-Towners." The Out-of-Towners' strategy quickly became evident, as they seized control of important infrastructure and key retail locations. They barricaded pharmacies, cordoned off gas stations, checkpointed hospitals and clinics, and commandeered public transportation. Radio stations were savagely overrun which then led to the loss of free information and public awareness. Any business with large refrigeration capabilities was seized which led to the loss of food for vast portions of the population. The clock was ticking.

The natives rose. Texans who had been quietly isolated as they sheltered in place coalesced into a massive militia. War broke out in the city, full-fledged street to street urban combat. One day at a time, one block at a time, one business at a time the locals re-took their city. Once the Out-of-Towners had all been dispatched or expelled new checkpoints were set up. The new Houston militia was truly a vision of what the Founding Fathers had envisioned. Middle-aged white men occupied the new checkpoints next to twenty-five-year-old inner-city African-Americans. Latin-American single mothers took turns looking after each other's neighborhood kids so that their friends may stand a watch beside Caribbean American migrant men who had sought refuge in the United States after oppression in their native lands.

La'Ron ended his isolation and inserted himself into the ownership of the community at one such checkpoint. Near his neighborhood, two arterials intersected where two pharmacies and a cancer clinic were located. Within La'Ron's local commute, this intersection was as strategic as any. Giving his time to help the community got him out of the house, gave him a purpose beyond work, and re-assured him that at its heart America was still the only place on Earth for him.

Adding to his philanthropic and patriotic purpose was an added compelling incentive, La'Ron met someone. A transplant like himself, Beth was a fair-skinned brilliant brunette from the northeast. Beth had attended MIT where she earned a degree in engineering which had parlayed into a highly rewarding career at NASA.

Beth and La'Ron struck up a friendship, providing each what they desperately needed; humanity. A reminder that decency and tolerance were still possible. Each had voted differently in the past election, many of their political views diverged. Inevitably their conversation often steered into politics, where an amazing thing transpired. Due to their newfound friendship, respectful exchanges of ideas transpired. There was no shouting, no bullying, no condescension. Just a good old fashioned exchange of ideas. More often than not conversations would inevitably end with one smiling and saying to the other, "I see your point."

It was beautiful. It was wonderful. It was America.

Now, the pair sat in front of La'Ron's massive windows just inside his house drinking merlot and devouring the Texas sunset. Just beyond the front room, back in the kitchen, a pot of gumbo simmered in a stockpot. Smooth jazz played low in the background through a Bose sound system. Thousands of feet overhead, a line of passenger jets descended on approach into George Bush Intercontinental Airport. Periodically the wash of helicopter blades could be heard beating the air, La'Ron knew they were typically news choppers though occasionally it would be law enforcement.

Beth's cell phone was unlocked, she had instinctively excused herself courteously to check on a text from her mother back in Massachusetts, only to sheepishly remember in her reflex that cell phone networks were now virtually worthless. La'Ron unlocked his own using the fingerprint identification feature and used it to dim the lights a little. He accessed the appropriate application and deftly moved his thumb to roll house lighting down slightly; *one click, two clicks....not quite dark enough...three clicks.*

The room went dark. Backlighting from his phone went dark as well. Confused, La'Ron pushed his finger onto the ID pad to unlock the phone, it did not respond. Then he tried pushing the button to the device's side to manually unlock it, no luck.

What the hell, I had plenty of charge. Why did it die? He began running through reasons in his head why turning the lighting down on his phone would have so dramatically drained the battery. There was no reason, he'd had the application on the phone for months and used it every night. *Had it become corrupted? If so, how did my phone manage to jack the lighting all the way off? Damn, it got real dark in here.* La'Ron couldn't even see his guest, it was so dark.

He moved to reassure Beth, "I'll get up and go turn the lights back on, sit tight."

Beth's voice answered kindly yet with the slightest hint of apprehension, "I think it's another blackout, La'Ron. The street lights went out too. Isn't it weird though that my phone died? I had a charge, what are the odds the battery goes dead the same time a blackout happens?"

Her phone went dead too?! No way is that a coincidence, what the hell is happening?!

Forcing himself to maintain a sense of control, La'Ron quickly worked the odd scenario in his brain searching for what he could do to diagnose why the phones would crash at the exact moment a blackout happened. *This isn't logical!* A solution struck him seconds later; *we need to charge these phones.* With a power outage in progress, there was just one solution available to him and Beth; the cars.

"Why don't we move out to my car and plug the phones in, then try powering them up again?" he offered.

"Sure we can do that."

La'Ron couldn't see his guest through the pitch-black but sensed her standing up. La'Ron stood and reached for her hand. Finding it, she accepted his hand warmly. Moving slowly he led her through the house, using his free hand to feel around wall edges until they finally came upon the garage door.

More groping around the pitch black garage helped him find a car door handle. La'Ron was troubled with renewed anxiety when the dome light failed to illuminate. Hopeful that he had inadvertently bumped the switch at some point, La'Ron forced the problem from his mind and settled into the seat. It took another few minutes of patting around before he located his phone's charging cable. He plugged the phone in while Beth waited quietly beside him.

"I'm sure this will take just a minute or so and then power right up," La'Ron assured her.

Anticipation made the seconds feel like minutes; or did the minutes feel like hours? La'Ron looked down at the phone in his hands. Usually, the screen would glow when charging, with a little lightning bolt inside a rudimentary battery. No such glow illuminated the dark. His fingers found the cable where they traced it back to the car's cigarette lighter. *Is it not plugged in all the way?* It was. *What am I missing?*

The realization hit him suddenly. *I need to give it power from the car!* La'Ron knew with the power being out he couldn't raise the garage door with his opener and start the car, but he could turn the ignition and run the battery, at least for a little while. At least enough to put some charge into the phones.

Reaching into a pocket he fished out the Audi's keys and fumbled to find the ignition. Movements feeling slow and awkward La'Ron felt compelled to explain to Beth his thought process. "Need to give the charger battery juice, I'll find the ignition and we'll be powered up in no time." It must have taken minutes he thought, thankfully the key finally found its way home. La'Ron turned it the requisite clicks to enable battery access.

Nothing. Not even a dim warning light. The Audi was drained, dead.

La'Ron's heart raced, his mind racing to grasp what exactly had happened and coming up with nothing.

Outside of La'Ron Buckner's house, commercial airliners plunged from the sky and slammed into the ground in even intervals from just beyond the entry to runways at George Bush Intercontinental back along approach avenues. For miles, the only light source observable was the fireballs where jumbo jets had violently impacted the landscape.

Houston Texas and the millions who called it home had been plunged into a state of absolute darkness.

EPILOGUE

Carlsbad, CA

Shelby O'Brien stood at the counter and emptied the boxes which contained her three-month supply of cyclosporine, one of the handfuls of medications that enabled her body to keep her transplanted organ by holding her immune system in check so that it would not attack her kidney.

Fifteen years with this kidney and Shelby had never had to count pills. She sorted the doses and whispered aloud to no one in particular.

"Six, seven, eight...nine. I have nine days left." That is, she thought, nine days left at standard dosage. Shelby considered rationing the pills to spread out her supply longer. Doing so would kick the can down the road so to speak, but not far down the road. The measure would also trigger irreversible damage to her fragile kidney, the extent of which would be determined by how soon she was able to obtain refills. Otherwise, she would just take the regular dosage for the next nine days and hope her prayers were answered.

Once she ran out, the clock would start counting down to kidney failure. What was causing this disruption in crucial medication re-supply would also serve to stifle her abilities to perform the necessary steps to stay alive once in kidney failure. She would need dialysis. Yet, if she couldn't make the simple half-mile drive to the pharmacy due to the obscene saturation of organized crime controlling the streets, she certainly had no hope of making the nearest dialysis center.

She was trapped, no, imprisoned in her own home; counting her days by pills and nights by gunshots. A community uprising had been savagely stifled just a few days ago when the meager force of gun owners was easily overwhelmed by the mob who had overrun the communities in northern San Diego County. It had been a veritable turkey shoot in the streets of Carlsbad, the slaughtered now rotted where they fell only to become feasts for feral dogs and crows.

Spirits crushed, those who had stayed within their own homes now feared daring to even crack front doors. Patrols by violent mobs of thugs had increased in the battle's aftermath, Shelby heard them roll past her home frequently. *Damn Henry for leaving me here alone!* She glanced at the handgun resting on the counter. Henry had taken her to the firing range many times, the weapon felt comfortable in her hands. Shelby would use it to defend herself. Risking a trip to the pharmacy however, was beyond her skills.

Shelby pushed her nine days' worth of medication back into the box and set the box back in the cabinet. She sighed deeply then walked to the pantry and opened it to examine her food situation. Fresh fruits and vegetables were now only a distant memory. Also gone was the bread and most meat products. Even non-perishables within the pantry were growing meager; meal planning now appeared to be reduced to pop tarts, saltine crackers, and stale whole-grain cereal she kept on hand which she told her friends she ate but didn't.

Even their black lab was suffering the strain. Thankfully Henry preferred buying their dog kibble in bulk. While at a glance the bag seemed over half full, still, Shelby started cutting his daily portions nearly a week ago. In response, the dog's begging grew bolder which in turn led to Shelby beating herself up in guilt. She would often give in and set her plate on the floor. Soon, even that wouldn't be an option. Shelby dreaded what decisions she may have to make when the food ran out, for both of them.

Shuddering, she strolled to the back door to let the dog outside to do his business. Shelby walked out with him. Away from the hell, which was life out in the community, her backyard remained an oasis, at least for now. A light westerly breeze felt heavenly on her face as it created the perfect balance of comfort with the San Diego summer sun. Melancholy seemed to be building; Shelby thought she might cry. Yet, as the storm of emotions gathered in momentum within her, the faint sound of an approaching helicopter approached from the north. Normally the sound of helicopters this side of Camp Pendleton was as ubiquitous as spring thunderstorms across the Midwest. Lately, however, they seemed absent. She hoped because they were occupied elsewhere.

Shelby tilted her head in the direction of the approaching helicopter. She had not yet spotted it, though her ears detected the audible signature of a second rotor wash. They grew louder.

Why can't I see them yet?

Seconds later, she realized why they had been so difficult to spot. The duo had approached at treetop level, so low that palm tree fronds danced up and down as the downdrafts passed over them. They were Cobras, or whatever the newer four-bladed upgrade was called these days, she thought. Shelby easily tracked them, now nearly on top of her house. Their noses were menacingly dipped forward, so close that she could see the pilot's faces. She could see streaks along the lightish gray paint where fuel had spilled down the side of the fueling port. She could smell the exhaust pushed down by the rotors, the sweet combusted jet fuel made her nostrils flare.

They had just passed over her, Shelby had only just spun on her heels to watch them go when each had unleashed a salvo of rockets. As the rockets shot from their pods the air was split with deafening *WHOOSHING* sounds, followed quickly by a series of explosions.

She could only barely just see the pair then roll onto their sides in turns. They were attacking something! It had to be this army of criminals savaging the neighborhood! Her heart soared, hope renewed. Shelby found herself actually yelling out loud. "Get the bastards!" she openly cried. Admittedly, it was still far too early in this ongoing evolution to know what the outcome would be, but she did know those were Marines overhead and someone was getting seriously fucked up. Ordinarily empathetic for basic human life, she found herself giddy. She felt joyful watching the beautiful helicopters pirouette above her, taking turns unleashing hell on her tormentors.

Amazingly, the attacks from above seemed to intensify in speed and ferocity. They seemed to set up a racetrack around the neighborhood, on the next pass the duo looked to be passing right over her head once more. This time as they approached, Shelby could see the 20-millimeter barrels start spinning. A split second later each aircraft launched a volley of lead in the direction of some well-deserving thugs.

370 · MATTHEW H. WHITTINGTON

The attack could only have been in progress for a minute or two when Shelby heard another sound; ground vehicles. She couldn't see them, but they had to be military. More Marines. What had been barely traveled roads for days, weeks, now filled with the euphoric sounds of humvees. Lumbering. Loud. Beautiful.

Shelby ran into her house, dashed across the floor faster than she ever had, and flung the front door open all in time to catch a Humvee streak by with a Marine standing tall behind a roof-mounted machine gun. That Marine hadn't seemed to notice her, though the one that followed did. A young man with bright eyes and a wide smile waved at her. Shelby didn't catch what he said but the younger guy had yelled something out the window. A moment later she heard vehicles work through gears to slow down while the rooftop machine guns rumbled to life. Where the helicopter cannons had unleashed smooth short bursts from their noses, the Humvee guns sounded more deliberate. More primal. It was as if each heavy chunk of lead left the barrel accompanied by a defiant middle finger. Shelby found herself hoping each report meant a corresponding degenerate was being sent directly to Hell for what had been forced upon her and the neighborhood. People died who shouldn't have, and Shelby hated those who caused those deaths more than even she realized.

The fight could not have lasted long. Even with her lack of combat training, Shelby could tell the fight was hilariously one-sided. Those who had terrorized the streets never saw this coming, they were comically outmatched and overwhelmed. Then, as quickly as the siege had begun, it ended. Heavy guns fell silent. Small arms from the Devil Dogs had been redirected to high ready and the sentries circling above eased back off their noses into slow scans, sounding far more tame than terrifying.

Scene secured, the couplet of choppers paired up and turned back north. A long silence fell over Carlsbad; the storm had passed.

Is it safe now, can I leave my house? Shelby wasn't sure. What if in her despair she plunged headlong into some rogue leftover checkpoint the Marines had missed? Still struggling with the internal debate Shelby then heard one of the humvees circle back her way. This time, only one came down her street and much slower. To her relief, this Hummer was occupied by the same Marine who had smiled and waved at her as they had charged into battle. Seeing that she was standing roadside, the vehicle slowly rolled to a stop. This time the driver side faced Shelby. The driver appeared to be in her mid-twenties, a female Marine. She put the Humvee into park and turned to face Shelby, "Scene is secure ma'am. Are you alright? Do you or anyone you know need urgent medical attention?"

Thunderstruck by the suddenness of her unlikely salvation Shelby's mouth dropped open and closed a few times before she could formulate a response. "I … I… I'm ok I guess. Low on critical meds, very hungry, but ok."

The Marine nodded curtly. "General King is down at the main street, ma'am, he's already working to restore critical ser-vices. There is much to be done. If you are in stable condition feel free to make your way to the town center and relate your needs to the triage stations already being set up. If you prefer I could arrange for transportation."

"I think I can manage, thank you. One question?"

"Yes ma'am?"

"Why now?" Shelby quickly realized the Marine would likely appreciate a more cogent query. "I mean, all this time...has been a nightmare. What's happened to finally bring you to me?"

The Marine seemed to take just a moment to gather an acceptable reply to set her mind at ease. When she finally spoke, Shelby nearly began crying again. "General King and the Marines of Camp Pendleton live in these communities too. Like you, the general is disgusted with what our communities have become. I can't speak for the timing, ma'am; he didn't share those details. I guess you could say he got fed up waiting on other channels to function as they should. It seems General King is resolved to take his communities back."

Tears streamed down Shelby's face. She nodded and smiled unable to push words through the tears. *Finally*, she thought. *Finally!*

Acknowledgements

This book has truly been a labor of love years in the making. I didn't just sit down one day and resolve to write this story. Hundreds of hours were soaked into research. Most of that time was invested into reading research material, 21 books in total along with dozens of articles, press releases and military periodicals. Additionally, I interviewed many people I trust as living encyclopedias in their own rights. I would like to thank the people who helped me understand my characters better and those who assisted with other aspects of this book here.

I interviewed men and women spanning a wide range of military disciplines during my research. I talked to airmen about how gunship crews function. I talked to a man in Army Special Forces to brainstorm how guerilla tactics might look on American soil. I interviewed Marines and Army soldiers. A handful of these warriors asked that I keep their names confidential. So, out of respect I will thank them collectively, anonymously as ONE. You will undoubtedly see your fingerprints all over this story. I sincerely hope that when you see ideas we spoke about, it brings a smile to your face. I was listening. I appreciate your time investment in me and I believe this story reads better because of your expertise. Thank you.

One of the coolest thrills during the writing process for me personally would occur when I would talk to friends about the book. A few asked me to be characters in the book! I cannot speak to what that would mean for them personally. What it meant to me was simply put, support. It was another human being saying, "Hey man this is cool and I want to be a part of it. I believe in you." This is important, more than they know. Perhaps more than support it meant accountability. On the days when I didn't feel "IT" and felt compelled to push this book to my personal back burner, it was people such as these who I felt obliged to satisfy. I could not fail to see this through. I suppose some might call them fans, to me they are so much more. Thank you for believing in me.

This book was edited by a highly talented woman, Heidi Owens. Anybody with basic computer skills can run a spelling and grammar check. It takes real talent to digest a manuscript and offer the deep cutting, brutally honest and above all indispensable feedback needed to take a story like this from good to exceptional. It is of course for you the reader to decide if my work reaches your personal level of exceptionalism, that is out of my control and I do not presume anything. What I can say with definitive clarity is that without Heidi's big red pen this story would have been noticeably lower in quality. Heidi, thank you for your considerable critical feedback.

Finally, I would like to thank my biggest fan, my wife Shannon. In no way is it possible to overstate what she has meant in bringing this book to life. She is the only person on this planet who has heard the audio version of this story before print. That is because as each chapter was completed, I read it to her out loud. Mostly I did this to hear my mistakes, yet her feedback along the way proved invaluable. I will concede her bias and say she supported me along the way as any best friend would. She also offered well-reasoned criticism, gently of course. Even before this story was completed, she identified spots where you the reader would want more or in some cases less. When during the creation process I would come across mental hurdles and jams she often talked me through the issues to clear mind clutter, thus reducing time spent in so-called "writer's block." Creation of this story was only one piece of the puzzle, getting it through the mechanics of publishing and into your hands was all Shannon and the CLC Publishing team. Thank you for all you do for me Shannon, my cup runneth over.

Author's Footnote

All technology depicted in this story is either real, in testing or plausible pending outcomes of projects currently publicly documented as being in testing. At no time have I sought out or inadvertently uncovered military secrets which would jeopardize national security. All tech depicted can be found using internet searches in either military press releases or technical articles. Locations described in this book are all real, yet at no time have I obtained direct knowledge of or described strategically sensitive areas. As with weapons technology, all locales described in my book can be read about using even the most simple internet search criteria.

I have used the names of two people I personally know in telling this story at their request. While their names appear in this book, character traits are not meant in any way to transfer from reality to fiction. Their own real life personal views do not necessarily align with that of the characters I have created.

This story was outlined and created prior to real life civil unrest centered around the 2020 United States Presidential election. Political figures described in Flashpoint are not modeled after any of their real life counterparts, any potential resemblances are purely coincidental and subjective from one reader to the next. Furthermore, scenes of unrest depicted in Flashpoint, especially those in the area of Washington D.C., were written more than a year before the real life events of January 2021. Flashpoint is a work of fiction. I do not personally endorse unprovoked violent acts such as those committed in January 2021. I do not harbor anti-government sentiments. Simply put, I am an American who believes in the freedoms guaranteed by the United States Constitution, strongly enough in fact that I once took the oath to defend it with my life. I state this to say I support all freedoms, and am not bound to nor do I support radical ideologies from either of the two major political parties. I wish more Americans would find the tolerance offered by the former middle. When that day comes, works of fiction such as Flashpoint will truly become fantasy rather than speculative fiction.

Thank you for reading Flashpoint.

Matthew H. Whittington